Earth Angel

Siri Caldwell

2013

Bella Books, Inc.
P.O. Box 10543
Tallahassee, FL 32302

Printed in the United States of America on acid-free paper.

First Bella Books Edition 2013

Editor: Katherine V. Forrest
Cover designer: Sandy Knowles

ISBN: 978-1-59493-346-2

About the Author

Siri Caldwell got her start in creative writing in high school writing notes from her parents explaining why she was absent. She has been a health journalist, hydrogeologist, yoga teacher and massage therapist. She lives with her partner outside Washington, DC.

Other Bella Books by Siri Caldwell

Angel's Touch

Acknowledgments

Thank you to Alexandra and Ric for discussions on angelic incarnation, to Krista for Reiki-ing the car, to Cynthy for information on harp therapy, and to Jennifer for everything.

Thank you to Karin Kallmaker for her enthusiasm, to Katherine V. Forrest for her clear-eyed editorial input, to Sandy Knowles for the beautiful cover art, and to everyone else at Bella Books who helped bring this book to life.

PROLOGUE

With a joyful laugh, the angel plummeted through the vast, singing void of space. She hurtled toward earth, her trajectory guided by a structure built eons ago using the technology of an extinct, alien race. Starlight blazed and vanished; galaxies spun.

Out of the corner of her eye, something caught her attention. Something subtly off. She slowed to a stop and reversed course, scanning for the source of wrongness.

There it was. She drifted closer to look. What was that? Not a…

She faded to a dim glow as she inched even closer. Not…

A fissure. Its edges shimmered with mathematical probabilities. Frayed threads on the verge of snapping sang dangerously off-key.

The angel shrank back. She'd seen this before.

And she'd hoped to never see it again.

CHAPTER ONE

Gwynne Abernathy had never seen so many angels in one room.

She sat at the end of the hospital bed massaging her mother's feet, willing her to wake from her coma. Gwynne's father sat nearby, holding her mother's hand, acting like it hadn't been years since their divorce. Maybe he'd come for Heather, her little sister. But Heather was already dead.

Her mother still had a chance, although her life force was so dim it was hard to believe anything could help her. Hard to believe, but not impossible. Not for Gwynne. She was good at this. With nothing more than a silent intention and occasionally an angel's help, she could manipulate energy currents and channel healing life energy into someone to stop a panic attack, lower high blood pressure, speed the healing of broken bones, ease the pain of cancer.

She could bring her back.

She could.

And, with or without her, so could the angels who floated around the room and crammed themselves into every available square inch of space as more and more angels continued to arrive. But not a single one laid her weightless, insubstantial hands on her mother to gift her with angelic healing light.

They wouldn't even try. They almost always helped with Gwynne's clients, but now, when it wasn't a stranger but her own mother…

"Why won't you help?" she whispered, her voice strangled from the effort to keep quiet. Generally she tried not to speak to angels in public, but right now she didn't care. She was doing her best, dredging her memory for every technique she'd ever learned and even those she'd forgotten, but her best was nothing compared to what an angel could do. What were they waiting for? If anyone deserved a miracle, it was her mother, and she was not going to give up until she got her one.

"Talking to your angel friends?" her father asked. He sounded exhausted. "Your mother always enjoyed listening to the stories you and your sister came up with. She loved that you had such vivid imaginations."

"She's not dead yet," Gwynne said. He didn't have to talk about her like she was already gone.

"I'm going to get coffee," he said, too much of a gentleman to argue. He pushed up wearily from his plastic chair. "Want any?"

"No, thanks."

He kissed his ex-wife's forehead with the same defeated gentleness he always had around her since the divorce, then lumbered out, forgetting to close the door behind him.

Gwynne dropped her head in her hands. It wasn't his fault. It wasn't the angels' fault, either. It was her fault. It was all her fault.

* * *

"You're not allowed back here," said the doctor standing in Abby Vogel's path, blocking her from entering the intensive care wing. "Medical personnel only."

"I work here," Abby said.

"No, you don't." The doctor took full advantage of Abby's petite stature to stare her down. She pointed to the travel-size harp strapped to Abby's chest like both she and her harp were dangerous viruses. "Get out."

Abby was pretty sure her hospital ID was buried in a pile of dirty clothes on her bedroom floor, still clipped to last week's shirt. "The nurses know me."

"I don't have time for this." The doctor hurried off, grabbing the first nurse she passed and raising her voice above the dull roar of beeping medical machinery and overlapping conversations. "Get that girl out of here."

The nurse glanced in Abby's direction as the doctor disappeared behind a curtained alcove.

"Abby." The nurse came over. "It's probably best if you skip the ICU today and go straight to the third floor. I wish…" She darted a glance over her shoulder, then checked over the other shoulder, clearly nervous. "I love your music, but it's probably better if you leave. She kills anyone who breaks her focus. Unless…"

Abby held her breath, hoping she could stay. The nurse looked around again, then motioned for Abby to follow her.

"Let's set you up at the far end. Maybe she won't notice you back there."

In the far corner of the ICU, Abby pulled up a chair at the bedside of a colorless old woman hooked up to a tangle of machines. The machines emitted a whining mechanical hum punctuated by incessant beeping that would prevent anyone from resting. She positioned her lap harp between her thighs and leaned the instrument against her chest. The beeping was a shrill B-flat. She picked out that note and gradually wove it into an improvised melody, taking that B-flat and changing it from a dissonant aggravation to part of the music.

She played the lullaby again, more slowly, matching the rate of the ventilator, watching the rise and fall of the patient's chest slow as the music helped her stop fighting the ventilator and wearing herself out.

Abby loved her little 27-string, seven-pound harp. It had a comforting, mellow tone that was perfect for hospital patients whose nerves might be jangled by a more tightly strung harp, and with it she changed respiration rates, she calmed frightened heartbeats, she created healthy rhythms in damaged tissues full of pain and chaos. All with music.

She let the last note linger and rose to leave.

"That music is so calming," said a passing nurse, one she didn't know well.

"Do you have anyone in particular you'd like me to play for?"

"Room 304 would be good. The doctor's threatening to sedate that man if he doesn't stop pulling out his IV. Other than that, take your pick."

The patient in Room 304 was not happy to see her. He tried to rise from his bed but only made it a few inches before he collapsed.

"I'm not dying yet," he bellowed from beneath his white sheets. "I don't need no angel here."

Ah, yes, the joke that never got old, that seemed witty and original to every patient who came up with it. Angels and harps. She supposed she should be happy it wasn't something worse.

"Cranky today, are we?"

"Goddamn nurses are holding me prisoner here. Help me escape."

"They're trying to help you get well."

"They're poisoning me is what they're doing. See this here contraption?" He fumbled ineffectively with the intravenous drip taped to his arm. "Poison. Keeps me weak so I don't fly the coop."

It had to be scary to not feel like yourself, but telling him so probably wouldn't help. "Would you like some music?"

The patient let loose with a string of violent curses. She could see why the doctor wanted to sedate him. Medical personnel didn't get paid enough to deal with people like this.

"I'll take that as a yes," Abby said.

"You're one of them! You're in on it! You're all trying to kill me!"

Channeling peace and calm through her music, Abby plucked the harp strings as softly as she could so he'd have to quiet down to hear her. It wasn't long before his accusations fizzled out and he closed his eyes and fell asleep.

She played awhile longer, then left her sleeping patient and made her way down the antiseptic-smelling hallway of the hospital's third floor, her harp supported on a wide strap slung across her back. At the far end of the hallway, a ball of yellow-white sunlight the size of a soap bubble floated through the bank of glass windows. It oriented itself, blazed like fire, and zipped past, all the way down the hall. Abby looked over her shoulder and the light zipped past her once again before it returned and settled at her side.

"Where to?" Abby asked. She didn't care who she performed for, and the nurses gave her free rein, but Sapphire, her favorite ball of light, liked to pick the rooms for her.

This way.

She wasn't quite sure what Sapphire was. An angel, she liked to think, but she had no way of knowing whether anyone else would agree. Since no one else—not even the few psychics she'd talked to over the years—could see or hear her otherworldly best friend, it was kind of impossible to compare notes. Sometimes she wondered if it might be more accurate to call her an alien life-form—or maybe, possibly, a figment of her imagination—but Sapphire called herself an angel, and that was good enough.

Sapphire floated down the hall and stopped in front of Room 311. The door was open. Abby peeked in. The room was blindingly bright, crammed wing to wing with angels. Or... whatever. Aliens. Figments. Imaginary photons. Take your pick. She cupped her hand over her forehead like a visor and squinted. A hospital visitor sat hunched in a flimsy chair with her head in her hands, her elbows on her knees, at the foot of the bed of an apparently unconscious patient. A forest-green chamois shirt was draped over the back of the chair and an empty paper coffee cup sat at the visitor's feet. Why were so many angels in the room? It wasn't unusual to encounter other angels at the hospital, especially at the bedside of dying patients, but this was the biggest crowd she'd ever seen. Generally a single angel was enough to ease a patient's fears, so they tended to spread out, one to a room. But not this time. No wonder Sapphire led her here—she wanted to hang out with her friends.

Abby wavered outside the door as Sapphire morphed from a ball of light into more traditional winged angelic form and mingled with the others. The woman in the chair didn't move—showed no sign of having noticed Abby's presence at the door—so Abby raised her hand to knock.

"Go away," pleaded the woman.

Abby jerked back, startled, before she could knock. "Sorry."

The woman whipped her head in Abby's direction. She was about her own age, with a face that was too angular to be feminine but too fascinating to be a man's. Her chestnut-brown hair was cut short and pixie-like and was plastered haphazardly to her head like she hadn't slept in a long time, and her limp white T-shirt and jeans looked like she'd been wearing the same clothes for days.

"Sorry," the woman said, her eyes widening. "I didn't mean you."

Obviously she'd been expecting someone else. Because who else could she have meant? She couldn't have been talking to the angels.

Who were suddenly conspicuously absent.

After an interminable silence, the woman closed her eyes and put her head in her hands. "I didn't mean you. I didn't hear you come in."

Abby tried not to think too hard about why those angels blinked out of the room so fast, almost as if they were the ones who'd been asked to leave. Because they hadn't been. No one could see them but her. This woman had been talking to whoever she thought was at the door, not to her crowd of invisible, ethereal visitors, because she couldn't have known they were there. That was simply not the way it worked.

"Would you like music? I'd be happy to play for you."

"No, thank you."

"Sorry to intrude." Abby slipped out into the hall, ready to glare at Sapphire and make her tell her what that was all about.

But Sapphire, like the others, was gone.

CHAPTER TWO

Gwynne Abernathy was sick of feeling like a fraud. It had been three weeks since Heather and her mother died, and working with clients was a struggle that showed no sign of getting better.

"I can't do this anymore," she told her friend Megan McLaren. She stared at a line of wispy clouds that hovered over the Atlantic Ocean, distant but still visible from the rooftop patio of Piper Beach's newly refurbished Starfish Hotel, rechristened the Sea Salt by Megan's partner, Kira Wagner, when she became the new owner. With the start of the summer beach season three months away and construction not yet underway on the pool that was scheduled to claim two thirds of the roof, they had the rooftop to themselves. "I can't let people convince themselves that paying me to heal them is going to do them any good."

"You're quitting?" Megan asked in alarm. The wind blew her dark messy hair in her face and she pushed it out of her eyes. "It's just temporary, right? You're so good at what you do."

"I wish everyone would stop saying that."

"Maybe everyone keeps saying it because it's true."

Gwynne gripped the wooden railing and the edge bit into her palms. She should have become a doctor, she really should have. She should be working in the ER, saving people's lives and actually making a difference instead of wasting her time on massage and energy healing.

"If I was that good, I should have been able to save my mother."

"Everyone fails sometimes. Doctors fail too. People die. You don't see doctors quitting just because their patients die."

"At least they know they have a chance of saving them. The energy healing I do…it's all bullshit. No offense," she added, since Megan too was in the same line of work. They'd met in massage school and taught each other all sorts of things their teachers never mentioned. Megan McLaren was the only person she'd ever met who could see angels, who worked with them to ease pain and heal illness, who truly understood what it was like to be both envied and ridiculed for seeing something no one else could see. But this time, Megan didn't understand. Megan was never going to understand.

"Just because you couldn't pull your mother back from the brink of death…"

"I asked the angels for help and they just…stood there. They looked at me like they felt sorry for me. Like I was deluded to believe they could help."

Megan leaned next to her against the railing. "Was there really anything they could do? Saving a person's life is a lot to ask. Does anyone really have that power?"

"I used to think so."

"Please tell me you haven't lost faith in your abilities."

Great. Now Megan felt sorry for her.

"What I've lost faith in is how useful any of it is. Yeah, I can help people, but help them do what? Get over the flu a few days faster? Relax a tight muscle? Sooner or later they'll feel better without my help."

"You do more than that."

"What, invite the angels in? The angels will intervene when and if they feel like it."

"They can't save everyone," Megan contended. "There's only so far anyone is allowed to intervene."

"My mother shouldn't have died. Neither should my sister. I should have been able to help them." One stupid accident and they were both gone.

"They were dying. We're facilitators, not fixers."

"Yeah, well, apparently I'm not a fixer *or* a facilitator."

Megan gave her a pained look. "You relieve people's suffering. You heal the pain in their souls."

"Do I?"

That just didn't seem like a particularly valuable skill right now. What good was it if they were still going to die? She should go to med school. There was still time for her to change careers.

Oh, who was she kidding? Megan was the one who'd been a whiz at anatomy, back when they were both in school. Gwynne had learned enough to pass the massage certification exam, but it hadn't come easily. Realistically, she knew she wasn't going to become a doctor anytime soon. Or ever. And let's face it, the doctors hadn't been able to save Heather and her mother, either. The doctors were as helpless as she was.

It was the angels who should have saved them.

"People die," Megan said. "Sometimes there's nothing you can do. Maybe what you wanted was impossible."

"It wasn't impossible. I should have—"

"What happened to them was not your fault."

Gwynne's legs tensed with an acute desire to stomp away, but Megan would just follow her with offers of help.

Megan meant well. But she didn't know what the hell she was saying.

* * *

In the crap acoustics of the basement of a guy she'd never met before, along with his two guy friends and one other woman, Abby improvised on her harp to the rhythm of the group's four guitars, at times reinforcing the beat, at other times weaving in and out of gaps between notes, becoming part of the bluesey, ever-changing soundscape.

"You're good. You could pick up guitar if you tried," said Bruce, the guy whose basement it was. "Once you try guitar, you'll never look back."

"I like the harp," Abby said.

"It doesn't sound right with our group. The harmonies are off."

It didn't sound right? It sounded great. No wonder they were all guitar players, if guitar was the only instrument the group's leader approved of.

"Do a solo instead," Bruce suggested. "Eight bars for an intro and then the rest of us take it from there while you sit it out." He fingered a chord. "Sixteen bars," he added with a smarmy smile that shone with self-congratulatory confidence that he was a good guy doing her a favor.

But playing a solo intro defeated the purpose of jamming with other musicians, of experiencing the joy of improvising and responding to what the others were doing and creating music that had a life of its own, an out-of-control momentum it didn't have when she played solo. She played solo all the time. This was supposed to be different.

"Her harp sounds okay," said one of the other guys.

"As a solo," Bruce corrected.

"Isn't it just about having fun?" Abby suggested.

Bruce's gaze lingered too long on her chest. Abby's hands tightened on the frame of her harp, which rested against her shoulder and partially blocked his view. Her chest was a healthy size, but aside from a minor hint of cleavage, it was completely covered by the bodice of her awesome dress. She glanced down to confirm that yes, the laces crisscrossing up the front through leather eyelets were securely tied. The dress was figure-hugging, yes, but not an eyeball invitational. It was true she might have been better off wearing jeans and a T-shirt, which were good for not attracting attention, but after twelve years of school uniforms, she'd found her own style, and she'd be damned if she'd conform to somebody else's ideas about what she should wear.

She liked this dress. All her favorite dresses accentuated her figure because she'd decided before she hit puberty that the way to spot a lesbian was to look for a girl who was off-the-scale feminine. They didn't care about boys, right? So it made sense that the way to attract one was to dress as differently from a boy as possible.

Never mind that the girl in her class she found herself fantasizing about was a rugged-looking tomboy.

Okay, so her theory was flawed. Slight change in plan.

But at this point it was too late to change what kind of clothes she felt comfortable in. It was probably too late even back then.

Bruce's gaze continued to linger. Maybe he didn't realize he was doing it. Abby narrowed her eyes at him and tried to relax her grip on her harp.

"If you're gonna dress like a wench," he said, "you might as well show some cleavage."

"Seriously?" Granted, they'd met only an hour ago, and maybe the women he was used to hanging out with didn't mind his brand of conversation, but she was here to make music with other musicians, not listen to this guy make an ass out of himself.

One of the other guys snickered.

"Come on, Bruce, don't be a Neanderthal," said the lone woman in the group. She clasped the hand of her boyfriend, the one who had shown his approval for Bruce's commentary by laughing.

Caught by his girlfriend's opposing view, he coughed up a "Seriously, Bruce."

Bruce shook his head in disgust. "She's got you whipped, man."

"Women don't like it when you call them wenches," said the snickerer.

"Women?" said Bruce. "Since when did you start calling them *women*?"

He shrugged. "Gertie educated me," he said, clearly wise enough to toe the party line as long as his girlfriend was in the room. It was actually kind of sweet.

"Whipped," Bruce said.

"Can we all shut up and play?" Gertie said.

Bruce sprawled on the sofa with his guitar in his lap. "Whenever loverboy's ready."

"Shut up," said Gertie's boyfriend.

"Abby plays the intro," Bruce reminded them.

Abby sighed. This was not going to work out.

* * *

Gwynne squinted into the sun from her perch on the Sea Salt Hotel's rooftop. She'd picked a good day to return—it was one of those freakishly spring-like days in February that reminded her the tourist hordes were on their way, and she and Megan and Megan's partner Kira were taking advantage of it by flirting with winter sunburns—something she'd be doing a lot more of now that she'd decided to take a job working for Kira in the newly opened spa located on the ground floor four stories below.

"Are you sure you want to do this?" Megan asked.

"She's sure," Kira said.

"I'm sure." Gwynne leaned back, balancing her patio chair on its two back legs, maintaining traction with the toes of her canvas boat shoes. Supervising massage therapists and managing a spa wasn't the clean break from her old life that she had hoped for, but it was certainly something she was qualified to do, and Kira was desperate for someone to replace Trish, her current manager, who was moving to Minneapolis. Megan was qualified too, of course, but Megan's clients came first, and she wasn't going to give up her thriving massage practice for anyone, not even for the love of her life and the spa they'd designed together. Unlike Gwynne, who had just given Megan her entire client list.

"Don't you want to take a few days to think about it?" Megan said.

"I never think before I act. Why start now?" Gwynne needed to stay as busy as possible so she wouldn't have time to think, because thinking led to wallowing, and wallowing led to dwelling on things that no amount of avoidance was ever going to let her forget. Maybe quitting her old job wasn't the best way to do that, but she'd never claimed to be logical.

Megan didn't look amused.

Gwynne rocked in her chair, testing how far she could take it off-balance. "You know it's true."

"But giving up your healing work," Megan said. "Are you sure?"

"Hey." Kira leaned forward and scooted her chair closer to Megan's, scraping it against the roof-deck. "Don't talk her out of it, honey. I need someone for that job."

Gwynne lowered her chair legs. "I'm glad I can help out."

"You're doing me a huge favor," Kira said. "I can't tell you how much I appreciate it." Yup, she was desperate.

"Don't speak too soon."

"You're perfect for the job," Megan protested, generously pretending she'd never been frustrated by Gwynne's limitations in the keeping-her-life-organized department. It wasn't the only hole Megan pretended to have in her memory where Gwynne was concerned. Which made it easy to be friends. Especially when they both were more than willing to forget they'd ever briefly dated each other. "I just don't want you to rush into it."

"I don't mind if you rush into it," Kira said. "Trish is leaving in a week."

"I don't feel rushed," Gwynne said.

"If you're sure…" Megan dragged the word out so long Gwynne thought she was going to run out of air. It was nice of her to worry, but she had to quit working one-on-one with clients before either her negative energy or her incompetence made someone more ill than they already were.

Megan finally took a breath. "If there's anything we can do for you…"

Like stop second-guessing her? But Gwynne knew how to get her to drop the topic. "Any chance you'd be interested in adopting a super-adorable rabbit?"

"Oh no, *another* one?" Clearly this was not the return favor Megan had in mind. "When are you going to stop taking in all those strays?"

"I only have two right now." *Right now* being the operative phrase. It was only a matter of time before her house filled up again, not that she needed to mention that. "I found homes for all the others."

"All your other animals," Megan clarified, "or all your other rabbits?"

"Okay, okay, I also have a kitten. And a guinea pig. But I'm working on it." Gwynne downed her water, avoiding the slices of cucumber that floated in her glass. Another one of Kira's experimental drinks to serve at the spa. "Want a kitten?"

Megan rolled her eyes. "At least it's only two rabbits. I'll never forget that time you had fifty of them running all over the house and they got into your treatment room while I was giving you a massage."

"It wasn't fifty." The most she'd ever had at one time was seventeen, when a whole litter of mini lops pushed her over her previous record of twelve. And that time that Megan was talking about, it was more like ten. Megan had refused to continue with the massage until Gwynne climbed off the table, naked and exasperated, and chased the rabbits out.

"Okay, less than fifty," Megan conceded.

"Thank you."

"At least forty-nine."

"Geez, Megan, thanks a lot. Kira's going to think I have a hoarding problem."

Kira refilled their glasses without comment.

Megan swirled her glass of cucumber slices. "You could have warned me the door didn't shut all the way."

"They weren't trying to scare you," Gwynne said. "They just wanted to see what we were doing."

"What *were* you doing?" Kira said.

"Jealous?" Megan cheered up and patted Kira on the thigh. At least that's what Gwynne assumed. If something more than that was going on under the table—which, judging from the sudden change in Kira's expression, it probably was—she didn't want to know. She was glad Megan was happy, though. Kira was better for her than Gwynne had ever been.

Gwynne emptied her glass in one long gulp. She might not be a massage therapist or an energy healer anymore, but she still believed in staying well-hydrated. Years of pressing glasses of water into her clients' hands weren't going to be undone in a single day.

"I think I have a rabbit phobia now," Megan said. "Remind me never to adopt one."

"How about a guinea pig?"

Megan's face softened, as she knew it would. Everyone loved guinea pigs. Until they realized how much cage cleaning was involved. Which Megan was apparently contemplating now, because that smile that said *aren't they the cutest* was already fading. She raised her palms with a sigh and slapped them on the table. "They're rodents."

"Well, technically…" Gwynne admitted.

"No pets, Gwynnie. I don't do pets."

"Okay, okay." She didn't want to give up the guinea pig, anyway. She'd named her Apple and she had the cutest tuft of hair that poofed out on the top of her head and hung over her eyes like bangs. It was totally adorable.

"If you think of another favor—a non-pet favor—let us know," Megan said.

"You don't have to do anything for me."

"There must be something…" Absentmindedly, Megan refilled everyone's glasses, even though only Gwynne's was empty. "How about music while you work? Kira's thinking about hiring a musician for the lounge."

Kira rose from the table and paced. "I haven't decided."

"If you're looking for a harpist, there's one up at the hospital in Lewes," Gwynne volunteered.

Megan grinned at Kira. "See, it's a sign."

Kira barked out a laugh. "It is not a sign." Ever since they'd met, Kira had become more and more open-minded about Megan's pseudoscientific beliefs, but she still had a ways to go.

"It is a sign," Megan insisted.

"There was that violinist we interviewed last month," Kira said. "She wasn't bad."

"Too screechy," Megan said.

"She was good," Kira argued.

"You promised there were going to be perks to knowing the owner," Megan reminded her partner.

Kira stalked toward her, oozing sensuality. "This is the perk you want? Veto power over the music?"

"Yes."

"When I made that promise, music was not what I had in mind."

"I know what *you* had in mind." Megan pulled Kira onto her lap. Kira was starting to go gray, but she still had the body of a twenty-year-old marathon runner—a physique that was not Gwynne's type, but that clearly was Megan's. "If you're going to call it a perk, it's supposed to be for *my* benefit. You get too much out of it."

"Oh, you'll benefit, all right," Kira murmured, shifting on her lap.

Gwynne squirmed and eyed the exit. Maybe they wouldn't notice if she left?

"No violin," Megan said, pressing her lips to the back of her partner's shoulder.

"I liked her," Kira said.

"You'll both like my harpist," Gwynne said, jumping into the conversation to remind them she was still in the vicinity before things got out of hand.

Megan turned to her politely as Kira slid off her lap. "Is she a hospital employee? Was she good?"

Those were both relevant questions, but admitting she didn't know precisely what the musician had been doing there, or what her harp sounded like, wasn't going to help her cause. "Uh..."

Megan looked at her sympathetically, probably assuming she'd triggered painful memories. "Sorry."

"No, it's not that." Gwynne had no idea why she was pushing for this. She was surprised she even remembered the harpist, considering how consumed she'd been by everything else going on, but there was something about her that had cut through the blind despair of those hours and imprinted itself on her memory. Something that made her want to see her again. And not just to apologize, although she wanted to do that too, because the apology she'd grumbled at the hospital had been totally inadequate. The harpist took it in stride, but that was because she was a good person. She had to have a good heart to work in a place full of people who were stressed and scared and not at their best. "You're going to like her."

"Uh-oh." Megan knew her too well.

Kira looked at Megan, then back at Gwynne. "Are you saying you've never heard her play?"

"I'm sure she's good," Gwynne said.

"Jesus." Kira paced over to the railing and back. "I can't believe I'm trusting you to run my spa."

"Of course you trust me. I have excellent instincts," Gwynne said.

"It's your years of experience with clients that I'm counting on."

"So, yay," Megan said. "We get music."

Megan grabbed Kira and kissed her on the cheek. At least Gwynne thought it was her cheek. She was doing her best not to watch. When she figured it was safe to look up, the two had returned to separate seats.

Kira looked a little dazed. "I need to run the numbers first."

Megan's voice deepened. "I can help you with that." From the light twinkling in her eyes, it looked like she was ready to "help" her right here on the table.

Kira riveted her full attention on Megan. "I think that might be a good idea."

"Go ravish her in another room, please, where I don't have to watch," Gwynne said, pushing back from the table before things went any further. "I'll be back later."

"No, wait," Megan said.

Gwynne left. On her way out she heard Kira say, "I thought it was my turn to ravish *you.*"

* * *

Abby hesitated at the edge of the softball field and watched a dozen or so women joke with each other while they casually warmed up, twisting and bending at the waist and swinging their arms. It was a rare Saturday afternoon when she didn't have a wedding to play, and she was determined to take advantage of it—get outside, do something different. She was always glad for the happy brides and grooms, and she appreciated the financial security of having so many paying gigs, but living through weekend after weekend celebrating heterosexual love couldn't be one hundred percent healthy. It would be nice to spend at least one Saturday feeling like she was with her own kind.

Not that she was a jock—far from it. She'd passed gym class by showing up for class and being a good sport about being picked last whenever they divided into teams, and by ignoring how much she hated feeling uncoordinated, hated the way she jiggled when she ran, and hated wearing sports bras that were too tight and too hot and still didn't stop her chest from hurting every time she bounced. But that didn't mean she couldn't give this a shot. Maybe without prepubescent boys in the mix, sports would be more fun.

Besides, she'd left Baltimore and moved over a hundred miles to the small coastal town of Piper Beach almost four months ago and it was high time she made some friends outside of the hospital staff. This was why she'd moved here, after all—because she was convinced that somewhere out there, if she could only find it, was a place that felt like home.

Bruce's guitar jam wasn't it. Maybe softball was.

She approached a pair of African-American women in softball-type outfits as one of them straightened up from tying her laces. Wow, she was tall. Tall and stunningly bald.

"What position do you play?" asked the stockier of the two, who sported a mass of braids.

"Oh, uh, anything. Whatever you need," Abby bluffed. She figured they wouldn't assign her to anything important until they saw her play and knew what she could do. Or, more to the point, not do.

"I'm Hank," said the one with the braids. "We're short players, so make yourself useful." She glanced pointedly at Abby's sneakers. "And next time, wear cleats."

The other woman poked Hank with her elbow.

Abby decided not to take offense. Hey, at least her hair was in a ponytail, right? That was about as jock-like as she was going to get. She adjusted her headband, a print with bold orange daisies that matched her leggings but teetered on the edge of clashing with her red hair, and fluffed her ponytail in an I-never-play-sports-that-could-involve-safety-helmets kind of way. She was not normally prissy about her hair, and she didn't even really mean it, but Hank brought it out in her—this weird cross between flirtation and defiance.

"Just so you know," Abby said, "I'm not good at sports."

Hank looked her up and down. "Don't be scared, little girl," she said rudely. "I'll teach you to play."

The woman next to her snorted.

Hank turned her head belligerently in her friend's direction, hiking up one shoulder. "What."

"*We'll* teach you to play," the woman said.

Hank dipped her chin. "Come on, Aisha, I didn't mean it like that."

The two of them got into an argument and Abby escaped and joined the rest of the group. Someone pulled her onto their team and soon she found herself up at bat.

Her first swing was a disaster. A couple of women cheered in a motherly way, supportive of the new girl who obviously sucked.

The next pitch, she could immediately tell from the change in the pitcher's windup that she was moving more deliberately, more slowly, tossing her a gentle, easy-to-hit target. Being nice to her. Bruce's attitude at the guitar jam was almost easier to deal with.

Abby tightened her grip on the bat. She swung, and missed. How could she be so coordinated at the harp and so uncoordinated with a bat? She had good hand-eye coordination, just not when it came to balls. And no, she did not mind if anyone snickered at that, because she meant it that way too.

Juvenile, yes. But true. When it came to balls—of any kind—she was not interested.

"Give it a good whack," the catcher encouraged her.

Another pitch came at her.

"Whack it!" someone yelled as the ball approached. "Pretend it's your boyfriend's head."

Abby clenched her jaw and swung, and as the ball thunked into the catcher's mitt, the bat flew out of her hands.

She didn't belong here.

CHAPTER THREE

Abby navigated traffic the way she played music—exquisitely aware of the location of all the players, whether they were cars and traffic lights and pedestrians on the street or strings and levers on a harp. She could sense where each vehicle was, feel it in her fingertips, feel a tug on the invisible strings that linked her to each driver when someone was about to come to a sudden stop or change lanes without using their turn signal, and she adjusted her speed accordingly, smoothly weaving around obstacles at well above the speed limit, one element in a coordinated whole. It wasn't mind reading; it was an innate *knowing*. She didn't understand how she did it, but she never questioned it.

Her driving mojo didn't carry over to other aspects of her life, but that was fine. Life without surprises would be boring. She thought about that when she arrived for her audition at the Sea Salt Hotel and Spa and wheeled in her five-foot-tall, 36-string harp and saw who was there to greet her.

It was the woman from the hospital. She no longer had dark circles under her eyes or that appalling look of utter exhaustion, but it was definitely her. The despair was still there, lurking in her eyes, weighing down her shoulders, but it was so well hidden that anyone who wasn't paying attention would think she was doing fine. Unlike the last time she'd seen her, her spotless jeans and unwrinkled emerald silk blouse under a matching jacket—besides bringing out the green of her eyes—did not look like they'd been slept in, and her short brown hair was styled into adorable pixie spikes. For a lot of people, a well-groomed exterior was a sign that they'd returned to normal. For this woman, she suspected it was an act.

"I'm Gwynne Abernathy," the woman said, not mentioning their previous run-in. "Can I carry something for you?"

Abby handed her the low wooden stool hooked over her wrist and followed her with her harp through the lobby and down a hallway.

"You're the one who recommended me for the job?" The hotel owner had mentioned Gwynne's name on the phone, but Abby hadn't recognized it. She'd dismissed the minor mystery as unimportant, since every year she performed for thousands of wedding guests whose names she'd never know.

But this wasn't an anonymous wedding guest. This was... *her*. The one she'd been obsessing about for weeks, wondering if she really had ordered those angels out of that hospital room, or if it had all been a weird coincidence.

She wasn't expecting it to be her. The woman hadn't even heard her play. And it wasn't like they'd talked, or made a connection. On Abby's part, yeah. Considering all the time she'd spent mulling over their awkward encounter, she'd have to say they made a connection. But on Gwynne Abernathy's part? Doubtful. But that was okay. If it got her an audition, she'd take it. And maybe afterward she'd pull her aside and ask her what had happened in that hospital room.

"Thanks for putting in a good word for me," Abby said.

"I'm surprised Kira mentioned it."

The hallway opened into an archway that led into a spacious lounge where Gwynne set down her harp stool. The room was uncluttered and painted white, designed to draw your eye to the hundreds of glass balls on the ceiling, each one lit from within, glowing with the pale blues and greens of sea glass. Glass pebbles in the same range of colors tiled the far wall, and an adjacent wall was painted with a mural of a mermaid sunning on a rock. The beautiful design barely registered, though, because the room was swirling with angels. They spun around her and Gwynne, unafraid to come close, and as one swooped toward her face, Abby tripped on her long skirt. She caught her balance on the hand truck her harp was on, leaning on it harder than she would have liked but managing not to jar the harp.

"Are you all right?" Gwynne asked.

"Yup, no problem." Abby spoke with a practiced glibness that came from years of denying sights that were clear as day to her but seemingly invisible to everyone else. Did angels follow Gwynne Abernathy everywhere she went? She didn't look terminally ill, and she couldn't think of another good reason why so many of them would be here. The place was positively angel-acious.

A blonde dressed in white linen pants and a clingy white sweater unfolded herself from one of the white sofas and padded over in bare feet. "Hi, I'm Megan McLaren. Kira should be here any minute for the interview. Do you need help setting up?"

"No, I'm good. I'll just need a few minutes to tune." Harps didn't like to be moved—any change in temperature or humidity meant they needed to be retuned, or at least checked.

Abby unstrapped her harp from the hand truck and unzipped it from its padded case, her hands passing through the illusion of angelic bodies. Usually she tried to avoid that, but there was no real reason to—they did not actually have bodies, not bodies you could feel or touch. It was easy to forget, though, because they were good about respecting physical boundaries and usually didn't crowd so close. She didn't know what they were so worked up about today. It had to be something to do with Gwynne.

"Look, I'm sorry I snapped at you," Gwynne said. "At the hospital."

Abby glanced up from her harp in surprise. "You didn't snap."

"I didn't know you were there. It wasn't you I was mad at."

She didn't volunteer whom she *was* mad at, though. A family member, a nurse, a flock of angels she had no way of knowing was there…

"You don't have to apologize. It's fine." Puzzling, but really, fine.

* * *

Abby Vogel was a tiny little thing, no taller than her harp, but clearly strong. She hefted her five-foot harp out of its carrying case like it weighed nothing. Her dress, however, screamed the opposite of tough. It was straight from a Renaissance faire—a red velvet dress that laced up the back and hugged her lush curves, then flared at the hip into a skirt that fell all the way to the floor. Her sleeves were the same way, clinging to her upper arms but draping loosely from the elbows so the fabric fluttered whenever she moved her arms and made it hard to look away. When she'd hiked up her skirt to avoid stepping on the hem on her way in, she revealed what looked like homemade knee-high deerskin boots lashed to her calves with leather laces. Her long, red hair was streaked with blond and gold and caramel highlights, and on her head sat a gold circlet that had gone out of fashion centuries ago.

Gwynne wouldn't be caught dead in a getup like that. On Abby, it looked romantic—and that was not a word Gwynne had ever used to describe anything.

Romantic? Try bewitching. Like Abby had emerged from a fairy mound glowing with confidence that this was how the natives dressed, and had no idea that if she wanted to, she could make a string of sexual conquests during her stay.

Gwynne swallowed—it was either that or drool. Obviously the deaths of her mother and sister had knocked out some of her common sense. She wasn't used to being turned to mush by a stranger wearing period costume.

Kira dashed in as Abby finished her tuning, saving Gwynne from further gooey, unexpected feelings. If she was going to fall apart, she'd rather not do it in front of Megan, her ex. Megan had seen enough of her mush.

"Am I late?" Kira switched from a jog to a bouncing walk for her last few steps across the room. Even when she wasn't late she was always running, always burning energy, making Gwynne feel like she should drop and do fifty pushups to prove she wasn't a slacker, even though she was. She was out of shape. People assumed she was fit because she was petite, but *fit* and *petite* were not the same thing. She used to make more of an effort to work out—she liked sports and she did play softball in the summer—but lately her idea of exercise was climbing onto a stepstool to reach the shelves of her kitchen cabinets.

While Kira introduced herself to Abby, Gwynne took the opportunity to brush a flutter of angel light away from her face. It was odd there were so many angels in the room. Either they liked the harpist or they liked her music, or both. Or maybe Abby was ill and they wanted to heal her? According to Kira, she'd had to reschedule the audition because of a doctor's appointment. For an ear infection, which didn't seem like it would be an angelic priority, but what did she know? They were here, and they certainly weren't here on Gwynne's account. And Megan they completely ignored—for once—so it wasn't her. No, it was herself and especially the harpist they were swooping around, for whatever reason. Not that they necessarily needed a reason. As far as angels were concerned, any day was a good day for swooping.

Before Gwynne could spend any more time contemplating their reasons, Abby began to play. She recognized the first tune, "Greensleeves." From there Abby moved from one haunting, aching melody to another in a seamless medley of ancient-sounding music full of aching loss, songs that sensed the grief in Gwynne's heart and lured it out of hiding. Was it her, or did this woman not know any cheerful music? She didn't know if she could listen to this every day. She'd either love it or end up an emotional wreck.

Far too soon, it was over. Abby's hands floated off the strings and down to her lap as the last bell-like notes lingered in the air and died out. For a minute no one said anything, still caught in her spell.

"That was beautiful," Kira said.

She nodded questioningly at Megan and Gwynne to gauge their opinion. They both nodded back.

"You've got the job if you want it," Kira said.

"Do I get to decide what music I play?" Abby asked.

"Absolutely."

"Then I'd love to."

* * *

"By the way," Kira said from across the desk in her office, handing Abby yet another employment form to fill out and sign, "there are some flakes who work here, but don't let it bother you. You won't freak out if Megan tells you she works with angels, will you?"

Abby's pen stopped, poised over the paper. "She thinks angels are real?"

It would be so great to talk to someone who understood, but she wasn't going to get her hopes up, because Megan couldn't see angels. No one could. Maybe what Kira meant was, Megan *believed* in angels. Lots of people believed in all kinds of crazy stuff. It didn't mean anything. She probably believed in ghosts too. Didn't mean she could see them.

There was that weird moment at the hospital with Gwynne, though, when she'd wondered if Gwynne had ordered the angels to leave. She'd asked Sapphire, her closest angel friend, about it afterward—when Sapphire finally deigned to reappear after abandoning her for the rest of her shift at the hospital that day—but Sapphire wouldn't answer. Since mysterious silence was typical for her, she wasn't sure she should read anything into that. But she couldn't forget the incident. The possibility that she wasn't the only one who could see angels was too compelling.

"Are you freaking out?" Kira asked.

"No, I—"

"You have that look," Kira said. "That look that says 'Get me out of here.'"

Kira didn't get it. "That's not—"

"I'm in love with her, so…"

"So you want to make sure I don't say anything to hurt her feelings?"

"Exactly. I'm not saying I want you to believe in the woo-woo stuff. I don't care either way. I just want to make sure this is not going to be a problem."

"It won't be a problem."

"Good. It'll be nice to have someone else around here who's down-to-earth. We can bond when the woo-woo factor gets out of control."

Abby noticed that she did not include Gwynne Abernathy in the "down-to-earth" category.

"So you're not a fan of angels," Abby clarified. She liked to know where people stood, especially when that person was her new boss.

"Let's put it this way. I don't believe in things I can't see. Megan's working on me, though." Kira looked pleased about that.

The thing was, though…it wasn't Megan the angels were circling during her performance. It was Abby and Gwynne. They liked Gwynne, and there might be a very good reason for that—a very obvious reason. The same reason angels flocked around Abby.

She'd never met anyone who could see angels. But she had a feeling Gwynne might be different.

CHAPTER FOUR

Abby looked up from her harp as Gwynne Abernathy greeted another visitor to Sea Salt. It was Hank, the first baseman from her embarrassing attempt to fit in with the local lesbians. Great. She hadn't even had a chance to get to know Gwynne yet, and already someone else was going to make that first impression for her. Someone who was dangerously dykey in her dusty work boots and dirty jeans that were the polar opposite of the fairy-tale dresses Abby loved to wear. No one would ever peg Abby as gay if they saw her next to Hank—not unless she and Hank were acting like best friends—and the chances of that happening were slim.

"I wondered where those shoulder muscles came from," Hank told Abby, acknowledging her presence for a split second before ignoring her again. Abby heard the words she didn't say: *Because they sure as heck didn't come from swinging at a softball.*

She wondered if working here was going to do anything at all to improve her lesbian credentials.

Probably not.

But it didn't matter. She liked having the freedom to play whatever music she wanted and she liked everyone she'd met here, even those who didn't understand there *were* other ways to get shoulder muscles. Try a feminine activity like playing the harp, thank you very much.

Not that she didn't understand why Hank didn't want to play softball with beginners. Performing music with struggling novices was not something Abby had much patience for, either.

"Thanks for the invite," Hank said to Gwynne.

"You should have told me your crew was doing repairs down the street. I would've invited you sooner," Gwynne said. "You didn't have to wait for me to drive by and notice you by accident."

"We only started today. Besides, I didn't know you worked here."

Gwynne poured Hank a glass of water and added a slice of cucumber. "You don't follow my every move?"

"Afraid not." Hank accepted the glass and plopped into an overstuffed chair. "Heard you quit the mumbo-jumbo business, though. How does it feel?"

"Hard to say."

"Right. Because you decide to take a job here in la-la land serving cucumber-laced drinks. You could've called me. I could've gotten you a job."

"Thanks, I appreciate the thought," Gwynne said drily. "Is this why you're visiting?"

Hank shrugged out of her jacket. "It's cold out. You have heat."

"Glad to know my company is so thrilling."

"Just trying to eat my lunch in peace," Hank grumbled. "This here is one of the shitty perks of road maintenance—if we want to eat, we have to hide, or some self-righteous member of the driving public is sure to report us to complain we're sitting around on our asses wasting the taxpayers' money. I'd like to see them out there freezing their toes off or frying in the sun, sucking fumes." She unwrapped a paper bag and started in on the burger that was her lunch.

"The guys give you a hard time for ditching them?" Gwynne asked.

"They think I have a hot date. Whatever."

"Why would they think that?" Gwynne said. "Did you fuck things up with Aisha? Because I swear to God, I'm going to make you apologize to her. Tell me you didn't break up with her."

"Shit, no."

"Then…?"

Hank finished chewing. "I don't talk about Aisha at work—period. The crew knows I'm not into guys, but I don't fill them in on my personal life."

"They're guys. They don't care about your personal life."

"Oh, they care all right. If it's something they can give me a hard time about, they care. And personally, I could do without their dating advice. I get enough shit from you already."

Abby watched them chatting, catching up on gossip about friends on the softball team. It figured that Gwynne played softball. She was probably great at it. Even if she *wasn't* great at it, she looked like she'd at least fit in. She was the cute, petite, less intimidating version of Hank, with a too-short haircut and a direct gaze that was not quite feminine. She'd swing the bat with a confident, graceful arc and she'd look perfect sliding in the dirt, her body tangling with another jock's and rolling from the impact.

And where did that thought come from?

She snapped out of it as Hank crumpled her trash and rose to return to work.

"When are you going to start playing with us again?" Hank asked Gwynne.

"I don't know." Gwynne's shoulders slumped. "I have a lot going on."

Hank swayed uncomfortably like she didn't know what to say. "I heard. Sorry about your mom and your sister."

Kira's partner had warned Abby about that—that Gwynne wasn't normally grumpy, but she'd recently suffered two deaths in the family.

"Thanks." Gwynne stared at her desk.

Hank stood silently for several long, awkward moments before edging toward the exit. "Come back anytime. We could use you."

"I guess," Gwynne mumbled unconvincingly.

"You too," Hank threw over her shoulder at Abby. It sounded like an afterthought.

Abby fingered the ends of her longer-than-shoulder-length hair. Maybe she would try softball again. Just because she didn't look the part didn't mean she couldn't learn to smack a ball. Her strong shoulders had to count for something.

Hank stopped in the archway and turned around. "And that chick you were dating," she told Gwynne. "The good pitcher?"

Gwynne frowned. "The red pushup bra?"

"Yeah, her. How come we never see her anymore?"

"Because we broke up." Gwynne sounded like it should be obvious.

"That doesn't mean she had to quit showing up."

"Her choice, Hank. Maybe if you guys had bothered to learn her name…"

"Maybe if you didn't call her *the red pushup bra*, we would've."

Gwynne folded her arms across her chest. "I'll let her know you want her back on the team."

"Great." Hank pulled on her jacket. "And do me a favor. Don't date anyone on the team. We can't afford to lose more players because of you."

"I gave you that player," Gwynne protested.

"Yeah, fine."

Abby didn't watch her go—she watched Gwynne. A red pushup bra? What was it that Gwynne had found so fascinating about her ex-girlfriend's choice of undergarments? Abby twined her fingers in her hair. Maybe she didn't want to know.

"When did you break up?" Abby asked instead.

"What? Oh, it's been a while," Gwynne said distractedly. "You should join the softball team, if you're interested. They need more players."

"You're assuming I can play," Abby pointed out. "You're the one she really wants."

"Don't worry about Hank. She's allergic to women who wear dresses."

"And you're not?"

Gwynne ran her fingers through her hair and made it spikier. She met her gaze for a long moment. "No."

Abby tried to breathe, pretending that gaze hadn't done anything for her.

"She's met me before," Abby said. "And I wasn't wearing a dress." The problem with Hank, if there was one, was not about her clothing choices and appearance. But if Gwynne wanted to act like it was, she'd go along with it. "I was wearing fleece leggings."

"Leggings?"

"It was too cold to wear shorts." She wasn't the only one on the softball field who'd thought so, either. "I didn't move here from North Dakota."

Gwynne shook her head and smiled. What, did Gwynne think she was missing some obvious clue?

"Maybe it's my hair."

"Maybe it's the fact that you call them *leggings* instead of *pants*."

No, it was the fact that Hank knew how terrible she was at Hank's favorite sport.

"Forget her," Gwynne said. "Your hair is beautiful. If anyone around here has problematic hair, it's me. *My* hair is a mess."

"It's not a mess. I like it." It did look a little hedge-clipper-gone-wild, but it was cute.

"Please. I got mad at my hair last night and hacked at it."

Abby looked again. She could tell it was different, but it didn't look terrible. "Going for the uneven look?"

Gwynne rearranged her hair into more spikes. "I may have been a little impulsive."

"It just needs a few days to settle in. Think of it as edgy." That was the thing about being impulsive—you had to have a positive attitude or it was all over. Even if the impulse involved scissors and already-short hair and anger you didn't seem to want to talk about with the friend you just had lunch with.

"*A few days to settle in*? I love that you're trying to make me feel better, but that is the worst white lie I've ever heard. Did you see the back?" Gwynne turned her head to show her the ragged cut that did, frankly, look a lot less intentional. "I have an appointment for tomorrow morning to get it evened out. They might have to shave that part."

"I'm sure it's salvageable."

Gwynne clasped her hands behind her head and leaned back in her chair. "I'm not worried about it. I can't see the back, anyway, and no one else cares what I look like."

She cared enough to get it fixed, though.

"Plus I came up with this great line about how it's edgy," Gwynne said. "Totally convincing."

"You didn't use it on me."

"I didn't use it because you seem like the kind of woman who would see through my B.S."

"I don't have to if you do it for me," Abby pointed out.

"I like you." Gwynne unclasped her hands and rubbed the choppy hair at the back of her head. "You don't happen to own a red pushup bra, do you?"

Abby opened her mouth in disbelief. Of course she didn't own a pushup bra, because there was no need to push anything up any farther than it already was. Not that Gwynne needed to know that. Besides, Gwynne was kidding—it wasn't a real question and she didn't expect a real answer. If Bruce the guitar guy had said it she'd be pissed, but with Gwynne, it was harmless. She just hoped she wasn't blushing.

"Was there anything about this woman you liked besides her bra?"

"One or two things." Gwynne gave a self-deprecating smile. "But she didn't see through my B.S."

* * *

The next time Abby saw Gwynne at work, someone had done some magic on her hair and turned it into a shorter version of her previous pixie cut that drew attention to her stunning, androgynous bone structure. She hadn't gotten close enough to see what the hair stylist did to the back, but she figured if she waited, she'd eventually get a chance to check it out without being obvious.

Or she could just ask, and hope that Gwynne didn't take it as an invitation to flirt with her.

Or hope that she did.

"Welcome to Sea Salt," Gwynne was saying in a warm, professional tone.

Abby continued to play her harp while Gwynne offered the guests—a stressed-out mother and a five-year-old boy—a glass of grapefruit-lime spring water that Abby had sampled earlier and voted much tastier than the cucumber water. The boy eyed the mint leaves floating in the glass and jerked away.

The mother corralled him into her arms. "My son has intestinal parasites that won't go away. A friend of mine said you do faith healing—"

Gwynne's face clouded over. "Energy healing."

"She said you were able to help her son."

"I'm sorry, I don't—"

"You have hands that heal. You cleared up his psoriasis when doctors could do nothing."

Gwynne's polite smile shut down. "I don't do healing anymore."

"Please."

Not another one. Abby wasn't sure why Gwynne got this constant parade of former clients and strangers coming through who were not here to visit the spa, but to visit her—or, more accurately, to beg her for help. They complained of fatigue, arthritis, fibromyalgia, infections, acid reflux, headaches…the list went on and on. They called, they came in person, and for all she knew they e-mailed, and Gwynne always turned them down. She wondered what had made her close the door on what by all appearances had been a spectacularly successful career as a healer.

"Can't you make an exception?"

It had to be so hard for Gwynne to say no to these people.

But say no to them she did, every single time. “You should see a doctor.”

The boy wriggled away from his mother and stopped in front of Abby and stared at her harp in awe. She switched to a medley of nursery rhymes she figured he'd recognize. At “Twinkle, Twinkle, Little Star,” he shrieked and ran back to his mother, then slumped against her leg.

His mother glanced at him distractedly. “You think I didn't do that first? The medication isn't working.”

“I can't help you,” Gwynne said tightly. “I wish I could. I really do. But it's beyond my abilities. You need to see a doctor and put your son on another medication.”

Abby segued into one of her favorite meditative tunes, hoping it would do something to help the mother. Gwynne looked like she could use it too.

“Please? My friend said what you did for her son was a miracle.”

But Gwynne didn't want to be a miracle worker. “Spontaneous remission. Conditions like that sometimes go away on their own.” She reached across her desk and touched the woman's hand in sympathy. “I didn't do anything.”

Spontaneous remission. Abby had heard that phrase tossed around by nurses in her vicinity. Because there was no such thing as a miracle worker. Not Gwynne, healing a little boy's tenacious parasites. Not a musician with a harp, easing patients' pain when the pain meds stopped working. There was no easy way to explain those recoveries, and *spontaneous remission* sounded more scientific than *we don't know*. Could Gwynne really heal?

“But what am I going to do?” the mother wailed.

“See a doctor.” It was killing Gwynne to turn her away—it was clear from the way her whole body was leaning in, her face troubled. But she wouldn't do it. “I don't want to give you false hope. If I treat him and that makes you hold off on seeing a doctor, he could get worse. I don't want him to get sicker than he already is because I let you believe I could heal him. Because I can't. I can't heal him.”

The mother pushed away from the desk. "I guess I'll just have to pray." Her son ran around her in circles and she grabbed him by the hand as he zipped by.

Gwynne bit her lip and watched them go. Once they were gone, she put her head in her hands, elbows planted on her desk.

Abby continued to play, flowing easily from one tune to the next. At first she tried to make Gwynne feel better, but soon she got caught up in the music and played for the pure joy of it. Music had always transported her, and with this particular harp, with its strong, even tone and its glorious resonance, that was even more true. Rees harps never went up for resale because once you got your hands on one, it sounded so good you never wanted to give it up. She could play this instrument forever. But eventually she did decide she couldn't play *forever*, and stopped.

"How's your ear?" Gwynne asked, not looking up.

It took her a minute to come back to earth and realize Gwynne was talking to her. "It's better. The doctor put me on antibiotics." Again. If only music could heal her ear infection as effectively as it soothed sick patients.

Gwynne grunted. "Finally, someone around here who's willing to go to a medical doctor for help."

* * *

"Please don't make me play the Wedding March." Abby leveled her gaze at her friend Penelope and sank her forearms onto the wobbly Formica table in the front window of her favorite ice cream shop. She leaned farther forward to emphasize her point. "Anything but that."

Back in college, she and Penelope had started their own rock band together. They amped her harp and Penelope sang soprano when she wasn't on the flute and Ramona and Natalie were on drums with an I'm-so-angry-I-have-to-scream-my-lyrics thing going on, and instead of being a loud disaster, it turned into a compelling, bizarre contrast of highs and lows that gave her chills. And now Penelope and Nat were getting married, and Abby couldn't wait to play the walking-down-the-aisle music for their ceremony and the nobody-listens-to-you-while-they're-socializing background music for the reception.

But not Wagner's Wedding March.

"It's traditional," Penelope said.

"It only premiered in 1850. What do you think people played at their weddings before then?"

Penelope pressed her fingers to either side of her forehead and stared. "You're trying to talk me out of it because you just don't want to play it."

"All right, that too." Gold star for Pennylongstocking.

Penelope squeezed her brow in frustration. "What else am I supposed to use?"

"A modern ballad," Abby suggested.

"Too cheesy."

"A Paraguayan folk tune. Their music for harp is amazing."

"I'm not Paraguayan."

"You're not German, either," Abby said. "Richard Wagner—the composer?—was German." She tried again. "How about Medieval and Renaissance music? It has more history than the so-called traditional stuff, and it's beautiful." She hummed a few bars of "Robin is to the Greenwood Gone." "And you could dress up your attendants—"

"No."

"No to the costumes?" But costumes would be so fun. She gathered her long hair off her shoulders and pulled it into a high ponytail as she contemplated her look. "I might have to wear a pointy wizard princess hat to your wedding."

"That's fine," Penelope said.

"I might actually do it, you know."

"I don't care. As long as you're there, you can wear whatever you want."

Abby released her hair. Pennywhistle was a better person than she herself would ever be. "What are you two wearing? White dresses?"

"Me? In a dress? No." Penelope folded a couple of paper napkins and ducked under the table and jammed the napkins under the central table leg to make it stop wobbling. "And I know this is going to be a big disappointment to you, but we are not wearing tunics or cloaks or sackcloth, either. Or pointy hats. Or whatever you delusional archaeology majors are wearing these days. I'm wearing a white tuxedo and Nat's wearing a black one." She popped up from underneath the table. "Is that nontraditional enough for you?"

"You'll look beautiful," Abby said.

Penelope scanned her face like she couldn't decide if she was serious or not. "White's not a problem for you?"

"I love that you're wearing what makes you happy."

"But you wouldn't wear white."

"Actually, I like white wedding dresses. The beading, the lace…What's not to like?"

"Stop. Just…please stop. You are *not* talking me into wearing a dress." Penelope shook her head in disbelief. "I should have known you liked those things. Would you really wear one?"

"Only if the veil was sewn to a pointy wizard princess hat."

"Really? A white dress?"

"Or maybe a Neolithic cavegirl leopard skin."

Penelope tested the stability of the table. "Yeah, good luck finding a girlfriend who will want her parents to see you in that."

The waiter arrived and Abby ordered a Kahlua-spiked milkshake. The waiter asked for her ID.

"You're carding her?" Penelope said.

Abby smiled tightly. One day this would stop happening, but that day hadn't come yet—even though anyone who bothered to look ought to be able to tell there was no way she was anywhere close to being underage. It was the round face that threw people off. Or maybe the freckles.

"Crow's feet," she said, pressing one finger to the outside of her eye as she reached for her purse.

"I don't see any crow's feet," Penelope said. "Give me a break."

Abby decided not to argue, because who was she to complain? As her grandmother liked to point out, eventually the worry lines would become a lot worse and she'd wonder what she'd been whining about.

"Don't you want to card me too?" Penelope asked the waiter.

"Do you want me to card you?" The waiter looked too exhausted and hung over to care that his tip was in imminent danger, but Penelope, who'd never been any good at reading men, pressed on.

"I'm younger than her," Penelope said, which was only marginally true. "You're making me feel old."

The waiter held out his hand and Penelope got out her purse. Turning thirty was hitting her hard if she thought being mistaken for a teenager, even out of an overabundance of caution imposed by this guy's law-abiding boss, was a compliment.

Talking about her wedding plans made it all better, though. Or maybe that was Penelope's vanilla milkshake with caramel sauce and a shot of Jack Daniel's. God knew alcohol was making it easier for Abby to listen to the endless details. She ran a finger down her list of possible tunes, humming a few bars and making suggestions for the reception music while the bride-to-be talked.

"It sounds like you've really kept in practice," Penelope said. "I'm jealous."

Abby sipped her shake. "You don't play anymore?"

"Not really. I take the flute out occasionally just for fun, but it's hard to find the time. You know how it is." Penelope swirled her straw in her nearly empty glass. "I wish I could have played professionally, but it's impossible to make a living as a musician."

"I make a living at it," Abby pointed out.

Penelope pursed her lips and wrinkled her brow. "Do you? Playing in a hotel lobby?" She sounded doubtful. "I assumed you had a real job and you played at that hotel—spa—whatever—resort—thing for fun."

"I play lots of places. Weddings pay the bills." At least they did when the check didn't bounce. Just last weekend she'd had to deal with a mother of the bride who was shocked—*shocked*—that she charged for her time. The bride had said her mother would have her payment ready, but with all the excitement, something obviously fell through the cracks, because when Abby asked for the check the woman became downright angry.

"You're charging us?" The bride's mother's hands had flown to her heart. "You can stay for the reception. It's open bar."

Party with a room full of drunken old men where she knew absolutely no one? Tempting.

"We have a contract," Abby reminded her.

"We'll feed you," the woman said earnestly. "I..." She glanced past her vaguely. "Rex! So good to see you."

Oh, good, the guests were starting to arrive.

Which was when Abby spotted the florist and chased her down. The florist would know who was in charge. She hoped. Because free food wasn't going to pay the rent.

Penelope folded another napkin and jiggled the table assessingly. "I never imagined you playing weddings. Isn't that...I don't know...beneath you?"

As opposed to not performing at all? If she had a normal job she'd come home from work and be too tired to play, and before she knew it she'd end up like Penelope, playing just once in a rare while, letting part of herself slip away. Instead she had the chance to make music her life. "I like weddings."

"But you were so good."

"Now I'm even better."

"You know what I mean. You could have played in an orchestra. Don't you feel like you're selling out? Weddings are so cheesy."

Abby tried not to be annoyed. "Didn't you just ask me to play at your wedding?"

Penelope closed her lips over her straw and looked up at her from beneath her lashes like an oversized kid trying to look cute in exchange for forgiveness. "I thought it would be like our old band getting back together, one last jam, having fun. I didn't know you did it professionally. If I'd known you play weddings every weekend I wouldn't have asked you. I don't want you to feel like it's work."

"It's okay, Pentachord. I want to do it." Penelope looked like she could use another milkshake, extra buzz, and Abby didn't want her to stress. "It'll be fun. Promise."

Penelope got a dreamy smile on her face that meant she was thinking of Natalie. That was good. Weddings were supposed to make you look dreamy. They weren't supposed to be about arguing with your old college friends.

"So…" Abby said. "Back to the question of what music to use for the processional."

"I have a friend who used Pachelbel's Canon in D at her wedding. That was nice," Penelope suggested.

Abby groaned. "Anything but that."

"You said anything but the Wedding March."

"I lied."

"Seriously, Abby. Maybe I should ask Ramona to play the drums. I bet she could do the Wedding March *and* Pachelbel's Canon," Penelope threatened. "Because I *like* them." Ramona was their fourth bandmate. She was coming to the wedding too, and was going to be part of the mini-comeback concert Penelope and Nat wanted to have after the traditional first dance.

"I can play Pachelbel," Abby said. "And the Wedding March." She would never argue with a regular client like this, so why was she doing this to Penelope? She loved getting the opportunity to play other music, but even when she didn't, no matter how many weddings she played, no matter how many times she rehearsed and performed the same old tunes, making music and creating a romantic atmosphere was always fun. "I'm sorry, it's your wedding. I'll play whatever you want."

Penelope let out a tired sigh. "What's so bad about the Wedding March?"

"No, it's your wedding. You choose."

"No, I want to hear this. I want to know why you care so much."

"Okay," Abby said, shrugging. "When you and Nat decided to get married, who proposed?"

"I did. I knew I wanted her, and—"

Abby interrupted her before they got sidetracked. She'd already heard the sappy details once and she'd love to hear them again—later. "You're a woman, and you had the nerve to propose?" She shifted in her seat, pretending to switch who was speaking. "That's right," she answered herself. "Because there was no man." Abby pointed at Penelope with her straw. "Not very traditional."

Penelope bit her lip and didn't respond right away. When she did, she spoke thoughtfully, weighing each word. "You know how in college, everyone said being gay was no big deal? I was so used to being out that it was kind of a shock when I got out in the real world and not everyone was okay with it, you know? And I want to prove to them that we're normal too. I want to prove that we can get married, and have the big, traditional wedding with the patriarchal walk down the aisle and the music everyone's heard a million times and the white cake that's chocolate inside because nobody really likes white cake. I want to be part of that. I want to be part of something bigger than me, part of the community, part of something that other people understand." She tossed back the dregs of her milkshake, holding the straw out of the way so she didn't get foam on her face. "When you take the plunge you'll probably hire a pagan priestess who'll offer an ancient Minoan blessing and you'll have the guests join you in a drumming circle followed by Gregorian chant, and I admire you for doing your own thing, but that's not me."

"Don't forget the woodland fairy princess costumes," Abby said lightly. She had no idea Penelope felt that way. It had been so long since they'd spent time together, and Penelope was right, life changed you, made you care about things you didn't know you were going to care about back when you were twenty years old. "I'd be honored to play the Wedding March."

"You won't regret this."

No, she wouldn't regret making Penelope happy. She could play the tune in her sleep, so what was three more minutes of her life? Being a professional meant performing the same music over and over again every weekend and finding something new to love about it each time. It would be fine. Penelope and Nat would be happy with their music, Abby would be happy being part of their celebration, and no one would know the selection had ever been in question. And when the day came that a bride requested a Paraguayan folk tune, she'd be ready.

CHAPTER FIVE

Gwynne dropped a butterscotch into her coffee and slumped behind Sea Salt's appointment desk, wondering for the umpteenth time how all her old clients and everyone they'd ever met seemed to know where she worked.

Her latest visitor approached her desk walking gingerly on the balls of her feet and favoring one leg.

"Are you Gwynne Abernathy?"

Could she get away with saying no? Except it wouldn't work, because she was already nodding yes.

"My friend Donetta told me I had to find you. Can you help me? The bottom of my heel hurts so bad it hurts to walk. It hurts to stand, even. The first doctor said it was tendinitis, and now the second doctor says it's a heel spur, except I have a spur on the other heel too, and that one doesn't hurt, so…"

"It could be a heel spur," Gwynne said. "But you need to see a massage therapist first before anyone talks you into surgery." The aura around not only the foot, but the entire leg, was an angry, irritated red, making her suspect there was more going on than a bone growth—a spur—on the heel. She scanned the room to make sure the other clients were waiting comfortably before coming out from behind her desk—getting sidetracked only briefly to rest her gaze on Abby at her harp. Turning people away hadn't stopped them from seeking her out. Maybe checking out their problem and *then* turning them away would be more effective. Maybe then they'd believe she couldn't help. "Have a seat on the sofa for a second and I'll take a look."

She touched the woman's foot, then her lower leg.

"It's my heel, not my leg."

Gwynne replied by pressing deeply into the calf muscle. The woman gasped and gritted her teeth. Yeah, thought so. People assumed heel pain meant the problem was in the heel, but more often than not, it stemmed from somewhere else.

"When you're driving, do you have trouble working the gas pedal?"

"You can tell that?"

"You have trigger points in your calf. Why don't I schedule an appointment for you with Megan McLaren? She'll be able to fix this."

"Donetta told me to ask for you."

"I'm not seeing clients right now." No matter how many times she said that, she just couldn't seem to escape her reputation. She cradled the woman's foot and ran a current of healing energy from her heart, through her fingers, and into the contracted muscle fibers, releasing the tension.

"No walking in the sand until this gets better," Gwynne told her.

"Is that what did it? I figured it was my high heels."

"That too. See Megan for a massage. And all these spots that hurt, work on them two or three times a day, and your heel should feel better soon."

"Can I come back in a few days so you can check that I'm doing it right?"

"Megan will check for you," Gwynne said.

"But—"

"Megan's good too," piped up Dara Sullivan, a client of Megan's and a massage therapist herself, from the sofa where she sat waiting for her appointment. "Her work is very similar to what Gwynne does."

"Used to do," Gwynne corrected.

"I can't believe you quit," Dara said. "You were amazing."

"But you like Megan too?" the woman who was *not* her client asked hesitantly.

Dara flashed an I'm-in-love-with-the-world-and-I'm-going-to-sell-you-on-massage-therapy smile. "Megan's awesome." She looked at Gwynne and her smile disappeared. "Not as awesome as Gwynne, of course. Her ability to manipulate energy fields is…I don't think anyone can do what she does."

I couldn't save my mother's life. Gwynne's stomach turned to granite, heavy and useless. Why she'd thought quitting her job would magically make everyone stop talking to her about auras and angels and all that happy horse poop, she didn't know.

"You're not helping." She needed to pull Dara aside later and ask her not to say stuff like that in front of the customers. "Megan is seeing my clients, and Megan is wonderful."

"Doesn't mean you're not wonderful," Dara retorted.

"Megan has a more compassionate presence. When she gives a massage, love radiates from her whole being. Me, on the other hand…I'm just a jerk with a skill."

"You need psychological help." Dara snapped open one of the random magazines that were lying around for the guests and vigorously flipped through it.

Megan emerged from the treatment room where she'd been finishing up with a client and looked straight at Gwynne, who was still on the sofa cradling the visitor's foot. "Gwynne. I thought you quit."

"I did." She sent a final burst of energy into the leg to integrate the healing.

The woman tried to sit up, but sitting up made her hold her hands to her head and fall back to the sofa. She'd be fine in a few minutes. Or ten. Or twenty. People always got dizzy when she channeled energy into them. She didn't have Megan's gift for gentle, beautiful healings.

Megan waggled her fingers like she was pretending to cast a spell. "That's what you call quitting? I could sense that healing from behind my door."

Gwynne stomped back to her desk. "Dara's your next appointment."

"Dara!" Megan said, mercifully letting it go. "Hope I didn't keep you waiting."

Dara slapped her magazine shut. "Could you please tell Gwynne she's not the big, bad jerk she seems to think she is? That people really do think it's worth it to be slammed around by her terrible, damnable energy? Because it works?"

"Dara…" Gwynne had known Dara a long time, and familiarity had not bred contempt. More like idolization. Besides massage, Dara was branching out into Reiki, a popular form of off-the-body energy healing, and she was always trying to improve her energy skills—especially now that her hands were in chronic pain and she needed a new career direction. She had made it clear that she would love nothing better than for Gwynne to teach her a few tricks, but Gwynne refused, even though she got tired of turning her down. Because honestly, saying no was doing her a favor.

"Is Gwynne beating herself up again?" Megan said, not sounding very concerned. She opened the file cabinet behind Gwynne's desk and pulled out Dara's file.

Gwynne shot her an irritated glance that Megan didn't deign to turn in her direction to notice.

"It'll pass," Megan told Dara. "Once she gets back on her feet she'll be back to having more than enough self-esteem."

"Back me up here," Dara said.

"Gwynne, you're not a jerk," Megan said dutifully. "Your channeling may not be subtle, but you're not a jerk."

"Although you are a jerk for not going out with me," Dara said. "If you ever change your mind about that, let me know."

Oh, yeah, let's not forget Dara also wanted a doomed sexual relationship with her. She'd feel worse about that if Dara wasn't already drowning her sorrows in the dating pool with someone else.

Megan slid the file cabinet shut. "You're not a jerk, Gwynne. You did Kira a huge favor by taking this spa manager job. If you were a jerk, you'd never have done something so generous."

"I needed a job," Gwynne grumbled.

"You could have looked for something else," Megan pointed out. "I think you wanted to help out."

"Believe what you like." She poured Megan a glass of Kira's latest concoction. "Ginger iced tea?"

"Thanks."

"It's got a kick," Gwynne warned. "Did you watch Kira make this? Because this is not just ginger, lemon and honey."

"Cayenne pepper," Megan said absently, taking small sips as she read over Dara's file.

"Right. Sure. Of course. That's what I was going to say." Gwynne put the pitcher away in the mini-fridge beside her desk. "It's not like ginger doesn't have enough kick on its own." Perhaps Kira could have informed her of the ingredients before foisting it on her customers.

A client came through the arched entryway and Megan slipped silently away like the professional she was, taking Dara with her. Gwynne switched on her customer service smile. She checked in the new client and then the one she'd just zapped returned to the desk and said, "I also have this pain in my throat when I swallow."

"Your throat hurts too?" Why hadn't she picked up on that?

She sank her focus into the throat's energy pathways, looking for patterns, cursing her instinctive need to check it out. She did *not* need to feed the rumor mill with more stories about her supposedly amazing abilities. At least Megan and Dara were on their way to Megan's treatment room and weren't watching, poised to accuse her of not being a jerk.

The truth about the client's pain floated effortlessly to the top of her awareness. "A medication is causing this. Something you're taking is burning your esophagus. What are you taking?"

"It's called…it's called…I forget."

"Do you know what it's for?"

"Uh…"

Gwynne sent a glow of healing energy into the woman's throat to soothe the inflamed tissues. "It's good that you're conscientious and want to protect your health, but try not to go overboard, okay?" Because it wasn't just the doctors, it was the patients, too, who ignored the risk of side effects and insisted on medical intervention instead of leaving well enough alone.

Yeah, like she was one to talk. Intervention should be her middle name. She closed her eyes and took a deep breath. Not *should be*. Used to be. No more trying to play God.

"Go back to your doctor," Gwynne said. "She can fix this."

"You did something to me, didn't you? My throat feels better already." She swayed and caught her balance by grabbing the edge of the desk. "I think I need to sit down. I feel dizzy again."

"Sorry, I should have warned you about that."

The client collapsed into the nearest chair. "What did you do?"

"Nothing, really. Can I get you a glass of ginger iced tea? You heard it has cayenne pepper, right?"

"Thanks."

When her dizziness passed, the woman left—limping much less—and then it was just her and Abby, who had said nothing the entire time and stayed busy playing her quiet background music, fingers flashing over the strings, seemingly incapable of hitting a wrong note.

Abby finished her tune and looked up from her harp. "Why don't you want to go out with Dara? She seems to like you."

Not the question she was expecting. At least she didn't ask how she'd made that woman's pain go away. She hadn't even been touching her when she eased the pain in her throat, and that kind of thing tended to make people assume there were no limits to her magic. Gwynne picked at a stray rabbit hair stuck to her sleeve. "Dara's still mad at me for something I did a long time ago."

"She's mad at you for turning her down?"

"How do you know that's what happened?" Gwynne countered.

"Please. I heard what she said." Abby rested her cheek against her harp and gazed at her expectantly like she was settling in to hear the whole story.

She had the most wonderful smile hiding behind all those freckles. Or maybe it was just nice for a change to see someone who wasn't in pain. Someone who didn't expect her to work miracles.

"She doesn't want me," Gwynne said. "She wants my healing skills. That's all she sees."

A hint of concern crept into Abby's eyes.

She didn't want her pity, for God's sake. She didn't *want* Dara to want her. Dara deserved someone who would appreciate her adoration.

"I'm not attracted to her. If we both pretend it's about my healing abilities, we can both save face."

"Hmm." Abby flipped through her sheet music. She seemed to sense this wasn't a conversation Gwynne wanted to have, and she was right.

"And she's dating someone!" Friends were always teasing them that one day she and Dara were going to give in to the inevitable, and the fact that Dara actually did have feelings for her—and that the attraction was completely one-sided—made those comments uncomfortable for both of them. Because if Dara felt anything for her at all, it had to hurt to be reminded.

Abby didn't ask for more details, but Gwynne volunteered them anyway. "I've never hidden my healing abilities, so anyone who goes out with me ends up either idolizing me or deciding I'm too weird for them. Except for Megan, but she and I were never going to work out because Megan—even though I love her dearly—takes everything way, way too seriously."

Abby stopped flipping through her music. "Kira's Megan?"

"I guess it's been so long, nobody cares anymore so they don't gossip about it. Or they've forgotten."

"And now you're friends," Abby said. "That's impressive."

"It's not that hard to do when neither one of you secretly has the hots for the other."

"Or hates each other," Abby pointed out.

"Megan's too nice to hate anyone."

"What about you?"

"Do we have to talk about me?"

"Maybe you're too nice to hate anyone, either."

"I wouldn't go that far." Gwynne leaned back in her chair.

"So you're saying you're a jerk, if I heard you correctly when you were arguing with Dara, but it seems to me you're not a jerk, because you don't hate Megan, except that's only because she's too nice?"

"I feel like I need to say something mean now to make you stop." How had Abby heard all that, anyway? Wasn't she focusing on her music? She must be good enough that the playing didn't take all her concentration.

"Let me know when you think of something." Abby turned to her harp and ran her index finger up the strings, creating a waterfall of sound that led into an enchanting, complicated melody that put an end to their conversation.

The tension in Gwynne's neck eased. The days that Abby worked at the spa had quickly become her favorite. Even full of clients, the lounge felt empty without her—without her cheerful presence and her bizarrely attractive fairy-tale dresses and her music. Her mood lifted whenever Abby showed up for work, and she was starting to wonder if that was because the harp generated a healing vibrational frequency—she could feel the air molecules pulsate—or whether it was due to Abby herself.

Gwynne closed her eyes and imagined the music seeping into her body, into every cell, making her feel alive, waking up the dead, numb places she hadn't felt in a long, long time. Was she kidding herself to think that someone else playing the same notes with the same perfection wouldn't make her feel quite the same? This wasn't the glow of music appreciation, this buzz that made everything more beautiful when Abby was around. This was something deeper.

Abby played on and on and on, until eventually, as the last note hung in the air, her hands floated to the wooden body of her harp and she hugged it to her chest.

"You're an amazing harpist," Gwynne said.

"Harper," Abby corrected with a quirky smile that was part apology, part sass. "Harpists play the pedal harp. You know, the kind you see in an orchestra. When you play the lever harp you're a harper. It sounds more Celtic-y."

"You're kidding. People really make the distinction?"

"Says the woman who calls herself an energy healer instead of a faith healer."

Gwynne quirked her brow. "You noticed that, huh?" Abby must have been paying attention when she talked to her former clients. She didn't remember the exact conversation Abby might have overheard, but it was true the faith healer label was one she was constantly trying to shake. She hated it when people put her up on the faith pedestal, like she had some special connection to God. Especially now. "Point taken."

"Every profession has its lingo," Abby acknowledged. "Gotta keep the riffraff in its place."

Okay, that was so not her reasoning, but if it was Abby's… "Maybe you shouldn't have told me about the harper thing. I don't want you to get in trouble with the other musicians."

"I'll take my chances." Abby's pale blue-gray eyes flashed with amusement.

Her eyes were…She'd never noticed before how compelling they were, how they sparkled like ancient starlight, a glint of something beautiful in the vast darkness.

Gwynne regrouped before she got lost in those eyes. "I didn't realize your harp was a different type. Although I did notice you don't have a Grecian column with all the sparkly, sparkly gold leaf." She'd never paid much attention to harps, but that was her memory of them.

"Not a fan of gold leaf?"

Not a fan of sparkly, Gwynne almost said, except everything about Abby was sparkly, lit up by her bright aura. Sparkly looked good on her.

"Watch." Abby plucked a string on her harp and then flipped one of the little metal levers near the top where the strings were attached. She plucked it again, and the note had changed. "Pedal harps do the same thing with pedals instead of sharping levers." She flipped more levers, her left hand flying across the instrument, and then began to play, her tapered fingers alternately curling into her palm and extending to pluck the strings with lightning-fast precision.

It was beautiful. As beautiful to watch as to listen to.

"You don't have to play when no one's here," Gwynne said. There was something about the look of crazy joy on Abby's face when she made music that reminded her of her mother, and she wasn't sure she wanted to be reminded. Her sister had had that same look when she was little, when she was playing tag and racing on her little-girl legs as fast as she could go. She didn't want to be reminded of that, either.

"There isn't no one here. You're here," Abby said. "I'll play something you can sing along with if you want."

"Trust me, your harp sounds a lot better without me." She smiled ruefully at the harpist…uh, harper. "But you can feel free."

"I don't sing."

"You too, huh? Never?"

"Not in public," Abby conceded. "I don't want you to run screaming from the room—you might not come back."

"My mother sang," Gwynne said, despite herself, embarrassed by the hint of wistfulness she was sure Abby could hear in her voice. "She would have loved to hear you play."

"What kind of songs did she like?" Abby asked, picking up on Gwynne's use of the past tense—if someone hadn't already told her what happened. "I'll play something for her. For you," she corrected herself. "For her memory."

"She sang opera. She studied voice when she was young."

"Opera. Okay. Wow. What do I know that would be…Oh! I know. How about *Lascia ch'io pianga*?"

"I don't know the titles, but…sure, okay. Maybe I'll recognize it. I mean, she could sing anything."

She sang along with the radio when she drove Gwynne and her friends to T-ball and later softball practice, singing the wrong words, making her die of embarrassment. She sang when she made dinner, belting out the recipe. She woke her for school by singing historical dates because she thought it would help, and the funny thing was, it did. Gwynne aced her tests because she'd hear her mother's ear-splitting opera voice in her head singing battle trivia. Come to think of it, she should have asked her for help in massage school when she struggled to memorize all those muscle attachments, but it never occurred to her. Her mother's singing had been an embarrassment. It was only now that she could admit to herself that her mother had a beautiful voice and a sense of fun Gwynne was lucky enough to have known.

"Was she the one I saw you with at the hospital? I don't remember if I saw the patient, if it could have been your mother or…"

"It was," Gwynne said dully, guilt twisting like a knife in her gut, tangling with the grief. Her mother shouldn't have died that day. Not her mother, not Heather. None of it should have happened.

"I'm sorry," Abby said.

Someone had definitely told her what happened, because she didn't seem surprised, just sympathetic. Which was good. It meant she didn't have to explain. It was too soon to talk about it to someone she barely knew, someone who would listen politely and make her feel worse. Even though there was something about Abby that made her want to tell her everything.

"Do you still want me to play the aria?" Abby asked. "I won't if you don't want me to, if you don't want to be reminded right now."

"No, it'll be nice. She always sounded so happy when she sang."

Abby started to play and Gwynne was glad it wasn't anything she recognized. It meant she wouldn't lose it.

* * *

Dara was back at the spa for her weekly appointment with Megan, early as usual because, Gwynne suspected, she liked hanging out in the lounge.

"Are you still doing magic shows?" Dara asked her. "My niece is turning seven and my sister's trying to figure out what to do for her birthday party."

"Are you referring to The Great Gwynnini, Illusionist and Rabbit Conjurer?" She hadn't performed as The Great Gwynnini in ages. "Sure." Gwynne handed her a glass of Kira's latest experimental beverage, a blend of grenadine, lime and coconut water. She gave one to Abby too, who was taking a break on one of the guest sofas. "I'm a little rusty, but I can do it."

"Fantastic!"

"I'd need an assistant, though." As soon as she said the words, Gwynne almost changed her mind, because it was her sister who had always been her assistant. Doing a birthday party magic show without her was going to be hard, emotionally.

"I'll be your lovely assistant," Dara said.

"You'll be busy with your niece," Abby interjected. "I'll be Gwynne's assistant."

Was that jealousy in Abby's voice? Hard to tell. Gwynne kind of wanted it to be, and that made it hard to be an accurate judge of what, exactly, Abby might be feeling. No, stop, she didn't need this right now. She didn't want to be interested in anyone romantically. There was no jealousy in Abby's voice. She was offering to help, nothing more. Gwynne was reading something into it that wasn't there.

"I always wanted to wear a top hat," Abby said. "Do I get to wear a top hat?"

"If you want to."

See? Maybe Abby was a fan of magic shows. Nothing to do with Gwynne at all.

"I can wear a top hat," Dara said.

"Wouldn't you rather spend the afternoon focusing on the kids?" Abby rose from the sofa and moved to a chair closer to

Gwynne, which to Gwynne's overactive imagination felt like she was staking a claim on her.

"Yeah, but…" Dara trailed off, looking conflicted.

"It's up to you," Abby said graciously, blowing Gwynne's theory. "Or we could flip for it."

"I guess I would rather sit with the girls," Dara decided.

"Great," Abby said. "I really want to do this."

"Why?" Dara asked.

Good question. Gwynne was interested to know the answer to that herself. Was Abby attempting to protect her from having to spend time alone with Dara? Because the alternative explanation would be that Abby was fighting Dara over her. Politely, subtly, so subtly as to border on imperceptibility, but nevertheless…

"You don't know what you're getting yourself into," Gwynne said, because if Abby thought a relationship with her was a good idea, she was not as smart as she looked.

Abby draped one arm over the back of the chair and swiveled to face her. Her eyes sparkled with curiosity. "You're not going to saw me in half or anything, are you?"

And if she was really smart and could read her mind, she'd just made a deliberate choice to misunderstand her.

"Not in front of little girls, no."

She was losing it if she thought Abby could read her mind.

"From what I hear, it's more of a live animal show," Dara said.

"Just rabbits," Gwynne clarified.

Abby's eyes widened, still twinkling. "So you're saying I just volunteered for rabbit poop cleanup duty?"

"They're litter trained," Gwynne said. "And I will clean up."

"So chivalrous," Dara murmured.

Gwynne shrugged it off. "Your job is mostly to distract the audience," she told Abby, as businesslike as possible. Her heart, though, was singing. "We can go over it the morning of the party."

"No rehearsal?" Abby said.

"You'll do fine." It would be easy to insist on days and days of rehearsal just for a chance to be alone with her, but the show didn't need days of rehearsal. Based on listening to her play the harp she knew Abby was comfortable improvising, so it was a good bet she wouldn't need much of a run-through. "If we mess up, we wing it."

She turned to Dara and winked, hoping Dara wasn't worried the party would be a disaster. "Don't tell Dara I said that."

CHAPTER SIX

Gwynne arrived early at Abby's apartment Saturday afternoon to help her lug her harp to the beach wedding of someone named Penelope. Abby had said if she wasn't dealing with sand she'd roll her harp on a hand truck, but in this case, she was going to have to hoist her instrument across the beach to the mini-platform that would be set up for her. Gwynne had volunteered to help because…uh…why *did* she volunteer? It just kind of happened. Well, why not? Nothing wrong with being helpful. There was also a stool and an amp to carry, but the main thing was the harp, which was apparently not the small one she used at the hospital nor the large one she played at the spa, but an even bigger, better one. "You have three harps?" she'd asked, and Abby had laughed and said, "Come to my apartment and I'll show you."

As soon as Gwynne walked through Abby's front door, she understood. There were at least a dozen harps spread around the room, with several folding chairs and music stands littered among them, leaving no room for the overstuffed sofa which had been relegated to the corner.

"I used to have a room called a living room," Abby said, smoothing the hem of a thigh-skimming crocheted sweater over her jeans and gesturing for her to come in. She laughed, seemingly not the least bit embarrassed to laugh at her own joke, and harp strings all around the room responded, resonating with her voice and filling the air with a burst of unexpected sound. For that one magical moment they sang on their own, without being touched, as if they were real, live beings.

"You have quite a collection." Gwynne picked her way through the room, careful not to bump into anything. "I had no idea."

"I know it's a lot, but I figure when you really love something, it's worth going overboard."

"They're beautiful." The harps were all different sizes and made of different types of wood. Some were decorated with intricate carvings or mother-of-pearl inlay; others were unadorned, elegant in their simplicity.

"This monster is the one we're dragging to the beach." Abby ran her hand lovingly over the gleaming cherry and maple. It was not dramatically bigger than the harp she played at the spa, maybe between five and six feet tall, but it had a lot more decoration. Nearly every surface was covered in swirling Celtic knots accented with—aack—gold leaf. And the most striking thing about the harp was the carved dragon that emerged from the wood like a gargoyle, clutching the pillar at the front.

"I have never seen a harp like that." She'd never even imagined a harp like that. It should have been the first thing she noticed when she walked in the room. She ran her hand over the dragon's scales. The workmanship was amazingly detailed. "Where did you find this?"

"I met the luthier at a summer music festival." Abby patted the dragon on the head. "Do you want to get going or can I introduce you to the others?"

"We have lots of time." Anything Abby wanted to do was fine with her. It wasn't like the wedding would start without the harpist…er, harper…what the heck, without the musician… and anyway, they really did have plenty of time. She had made a point of being early.

Abby turned to the harp closest to the door. "This is the one I use at the spa, of course. It has gorgeous resonance, which is perfect for meditative music, although the sound can get muddy when I play fast." She ran her index finger up the strings and a blur of notes filled the air. "The one I'm playing tonight has a tighter feel."

She went from harp to harp, pointing out differences in tone that Gwynne didn't have the ear to appreciate, never mentioning anything she didn't like about any particular harp. Despite the sheer number of harps she owned, it was clear she loved each one.

"Listen to this one." Abby sat on a folding chair and rested a diminutive harp between her thighs. She played a lullaby that rung like crystal raindrops, clear and high-pitched. "It's fun, even though it's only twelve strings, which is useless. You can't get any low notes when the strings are so short." Reluctantly she set the harp on the floor and gazed at it longingly. "I rescued it from a client's neighbor's basement. Stringed instruments lose their tone if you abandon and ignore them. But the richness is starting to come back." She reached down and plucked a few more notes. "I should get my stuff together so we can go."

"No rush," Gwynne said. She could listen to her play all day.

"I don't want to be late. What time is it?" Abby checked her watch. "Oh, we have plenty of time. I could give you a tour of the rest of the apartment, if you want."

She'd rather listen to her play, but she supposed she could do that at work. Resigned, she followed dutifully through the kitchen, the bathroom, and to the door of the one room she most didn't need to see: the bedroom. While Abby waltzed in, Gwynne hesitated in the doorway. A polite glance revealed a sewing machine on a desk, a bed she averted her eyes from, and a wall lined with a series of framed charcoal drawings of angels.

"You collect angels," she observed neutrally. Lots of people collected angels, she reminded herself. It didn't mean anything.

"I know, a harper who collects angels. What a surprise, right?"

Gwynne didn't want to enter any farther into the room, but she also didn't want Abby to think she was uncomfortable coming in. She could act cool. It wasn't like she'd never been in a woman's bedroom before. She strolled over to the drawings to examine them more closely. The angels were all gossamer, their shapes suggested by a few areas of shading and smudged lines that made them disappear into the paper, barely there. They were simple, but they radiated raw emotion: Wistfulness. Compassion. Pure joy.

"Did you draw these?"

"Yeah. I took an art class in college. All except for that one on the other wall—my friend Penelope drew that one for me. She's a lot better than I am."

"No, you're good. You really captured that feeling of unreality about them, the way you can see right through them."

Abby was looking at her funny. Why would she look at her like…She knew Gwynne could see angels, right? Anyone who spent more than an hour with her at the spa would have picked up on that popular piece of gossip.

"You're not even looking," Abby said.

"At what?"

"At Penelope's drawing."

Abby swung her arm like a traffic cop in exaggerated circles and pointed at the far wall to another framed drawing, this one done in black ink. The angel had tattered butterfly wings and wore demon-kicking thigh-high boots with lots of buckles drawn in painstaking detail. More fairy than angel, to be honest. Her wings partially obscured her torso while simultaneously making it quite clear she was otherwise nude.

"She's good," Gwynne admitted despite herself. "Your friend's got quite the imagination."

"She said my angels didn't have big enough boobs. I think it was a joke."

"Or a come-on." If someone drew Gwynne a picture like that, she'd definitely read into it. "Were you dating?"

"We were just friends."

"Are you sure?"

"Yes, I'm sure. It's not like I have so many ex-girlfriends I'd get confused and not remember sleeping with her."

"I have a hard time believing you don't have women falling all over you all the time."

Abby's face twitched as if she didn't know what to make of her compliment. And who could blame her? It was the type of charming, insincere comment that anyone who detected that note of bitter bewilderment in Abby's voice would feel compelled to make. But Gwynne wasn't insincere—she meant it. There was something irresistible about the way Abby's freckled, heart-shaped face glowed with innocence. Something desirable about the faint crinkles at the corners of her eyes. Why hadn't she dated more? Or had Gwynne simply misunderstood her comment?

"Believe it." Dismissing further debate, Abby walked to her closet and pulled out her performance dress and hung it on the back of the closet door. The dress had a navy blue satin lining with a gauzy lavender see-through overlay and navy sequins. Gwynne would not be caught dead wearing sequins, but she was positive Abby could pull it off.

Abby hunted through a chest of drawers, rummaging through a jumble of bras, underpants and tights. "If you were my navy blue bra, where would you be?"

Oh, dear God, she was definitely not answering that. *If I were your bra…*She attempted to search the room so Abby wouldn't look at her face and see the whole list of inappropriate answers that crowded her brain.

"I thought musicians wore black," she said stupidly. This wasn't an orchestra gig and she'd never seen Abby wear black.

Abby tucked her hair behind her ear. "Black is boring. When I perform, I put on a show."

She didn't need to. People didn't hire her because her dress was nice or because her harp looked like a dragon. They hired her because her skill was breathtaking and her music sang to the vulnerable places in her audience's hearts.

"Besides," Abby said, "that way if somebody hates my music, and they come up to me after the performance because their date dragged them along and they're smiling nervously, trying to think of something to say while their date is going on and on about how great I was, they can always say *I love your dress*."

"A pity gesture for your non-fans? That's sad." And Gwynne didn't believe it for a minute. "What if they don't love your dress?"

"What, you don't love my dress? Everyone loves this dress." Abby arranged the gown against the closet door to admire it. "If not, they're welcome to lie."

"Then I definitely love your dress." She didn't have much of an opinion either way. Pretty? Yes. Over-the-top? Also a yes. Lust-worthy? Not unless Abby was the one wearing it.

Abby fanned the skirt of her gown and fingered the hem. "It took forever to sew, but I love this old-fashioned glamour."

"You made that yourself?" Gwynne didn't sew, but it was obvious, even to her, that this was not a beginner's project.

"I spend all my money collecting harps. I don't have any left over for costumes."

"I have to say the dress looks amazingly intricate." It was the polite thing to say, and it was true too.

"And sexy?"

"Um…sure."

"I know I said you were welcome to lie, but…you don't have to lie. I'm aware that this dress scares women off." Abby let the fabric slip through her fingers. "No one ever says *You look hot in that dress, can I ask you out?* Because women who date women would rather date someone who doesn't wear sequins."

"Then you haven't found the right woman." One who would be insane to care about her sequins when she could be looking at the way her hair fell across her face while she leaned over her harp, or the way she lit up when she smiled.

"I want to date someone I can talk to, and most women are…I don't want to say aliens, but…okay, aliens. I don't get them. I know I'm supposed to understand how women think, but I don't. I don't get how they think." She kicked at a pile of laundry beside the closet and brightened. "I knew I'd find it!" She fished out her missing bra and dangled it overhead like she was waiting for applause.

Gwynne tried not to choke. Abby was so right—she did *not* understand how women think. A bra at Macy's was an innocent item of clothing, but a bra in the hand of a woman you found attractive was a health hazard.

"Good thing that's a pile of clean laundry," Abby said, directing her comment to her lingerie.

Gwynne crawled onto the bed because, one, there wasn't anywhere much else to be with all the clothes strewn across the floor, which was something she couldn't get away with in a house full of nibbling rabbits, and, two, if Abby was going to act like she was straight and it was safe to wave her bra around, then Gwynne was going to remind her what she was dealing with. She leaned back on the daisy-patterned quilt and made herself comfortable, daring her to acknowledge that bringing her into her bedroom wasn't one hundred percent safe.

Abby hung her bra on the hook on the back of her closet door with her dress and ignored her. Gwynne stretched out her legs, letting her feet hang off the end of the bed so her shoes didn't touch the quilt. What did they call this size bed? A full? Smaller than a queen-size, anyway. Whatever it was called, she didn't understand how Abby could sleep with anyone in such a narrow bed. They'd have to lie on top of each other to fit.

Maybe that was the idea.

Her legs heated and abruptly she swung up to a seated position, her feet connecting with the floor. "You'll find someone." Maybe sooner than she thought, if they were both lucky. "Somewhere out there, there's got to be a non-alien life-form who gets you."

Abby shook her head and smiled. "When you put it that way…"

"It sounds too good to be true, right?"

"It sounds like an alien plot, is what it sounds like."

"Are you suggesting *I*…"

Abby positioned her hands on either side of her head and pointed her fingers like dancing antennae. Gwynne mirrored her, adding beeping space creature sounds.

"Another alien! I should have known." Abby crooked her antennae fingers in excited but unintelligible alien sign language.

"Plan B—you try kissing a space alien to see if she'll turn into a princess," Gwynne joked.

Abby's antennae fingers slowed, one awkward pointing move at a time, then stopped. "I believe that's supposed to be a frog."

Oh, crap. She'd gone too far. "How about—" Gwynne cringed at herself, but she couldn't stop. "—an alien frog?"

"An alien frog." Abby sounded dubious.

"A *cute* alien frog?"

Abby frowned. "I gave up alien frogs for Lent."

"Too many princesses following you around?"

"Too many frogs."

All goofiness abandoned, Abby knelt beside the bed and twisted her body to look underneath the bed skirt. Her toes bumped into Gwynne's shoe which, despite the frog comment, caused another spike in her blood pressure. Gwynne snatched her feet out of the way.

"You don't need to move," Abby said with her head halfway under the bed as she dragged out shoes and flung them behind her like a cat scattering kitty litter.

Gwynne balanced on her tailbone, her feet hovering an inch above the bed. "Do you want me to start taking stuff to the van? The dress?"

"No, thanks." Abby straightened and surveyed her choices with a critical eye. She picked out a pair of plum-colored strappy heels and pushed the rest of the mess in a jumble back under the bed. "I'm going to change into my dress before we go."

She was? Like, right now? Gwynne lowered her feet to the floor and ran her palms along the stitched seams of the quilt. This was what she got for being prompt. No, not prompt. Early. She'd made a point to be early because it was either that or be late, because she wasn't good with clocks. She'd always figured life went more smoothly for responsible people who showed up on time, but it seemed she'd been gravely mistaken. Because if she'd been late, Abby would already be dressed. Instead, Gwynne was going to wait in the other room and hope a certain frog-hater couldn't sense her imagination was running rampant.

"Where did you think I was going to change?" Abby said. "On the beach?"

So she'd forgotten that tiny detail, what with all the bra waving. Bras always distracted her.

"Guess the sandy public restrooms aren't going to cut it," she acknowledged. "I'll get out of here."

"Stay. I'll just be a minute." Abby had turned her back to her and was already pulling off her crocheted sweater.

Gwynne jumped off the bed and tripped over a belt and a dirty sock in her haste to face away from her. She should leave. Abby had told her to stay, but…she should leave. She spotted a gold circlet lying on top of a pile of hair accessories on top of the dresser and fumbled for it to give herself something to do so she wasn't standing there, motionless, like an idiot. Abby should have kicked her out. She shouldn't just pull off her clothes like there was no attraction between them. Either Abby was oblivious, which she doubted, or she was pushing her. Or she was oblivious. Gwynne's thoughts circled dizzyingly. She had to be oblivious.

She turned the circlet in her hands, studiously keeping her eyes away from the mirror above the dresser so she wouldn't see Abby's hands go to the button of her jeans. Too bad she couldn't cover her ears too, because hearing her step out of her clothes was almost as unnerving as she imagined watching her would be.

Fabric rustled, making her imagine the satin skirt brushing against Abby's legs. She glanced in the mirror. She couldn't help it. Abby was contorting her arms behind her, struggling with the mile-long zipper down the back of her dress, muttering about having gained weight. She wiggled and hopped and sucked in her stomach, but the zipper went nowhere.

The dress looked completely different now that it was on her body. The wisps of color looked great against her skin tone. And because Gwynne could see her aura, she could appreciate how the dress complemented the full spectrum of her personal coloring to dazzling effect. And the wiggling—the wiggling was hard to look away from.

"How does this tiara thing stay on your head?" Gwynne asked, her voice gruff.

Abby looked over her shoulder and steadily met her gaze in the mirror. "Bobby pins." The *Duh, what else would I use?* went unspoken. "You didn't have a very girly childhood, did you?"

"No bobby pins, or, obviously, tiaras, but I did go through a fairy princess phase."

Abby's eyes twinkled. "Hard to believe."

"Yeah, I know. All that frog-kissing talk gave me away." She might not have been girly, but fairies and magic had fit right in with her real-life angel friends. And who was wearing the fairy princess dress right now? "I'm sure you had princess fever worse than I ever did."

"Oh, yeah. There was hot pink crapola all over the house."

"And Barbie dolls?"

"You think I'm going to admit to that too?"

"I'll admit to it," Gwynne said. "What I can't figure out is why I wanted to undress them so much." She'd developed early, what could she say.

Abby gave up on her dress and dropped her arms to her sides. The dress hung precariously on her shoulders, the back gaping open, just waiting to slide off. "Can't you?"

Abby was going to have to work on her outraged face. Right now it was hard to distinguish from her come-hither pout. Her voice was kind of breathy too.

"Just this inexplicable fascination, I guess."

"You are something else."

Gwynne decided no apology was necessary. "I'm not the only girl in the world who changed her dolls' outfits a lot."

"How convenient. You can help me zip up my dress."

Oh, no, not that. Abby had played right into her hands and now she really wished she had kept her mouth shut. She should have left her bedroom the minute Abby started to get changed. She was crazy to have stayed.

Gwynne replaced the circlet on the dresser with a clink. Of course she stayed. Anytime Abby was around, Gwynne stayed. It was like a compulsion, the way she needed to be near her.

"So, Gwendolyn?"

"It's Gwynne."

"No feeling me up."

"I wouldn't dream of it."

"I noticed that about you, Guinevere. You're very polite."

Abby wouldn't say that if she knew Gwynne was imagining what it would feel like to pop open her bra and slide her hands into the back of her dress and around to the front and impolitely cup her very lovely breasts.

"It's just Gwynne."

"Is that short for something?"

"No."

Abby's lips curved in a bewitching, not-so-innocent smile. "Okay, have it your way, Gwynnosaurus." She turned her back to her and swept her long hair out of the way, exposing the delicate column of her neck.

Gwynne's laugh came out hoarse and bothered. That freckle-covered neck looked quite kissable. So did the curve of her lower back, laid bare by that too-long zipper. She reached for the zipper. She could stand behind her forever, stroking the hollow of her spine and kissing the back of her neck and making her very, very late for her gig.

Why did Abby have to wear a dress? Blouses were nice. They came in a range of colors and they had the added bonus feature of buttoning in the front, making them easy to close without requiring assistance from friends. She could have worn a blouse with a long skirt instead of this handmade dress that had a tight bodice and a tricky zipper. Then Gwynne wouldn't be in this situation, fantasizing about the softness of her skin against her lips instead of already on her way out the door.

It wasn't too late to refuse to help. She could say no. But she'd seen Abby struggling with the tight closure, and refusing to help would be rude.

Rude. Sure. Talk about a rationalization.

It was clouding her judgment to stand this close to her, close enough to breathe in her lilac scent, close enough to unhook her bra. The wide expanse of her back begged to be freed. Abby stood very straight and Gwynne leaned in.

Stay away from her bra, Gwynne.

The closeness was making her crazy. Abby breathed faster, audibly, reacting to her nearness, or possibly to her very careful hand placement, one hand tugging on the zipper tab and the other holding down the fabric for counterbalance at her sacrum, a.k.a. her ass.

She got the zipper halfway up before it got stuck. Abby squeezed her shoulder blades together to help make it easier, but even so, Gwynne had to step even closer to pull the two sides together. She accidentally grazed the edge of her protruding shoulder blades. Her fingers shook.

If there was a God, Abby did not own a single blouse.

"There's a hook at the top," Abby said softly, her voice a caress.

"I know."

She pulled the zipper the rest of the way up and fit the hook together. She tucked the edge of a wayward bra strap out of sight and smoothed the neckline and reluctantly stepped back, hoping Abby couldn't hear that she too was struggling to breathe.

God, they were both a wreck, and they were going to be late to Abby's gig if they didn't get a move on.

But the next time she touched this dress, she was taking it off.

CHAPTER SEVEN

March was not the warmest time of year to hold an outdoor wedding, but Penelope had her heart set on a romantic ceremony by the sea, and off-season was the only time of year anyone could get a beach permit. Abby felt a little chilly during the ceremony, but she poured her heart into the processional music, and afterward, as the light started to fade, they moved into a heated tent where Abby was stationed near one of the space heaters and played background music while guests mingled over drinks, scouted for their place cards, and admired vases overflowing with giant poofball alliums and white snapdragons atop magenta tablecloths lashed to the table legs with white ribbon.

"You're an angel."

At the sound of the ethereal voice cutting through the babble of chatting wedding guests, Abby glanced up from her harp. An angel shimmered in front of her—an angel she didn't recognize.

"Funny." Abby continued playing.

"I'm not joking."

Abby substituted a different chord progression for the left hand. She was used to angels popping in and out, especially when she played. They usually didn't talk. Sing, yes. Converse, no.

"If you're looking for Gwynne Abernathy…" She needed to concentrate on her playing and besides, angels seemed to like Gwynne.

She spared a moment to glance up from the strings to scan the crowd and spotted her in her cute server uniform. When they'd arrived at the tent to set up her harp before the guests arrived, the frazzled caterer was having a meltdown because two of her waitstaff had failed to show up, and Gwynne had stepped in and generously offered to help and been hired on the spot. She'd dashed home in Abby's minivan to change into black slacks and a white button-down, long-sleeved shirt, and with a black vest from the caterer, she looked convincingly official. She was carrying an appetizer tray on her shoulder like a pro, and whatever the appetizer was, it appeared to be delicious, because guests were crowding around her, following her for seconds. Kind of the way angels followed her around.

"She's over there." Abby nodded in her direction and continued playing.

The angel stayed put. "I'm looking for you, Abigail."

"I'm kind of busy right now." Abby angled her head closer to her harp. Not that anyone would notice, with all the noise, that she was talking to herself. Leave it to the chatty one who knew her name, although she pronounced it oddly—*Abigay-el*, like all the biblical angels whose names ended in "el"—to have bad timing.

The angel swept a glowing wing over Abby's face, momentarily blinding her.

Unable to see, Abby transitioned seamlessly into an arpeggio, a harp-y musical effect which people always loved and which, fortunately, she could do with her eyes closed. From there she moved into a glissando, which was even easier, just gliding her finger up and down the strings to create the most basic of harp sounds. The show must go on and all that, and if this angel insisted on being rude with her wattage, she could compensate for a few minutes, cover with favorite tunes she could play by feel, and then call on Sapphire—an angel with better manners—to play bouncer and get Ms. Sunshine out of her face.

"I'm Elle," said the angel. "We need your help."

"Can we talk about this later?" She really didn't want to play blind all night, and even if the light stayed out of her eyes, this was not the best time to be having a conversation, especially with a creature no one else in the crowd could see.

The angel made another pass at her forehead, forcing Abby to squeeze her eyes shut.

"The bridge that connects the Angelic Realm to earth is breaking down, and we need your help. We need you to come home."

"I'm going home in a few hours." If she didn't get fired first for not providing music.

"Home to the Angelic Realm," the angel said.

"You're delusional," Abby said dismissively. She might see angels but she wasn't crazy.

"I'm not delusional," Elle said.

"Or maybe *I'm* delusional, to be having this conversation."

"You're not delusional, either—not in the way you think you are."

"How reassuring."

"Return to the Angelic Realm," Elle commanded. "You're an angel."

"I'm not."

The noise of the party seemed to fade away, replaced by the angel's sharp inhale. "You don't remember." Her shocked whisper hung in the air.

Abby felt a flicker of interest despite herself. *Not a good time to be having this conversation*, she reminded herself, but there was so much about her early childhood she didn't know, and her curiosity got the best of her. "Remember what?"

"It doesn't matter," Elle said firmly. Abby wasn't sure which one of them the angel was trying to convince. "We can still do this, even if you don't remember. Remembering is not a requirement."

"I'm not an angel." This was starting to get annoying. She flipped some levers to change key and switched to another tune.

"You are."

"If I really am an angel," Abby said, trying to sound reasonable, "why don't I look like one? Why don't I glow?" If she acted like she believed her, went along with this for a few minutes, maybe the crazy angel would go away and let her finish playing her set.

"You're an incarnated angel—an angel in human form."

"So…I'm human."

"You're an angel."

"But I have a human body." Abby's protest came out louder than she intended, making her cringe. It was bad enough having to state the obvious; it would be worse if one of the wedding guests overheard her having this bizarre conversation with herself. "See?" She poked at her thigh with one hand while her other hand continued the melody. "I have a physical body."

"So it would seem." Elle's low opinion of the powers of human perception was clear.

"So that makes me…what? A fallen angel?"

Elle snorted. "Oh, please. Angels don't fall. Incarnation is hazard duty. We volunteer for this."

The safe thing would be to not talk, to pretend the angel wasn't there. The safe thing would be to act normal in front of the one hundred and fifty guests who, although they did not seem to be paying any attention to her, would choose the exact wrong moment to notice she was talking to herself. Unfortunately, on any given day, *safe* moved up and down her list of priorities, and today it was not high on the list.

"So how does that happen? I materialize on the earth plane one day and no one notices I never existed before? I have human parents, you know."

Elle just hovered there, listening to her hash out the logic of it, and suddenly Abby got a sick feeling in her stomach. It was true she had been raised by two very human grandparents, but she didn't know much about her parents. Her mother, like Gwynne's, was dead, and her father was a mystery, supposedly a drug addict her grandparents had never even met.

"I did have human parents, didn't I? My father wasn't..."

"That's not how it works." Elle glanced heavenward and rubbed a hand over her glowing face as if the idea gave her a headache. Her golden light became tinged with a lurid shade of green.

Abby felt oddly relieved. Somehow the thought of an angelic father getting it on with her human mother made her just as ill as it seemed to make Elle.

"Besides," Elle said. "We only manifest as female."

"You're saying my *mother* was an angel?" That didn't make sense, either.

"Of course not. Your mother gave birth to some human DNA. You appropriated it and said thank you very much."

Abby was aghast. "What happened to the human soul who was supposed to get my body?"

"She was matched with another body, I suppose. There's plenty to choose from."

That made her feel mildly better—if it was true. "So biologically, I'm human."

"Biologically—physically—yes. Your energy field is not entirely human, though. There are telltale patterns in your aura that can be identified if a person knows what she's looking for."

Abby's fingers slowed on the strings. Evidence. What a concept. Gwynne was an energy healer. Had she noticed anything different about her? Would she tell her if she had?

"It would be a lot easier to believe you if I had any memory whatsoever of some previous angelic existence."

"When you incarnate and take on human form, your memories are suppressed and your angelic powers are blocked. It's the only way the process can work. We have to make sure you believe you're human so you can fully experience what it's like, because the better we understand the human condition, the better we can help. But now we need you to return to the Angelic Realm."

"Okay," she said, curious. A visit would certainly be interesting. She'd always wondered what Sapphire's home was like. "Do you whisk me away or what?"

"You kill yourself."

Abby fumbled her fingering. She stopped mid-tune and put her harp down oh-so-gently. Then she scooted off her stool and started backing away. "Um…That's not going to happen."

Okay, so every time a bride wanted to hire her to play at her wedding she promised she'd shoot herself if she had to play Pachelbel's Canon in D one more time, but come on. She wasn't serious. She'd shoot the bride before she shot herself.

"We need you to kill yourself so you'll revert to your true angelic form."

"How is that supposed to work?" She had no idea whether Elle could physically force her to do anything, but it seemed smart to play for time, get more information. "I get reborn as a baby angel?"

"No, you resume the form you had before you chose to be born as a human."

"Sapphire?" Abby said under her breath as she continued to back away, hoping her friend would hear her urgent mental call. "Sapphire? Are you around?" Most of the time she did show up when she wanted her.

Fortunately, this was one of those times. Sapphire appeared in her favorite form—a baseball-sized ball of light—and hovered at her shoulder. If the crazy angel posed any danger, Sapphire would protect her. Even if the crazy angel was a symptom of Abby's own psychotic break.

"This…" Abby began. This…what? Angel? Maybe Elle wasn't what she appeared to be. "This…*apparition*…says I'm an angel," she told Sapphire. "Why would she say that?"

"Because it's true," Sapphire said.

Abby choked. Now she tells her. After thirty-one years of friendship, now she decides to divulge this life-changing—or perhaps she should say life-ending—piece of news.

"And you didn't tell me?" Not that she actually believed her. It was too bizarre. And yet…part of her—the part that she kept firmly locked up, because that was what you did to the voices in your head—wanted to believe. "Why didn't you tell me?"

"You asked me not to," Sapphire said.

"When?" Abby demanded, flabbergasted.

"Before you incarnated. The point of living as a human is to believe you're human, otherwise you can't fully experience human suffering."

Exactly what Elle had said. Abby felt thrown off-balance. She'd wanted Sapphire to tell her Elle was an imposter, or simply lying. Or confused. Insane, mistaken, or talking to the wrong person. Instead, Sapphire was agreeing with her.

It had never occurred to her that Sapphire would gang up against her with another angel. She trusted Sapphire. She'd known her forever. They were friends. At least she thought they were friends.

Abby squinted into Elle's brightness. This was Elle's fault. She must be coercing Sapphire to back her up. "Who did you say you were?"

"Gabringingelle." The angel's voice vibrated like a crystal bowl sitting on a metal-strung harp, creating a cascade of exquisitely pure notes that were almost painful.

Abby tried to repeat it. "Gabr–"

The angel cut her off. "Just call me Elle. No one's ever able to pronounce it correctly."

No kidding. No human being alive could make a sound like that. "Sounds more like Gabriel than Elle," Abby said suspiciously. The patriarchal nitwits from two thousand years ago wouldn't have listened to a female angel, but angels could shape-shift, and besides, people saw what they wanted to see. "Or Gabrielle?"

"I prefer Elle," the angel said, her voice still vibrating at a humanly impossible register.

One of the wedding guests, a woman in an expensive suit and sturdy heels who seemed blissfully unaware of the angels' presence, marched right into their midst to shake Abby's hand. "You're Abby Vogel, right?"

"Yes." Abby kept a nervous eye on the two angels as they spun close overhead.

"I heard you were a hit at Candace's open house on Owl Street last Sunday. The offers she received on that home were much higher than I expected." The woman presented her business card. "I want to hire you to do some open houses for me too. Do you have any Sundays free this month? I'll pay double whatever Candace is paying."

"She sold the house already?" Abby said feebly, trying to focus on the real estate agent in front of her and not on the giant angels above her.

"It's under contract. Didn't she tell you?"

Abby shook her head.

"Word is out that you create a high-class ambience, and that's what selling a luxury vacation property is all about. I've got two listings that aren't moving as fast as I'd like, and I need you."

Amazing what people thought a musical instrument could do. "If I don't have a wedding that conflicts, I'd love to." The Christmas party circuit was well behind her for the year and she could use a few extra hours of work.

"Wonderful."

"Are you a friend of Penelope's or Natalie's?" Abby asked, making conversation.

"Who? Oh, you must mean the brides. I'm not here for the wedding. You can't exactly keep people out when you celebrate on the beach, now can you?" She gave an embarrassed laugh. "I heard you were performing and I had to hear you for myself. Definitely worth it."

"Thanks." Abby wondered which part she'd heard—the part before the arrival of her distracting angelic visitors or the part after. If it was anytime during the past ten minutes, she was going to be in for a pleasant surprise when she heard what she could really do. "I'll give you a call tomorrow when I have my calendar in front of me."

As soon as the real estate agent left, Elle moved into her line of sight. "You have to kill yourself."

Abby shaded her eyes. Maybe she was hallucinating. That would be nice. After all, everyone she'd ever mentioned her angel friends to seemed to think she was imagining things. Maybe she'd been wrong all these years and they'd been right. If so, her hallucinations were really getting bold these days. She cracked her knuckles. As long as Elle didn't tell her to buy a gun and shoot up the hospital patients, she should be okay. She was still in control of her mind. Probably.

"Isn't there some other way I can help? Why don't I continue on here in my job of learning about humanity?"

"We're all grateful there are angels like you who aren't afraid to volunteer to live as humans, but we have another job for you now that's even more important."

"The bridge."

"Exactly."

"I'm more valuable to you here," Abby said, hoping she sounded convincing.

"You're no good to us here. You're working at a hospital trying to do an angel's job of comforting the sick and helping the dying make their transition. Harp therapy is a worthy occupation, but living as a human, your light is masked. You could help people much more effectively in angelic form."

"No, thank you."

"The attachment you feel to your life on earth is nothing compared to the love that will flow through you constantly when you join us. If I could only help you remember, you'd understand."

"How convenient that there's nothing you can do to make me remember."

"Convenient?" Elle smoothed a wayward feather. "If you must know, your incarnation has been disappointing. You were supposed to choose a mother who would make your life difficult. You chose the wrong human to be born to."

"I was born to a drug addict," Abby said flatly.

"Who died," Elle said. "Your grandparents provided a loving home."

"And you're blaming me for that?"

"This is more important than your personal feelings," Elle snapped. "The other angels and I could retreat to the

Realm instead of taking a chance that we'll be stranded here on earth when the bridge does collapse, but we haven't. If you remembered who you really are you'd understand. The whole planet is in danger if the bridge collapses. Not just the angels, but all of humanity as well. If we're not around to avert human suffering, the earth you care so much about will become a much darker place."

"Darker, how?"

"2350 B.C.," said Elle.

"536 A.D.," said Sapphire.

"Thanks, that clears everything up." It probably wasn't such a smart idea to be sarcastic with two angels discussing her imminent death, but she couldn't help herself. It was hard to take them seriously. And there'd been no smiting yet, so she'd decided—perhaps foolishly—that they'd rather talk than kill.

"In the year 536," Sapphire explained, "what the Chinese called 'a dragon in the sky' hit the atmosphere."

"A comet fragment," Elle said. "Ever hear of Tunguska? 1908?"

"No," Abby said.

"You can't compare the two," Sapphire said. "Tunguska was nothing."

"True," Elle agreed. "But remember how pretty the noctilucent clouds were, lighting up the night sky thousands of miles away?"

"As I was saying, there was an explosion," Sapphire said. "In 536."

"And in 2350 B.C.," Elle interjected. "And in—"

Sapphire pulsed with impatience. "There were only a few of us here on earth, trapped on this side of the bridge after it failed, and we weren't strong enough to deflect the debris."

"You mean the debris from the comet, or are you saying the debris wasn't from a comet at all, it was debris from the collapsing bridge?"

"The so-called 'dragon' crashed through the atmosphere and vaporized trees across half the continent," Sapphire said, ignoring her question. "Everything caught fire. Soot blanketed the globe and blocked out the sun for a year. Crops died. People starved. Five years later the Justinian plague swept through Central Asia, Europe, Arabia, Africa…Half the world's population was gone before we were able to fix the bridge and return to help."

"You modern-day people are so arrogant," Elle said, "thinking your forebears were ignorant and superstitious to fear comets and believe they were omens of bad luck. They remembered what you've forgotten—that comets and asteroids have destroyed civilizations. Asteroids and plagues and volcanoes and—"

"Then there was the Black Death in the fourteenth century," Sapphire added.

A plague would be bad, of course, but with modern medicine, even if there were no angels around, was that really a risk? The nurses at the hospital had been talking about the latest pandemic scare, debating whether it was all drug company hype. A few were worried they'd be the first to die, but most insisted the threat was overblown. These two angels, however, were definitely trying to scare her.

"Are you going to kill me if I don't cooperate?"

Elle looked so taken aback she couldn't be faking it. "I can't kill you."

"Why not?" On second thought, maybe daring an angel to kill her wasn't her best move. Not that she was convinced any of this was real.

"I'm an angel," Elle said. "It's not in my nature to kill."

"But it's okay for me to kill someone?"

"Suicide is not the same thing."

"Sure it is."

"Look, the point is, we're all taking our lives into our hands every time we touch that bridge. We can avoid the potholes, but the whole thing could collapse at any time. We already lost one angel."

"You…lost one?" Now that Abby wasn't worried about her imminent death at Elle's hands, she could hear the grief in her voice.

"A piece of the walkway broke off and she tumbled off the bridge and died."

"But you can fly. How could she fall?"

"The bridge isn't located in space. It exists *between* space. Between dimensions. If an angel falls off..." Elle grimaced. "We assume she's dead."

"I didn't think angels could die."

"Our lifespan might seem like an eternity to you, but yes, we eventually die. We're beings, not gods. We were created, so one day we will die, and we look forward to that day when we'll have evolved beyond the need to evolve and are ready to return to God and we will all finally be free. It will be glorious."

"Huh."

"Don't worry, the human race will die out one day too," Elle said breezily. "Their suffering won't last forever. Their end will be a glorious day too."

Abby shrank back. That was one dangerous angel. Definitely had a sharp edge. She'd always thought of angels as saving lives, easing suffering, and spreading love. Even though she'd spent a lot of time with people who were dying, and the angels who guided them, she'd never seen this side of them.

"I thought you were upset that an angel fell off the bridge."

"We are. Because now is too soon. Now is not the end of time. Not yet. Not now. We're not ready yet."

So much for not worrying.

"Why do you think I'll be able to fix it? I don't know anything about bridges."

"Not a problem!" Elle's abrupt switch to perky salesperson mode was a little scary. "All we need is your presence."

"My presence? That's going to fix the bridge? How is that going to help?" It sounded fishy.

"This is not the first time we've had difficulties with the bridge. We discovered eons ago that all we need is for all the angels in existence to gather on the bridge and it will fix itself. It couldn't be easier."

"Isn't there any other way?" Abby shot a glance at Sapphire, who was not coming to her defense.

"Not that we know of," Elle said.

"Really, it's easy," Sapphire said.

Abby tried a different tack. "Don't you have engineers who could take a look at the thing and figure something out?"

Elle's fake perkiness vanished. "We're not builders," she said flatly. "We dedicate our lives to healing and music and comforting people in despair. Understanding technology isn't important."

Funny, it seemed kind of important right now. "Maybe a human engineer could take a look at it for you."

"They wouldn't be able to see the bridge or even detect it with their instruments. Nor would they understand how it was built or how to fix it, any more than we do. It is a mystery far beyond anyone's comprehension."

"Someone must understand it."

"No one does." Elle muttered something under her breath that sounded like *frickin' malfunctioning alien technology*. "But we know how to fix it," she insisted. "All we need is your cooperation."

"Maybe someone else could do it?" It wasn't noble, but it had to be said. "Maybe another incarnated angel who remembers and understands what you're talking about? I can't be the only one, right?"

"We have to wait for *all* the incarnated angels to die and return to angelic form so together we can fix it. Any number fewer than the full complement is ineffective."

"I'm not willing to kill myself." She couldn't believe she was even discussing this. She'd learned a grand total of one indisputable thing today—that Elle and Sapphire were as good as she was at remembering random historic dates. Which meant nothing. Lots of people were good at trivia. It didn't mean she had anything else in common with these two. "Even if you could prove to me that I would absolutely, positively become an angel, I'm not doing it."

Elle and Sapphire exchanged meaningful looks.

"We'll talk later." Sapphire flew off into the crowd of wedding guests, circled Gwynne, who was weaving her way around tables and heading in Abby's direction, and disappeared.

"And one more thing. Don't go out with Gwynne," Elle warned.

"Excuse me?" Abby blinked at the sudden change in subject.

"Don't date her."

Elle was full of advice, wasn't she? Irrelevant, unwanted advice. "I wasn't planning on it," Abby said coldly. Was there no privacy around here? What difference did it make who she did or did not date, anyway? It wasn't like it was going to be an issue if she was dead.

"Good," the angel said.

"Why is that good?"

"I don't want any other complications." Elle shrank to the size of a butterfly and blinked out.

Dating Gwynne was a complication? Why? Oh, who cared. Elle was gone and Gwynne was almost at her side. She could worry about dating Gwynne when and if the issue ever came up. She sat on her stool and pulled her harp to her shoulder. She was supposed to be providing music, not gabbing with uninvited guests—invisible or otherwise.

Gwynne came to a stop beside her. "I have a song request," she said cheerfully. "'Another One Bites the Dust.'"

Abby glanced around to see if Elle was back yet. She would definitely be back. "I don't know if the brides would appreciate that."

Gwynne angled her head to one side and gazed at her steadily, probably wondering what had Abby so distracted that she didn't laugh at her comment. "How are you holding up?"

Abby leaned her harp away from her body and gently lowered it so it was balanced firmly on its base. She rolled her shoulders and stretched her arms behind her back, considering how to answer. How about: *While you were gone I was offered a job? Two jobs, actually, but one was volunteer, and the working conditions were not up to OSHA standards, which probably frown upon on-the-job deaths. And is it true you can really see angels?*

She settled for a less complicated response. "My shoulders are sore." She twisted her neck at various angles until it gave a satisfying crack.

"May I?" Gwynne positioned herself behind her and placed her hands on her shoulders.

"Mmm."

She wasn't sitting in a chair with a back, she was on a stool, so there was nothing between her and Gwynne but a few inches of empty space, a few inches that made her back tingle with awareness and reminded her of Gwynne pulling her zipper. Careful of the material, Gwynne massaged her shoulders and her back through the layers of her dress, her thumbs releasing the tight spots that came from playing the harp for too long and twisting to reach the strings.

"That feels fantabulous," Abby said. "I should schedule a massage with Megan or Yolanda."

Gwynne tensed. She felt it in Gwynne's hands.

"I went to massage school too, you know."

"Did you? No wonder you're so good at this." She hadn't meant to offend her. She wasn't sure exactly what Gwynne did to all those people who kept begging her to help them with faith healing or energy healing or laying on of hands, but she wouldn't call it massage. "Are you taking clients?" All she ever saw her do was turn her old customers away and tell them she quit, but if she ever changed her mind…

"If it's you—yes."

Abby leaned back against Gwynne's body and let her head fall back too, because God, she was leaning against her breasts and it felt like home. She had no shame. None. She was taking advantage of a sweet gesture and Gwynne was going to gently but firmly push her away any second, but all she could think was *Please, don't let this end.* She didn't want to think about plagues or exploding comets or anything else except how wonderful it felt to have Gwynne's hands on her, making her feel safe.

Gwynne didn't push her away. Instead, she looped her arms around her shoulders in a loose hug and held her close. Abby turned her head to one side, snuggling more deeply into the softness of her chest. Gwynne didn't budge. She stood solid and warm and welcoming, and although she could feel Gwynne's breathing had changed pace, she was pretty sure there was still air going in and out. Which was more than she could say for herself, because she herself was holding her breath, praying neither one of them would move or freak out or remember this wasn't the kind of relationship they had—at least not yet.

But after a minute, something in Gwynne's energy shifted. "Looks like we have company," Gwynne said.

Abby jerked her head up and saw that Sapphire had reappeared, but there was no one nearby paying them any attention, so who was Gwynne talking about?

"Who's your friend?" Gwynne asked.

Abby looked at Gwynne and Gwynne nodded in Sapphire's direction. But she couldn't be talking about Sapphire. No one could see Sapphire. Not even Gwynne, no matter what people said, no matter what she thought she saw at the hospital the day Gwynne's mother died.

Sapphire whizzed threateningly around Gwynne's head.

Gwynne should have looked unperturbed. She shouldn't have been shooing at Sapphire like she was under attack by gnats, or crossing her forearms protectively over her forehead.

"Charming little fireball, isn't she?" Gwynne said.

Abby shot up from her seat. She felt like she'd entered some alternate universe and didn't know how to get out.

"You can see her, can't you?" Gwynne drew her eyebrows together and frowned.

"*You* can see her?" She'd suspected Gwynne could see angels. She'd heard other people talk about it, she'd heard Gwynne talk about it, and part of her wanted to believe it was true. But believing wasn't the same as *knowing*. She'd never fully believed—never known for sure—that Gwynne could see *her* angels—that Gwynne could see Sapphire. No one could see Sapphire.

Still, there was no reason to feel light-headed. There was no reason to overreact. No reason at all.

Her vision tunneled and blurred. Through the ringing in her ears she heard Gwynne say, "Of course I can see her. Didn't we go over this already? I can see angels."

In a last-ditch effort, Abby stiffened her knees and tried to clear her head, but gray spots rushed in and swamped the tent.

* * *

Gwynne knelt by Abby's side and felt for her pulse. She was lucky she'd fainted onto the sand without hitting her head on the edge of the low wooden platform or falling onto her harp.

Abby's eyes blinked open.

"Are you all right?" Gwynne asked.

Abby grimaced and rolled to her side. "I need to get up. People will wonder what I'm doing on the ground."

"Everyone's having too much fun to notice. They can wait." She gave her a butterscotch candy from her secret stash in her pocket. Sugar was good for fainting. So was not rushing to get back on your feet.

Abby popped the butterscotch in her mouth and sat up and shook sand out of her skirt. Gwynne helped her brush sand off her back and made herself not think about the promise she'd made herself about what she'd do the next time she touched her dress.

"Do you want to talk about what just happened?" Gwynne asked.

"Nothing happened."

"I won't think you're crazy." She had to know that already, but she said it anyway, because apparently Abby had been covering up her abilities, pretending not to notice angels when she was around other people.

Abby squeezed her eyes shut.

Like that would help. Poor thing. "There's more to reality than most people know."

Abby opened her eyes a slit. "Maybe we're both crazy."

"We're not crazy. Believe me, we're not." She wanted to hold her, tell her it was okay, kiss her until she stopped worrying about it.

She wasn't sure Abby would appreciate that.

"I have to get up." Abby rocked forward onto her knees and rose an inch before pressing her hands to her head and changing her mind.

"Someone really did a number on you, didn't they? Someone convinced you angels aren't real."

Abby looked like a cornered rabbit weighing the odds of escape. "Didn't anyone try to convince *you*?" She squeezed her head and started to get up, but she still couldn't manage it.

Oh, no. She shouldn't have assumed Abby was comfortable with the weird, angel-filled reality they shared. Holding her by the shoulders at her harp had muddled her brain, made her say things she shouldn't. But hadn't Abby ever talked to anyone about her ethereal companions?

"You must have told your parents when you were little, right? And your parents told you the angels you saw were imaginary."

"Not my parents, my grandparents. They raised me," Abby said. She still looked pale, but at least she wasn't trying to get up. "They sent me for psychiatric testing."

"Yikes." Gwynne sat back on her heels. "Isn't that taking it a bit far?" No wonder Abby didn't know whom to trust.

"They were worried I'd turn out like my mother. They felt like they failed her, and, no matter what it took, they weren't going to fail me." Abby pushed herself up from the ground and stood. "It's not that I don't believe angels are real," she said. "I do. Sort of. I mean, they seem real to me. It's just that I've never met anyone else who can see them."

"We're pretty rare." That had been surprising, watching Abby have a conversation during the wedding reception with a being she shouldn't have been able to perceive. Gwynne had stared at her for far too long, trying to figure out if she was really observing what she thought she was observing. "Megan sees them too."

"Yeah, I guess that's what Kira was saying. She really can?"

"Yeah. And Kira won't think you're wackadoodle, either, even though she can't sense them herself. It's pretty funny watching her make small talk with thin air ever since Megan told her she sicced one of her angels on her. And you—you've got hordes of them following you around. More than I do. I think they must like hanging out with people who know they're there."

"You really saw Sapphire? The one who was circling you?" Abby's face lit up, so innocently delighted that Gwynne couldn't bear it.

What was she doing, talking to Abby about angels? She'd assumed Abby could see them. It hadn't occurred to her that Abby would doubt the evidence of her own eyes. And now Gwynne had just gone and confirmed for her that no, she was not crazy, and yes, angels were real. Perfect. Just freaking perfect. As if getting Heather killed because of this exact same information wasn't enough. When would she learn to keep her mouth shut? She should do it for the good of humanity.

She couldn't stand the look on Abby's face. She looked so happy, and all Gwynne could do was wish she'd never met her.

Because Abby would have been so, so, so much better off believing angels were not real.

CHAPTER EIGHT

Potential hallucination or not—with a strong vote for *not* from Gwynne Abernathy—Abby didn't completely trust Elle. She needed proof.

Penelope had assigned her a place at one of the tables for the wedding dinner and told her not to work the whole evening, but she wasn't hungry. Instead, while the guests enjoyed grilled tuna steaks and chicken cordon bleu by candlelight flickering in hurricane lamps, she walked down the beach, away from the tent, and phoned her grandmother.

"Grams. Do you remember me talking about angels when I was little?"

There was a long pause, just as she expected. The pause had been honed all through Abby's childhood to give her plenty of time to feel guilty.

"I thought we'd put this behind us."

We. Like it was Grams's problem too.

"When are you going to outgrow this, Abby? This unhealthy fascination with the supernatural?"

"Can't we talk about it?"

Another silence. Abby rubbed her ear. The infection was back. She needed to go to the doctor and get more antibiotics, but she never could get around to making the time to do it.

Was Grams going to say anything at all? Maybe she was doing the wrong thing by bringing this up. She'd stopped talking about her so-called hallucinations long ago and discovered it made her relationship with her grandparents go much more smoothly.

"I know you don't like to talk about it…"

Her grandmother cleared her throat. "You were such a tiny little thing when you lost your mother. Such a precious little thing. Only three years old. You were too young to know the difference between fantasy and reality. And you'd been through a terrible shock. We weren't surprised when you clung to these…stories. It was a coping mechanism."

"What stories?" Abby said quickly, biting her lip and hoping she didn't sound too eager.

"The problem came when you were nine, ten, eleven years old. You should have outgrown it by then. After what happened to your mother…"

Grams was getting sidetracked. "What stories, Grams?"

"Never mind."

"Grams!"

"Does it really matter?"

"Yes!" So much for not sounding too eager. She hoped she hadn't just screwed her chances of getting any helpful information out of her, because it felt like she might actually be on the verge of getting an answer instead of a lecture.

Her grandmother sighed. "You seemed to believe you lived with a family of angels."

Abby almost laughed. This was the big, terrible secret her grandmother never wanted to talk about? That she thought she lived with angels? Of course she thought she lived with angels. She lived with angels *now*. She'd always been able to see angels, as far back as she could remember. Which meant she must have been able to see them even when she was a child. Which explained the stories.

Unless the real explanation was that her younger self was babbling about a previous incarnation in another world that she could remember at age three and still talked about at age ten, but had since forgotten? That was Elle and Sapphire's take on it. It certainly wasn't her grandmother's.

"Did I ever say I *was* an angel?"

"I'm sure I don't remember."

"Please, Grams, try."

More silence. Abby waited patiently.

"Seeing your mother unconscious from drugs, maybe even seeing her dead…We hoped you'd forget what you'd seen. It was a mercy you were too young to understand what was going on. We thought you'd forgotten all about it."

"I did forget."

"It's better that way. It was such a relief when you stopped talking about your mother and those fanciful angels."

"But what did I say about them? Aside from the fact that I lived with them?"

"Who can remember? It was all childish nonsense." Her grandmother sighed again—a feeble, put-upon sigh. "You can come see for yourself. We saved some of your things in the attic."

* * *

"I need to talk to you."

Gwynne turned at the urgency in Abby's voice. It was after midnight and the wedding was winding down, and Abby could have gone home a long time ago, but hadn't, because it was her friend's wedding, after all, not some stranger's.

"How are you feeling?" Gwynne asked.

Abby's fainting had her worried, but after a short break, Abby had returned to her harp as if nothing had happened, as if she wasn't the least bit wigged out. She'd even performed with the two brides and another woman in some kind of college band reunion, and to look at her, all jazzed and flinging her arms around like a crazed rock star whenever her hands left the strings, you'd never guess she had anything on her mind other than the music.

"Do you want to walk on the beach?" Abby asked.

"Sure." She was done with her serving and cleanup duties. All she had left to do was help Abby carry her dragon harp and her amp and what all back to the minivan. "What about your stuff?"

"Ramona said she'd keep an eye on it." Abby took Gwynne's elbow and pulled her away from the tent and the guests who spilled onto the beach. She stepped out of her dressy, impractical heels and shivered.

"Are you cold? I have a sweatshirt in my beach bag that I left in your van, if you want to borrow it."

"Will it fit?"

"We'll find out."

They changed direction, away from the beach. When they reached the van, Abby slipped Gwynne's hooded, kangaroo-pocket sweatshirt on over her dress and Gwynne tried not to think about how good it felt to see her wearing it. Before her personal energy field could become any more protective, Gwynne turned away and rummaged in her bag for the flyers and stapler and roll of duct tape she took with her everywhere she went, just in case, because there were always good places to post her flyers, which currently featured a great photo of her calico kitten posing with the two rabbits, looking all Dr. Doolittle and peace on earth, which to tell the truth was not exactly the normal state of affairs at her place.

"I liked your band," Gwynne said with her head practically inside her bag. "Interesting instrumental mix."

"Penelope wanted to start a chamber ensemble—flute and harp and a couple other strings—but I was an archaeology major and I thought it would be more fun to have drums, because flute and drums are the oldest instruments. Not counting sticks. Which we also had. We also had a gourd rattle at one point."

Gwynne upended her bag and dumped the contents onto the seat. "Did I see sticks?"

"You know, hitting two sticks together. It's believed to be the oldest instrument if you don't count the human voice."

Oh yeah, the drumsticks they were high-fiving each other with.

"I thought it would be fun to teach myself the lyre," Abby continued, "but they're not easy to find, so Penelope researched it and said what would be *really* cool would be if I played a hunter's bow like the cavemen, but I said, 'What the crap am I going to do with a one-stringed instrument?' and then Nat jumped in and volunteered to learn because she was always trying to impress Penelope and she didn't care that she was being obvious."

"Seems like it worked out," Gwynne said.

"Their relationship, yeah. The musical cave bow, no. We never could get it to stay in tune and even when it was in tune, it sounded…not good. The rest of it, though—it was a great band. I miss it."

They headed back to the beach and Gwynne scouted for potential flyer locations along the way. It didn't take long before they reached a lifeguard stand dragged up beyond the high tide line and tipped upside down for the night. Gwynne stuck a flyer on it and taped it down so it wouldn't flap in the wind. Some of the lifeguards would remove her flyers in the morning, but not all of them. It was worth a shot.

"Look how cute Peter is with his head resting on his paws," she told Abby. "Who could resist?"

It was hard to make out the photo in the dark, so Abby took an extra flyer from her hands to get a better look. "Which one is he?"

"The black rabbit."

"He is cute," she agreed. "I can't wait to meet him tomorrow at the birthday party."

"Do you want to adopt him? He's really sweet."

Abby handed the flyer back. "Megan McLaren has met your rabbits, right?"

Uh-oh. Any mention of Megan in the same sentence with the word *rabbits* was not a good sign.

"Not these ones," Gwynne assured her.

"Huh."

"Why?" she asked innocently. Not so innocently. Oh, come on, what did Meg say about her rabbits this time?

"Because every time she walks by your desk and sees the photos of your rabbits she gets this look on her face."

"What kind of look?"

Abby sounded apologetic. "I think she's cringing."

Gwynne waved her hands dismissively, the roll of duct tape bouncing around her wrist. "Meg's not a rabbit person."

"Apparently not."

"But *you* might be."

Abby gave her an understanding smile as she slowly shook her head. Gwynne stumbled in the sand. That smile was dangerous.

She rolled her flyers into a tighter tube. "You could adopt a different rabbit if you don't like these. I'm always fostering new ones, and it'll get worse after Easter—that's always a busy time of year."

Abby kept shaking her head. "Where do they come from?"

"Oh, here and there," Gwynne said vaguely.

Was it her imagination, or was Abby standing closer? She'd switched her high heels to her outside hand as they walked side by side, and her empty hand swung freely between them, close enough to accidentally brush against Gwynne's leg. Not that there was any accidental brushing going on. But there could be. The possibility was all she could think of. She swore she could feel the pressure of the space between them, aura pushing against aura.

"Why don't you keep them?" Abby asked. "Your rabbits. If you love them so much."

"I'd like to, believe me, but I can't keep every abandoned rabbit who comes in my door. It's the only way to keep the influx under control. I'm a regular rabbit homing signal."

"So you're completely blameless. Rabbits mysteriously show up at your door."

"Kind of like you and all your harps," Gwynne retorted.

Abby's path drifted off-center, widening the distance between them. Good. Distance would lessen the tingling that threatened to overwhelm her senses. The high heels were switched to her other hand, adding a physical obstacle in that empty space between them.

"They call out to me and I can't say no," Abby said.

"I can say no."

"Oh, suck it up and admit you can't."

Gwynne thrust the flyers toward her and unrolled them so Abby could see and stabbed her finger at the words *Free to Good Home*. It killed her to look at those words. She hated saying goodbye, but she made herself do it over and over again. She'd love to keep every single one of her bunnies and the occasional cat or guinea pig, but that wouldn't be healthy—for her or for the animals. They were better off living in homes that weren't overrun by furry creatures, where they could each be the center of attention.

"I can," Gwynne insisted. "I give them away."

Abby gently relieved her of the flyers and rolled them up, her movements so unnaturally calm and deliberate that Gwynne got the feeling she was being treated like a crazy person waving a knife around. She wasn't that bad, was she? Maybe she got a teensy bit emotional about the rabbit situation, but it was under control. So sue her.

"I'm sure it's not easy to give them away," Abby said.

"It's not."

"You could give them to the animal shelter," Abby suggested.

Gwynne frowned at her. "Bunny killers."

"Not that you have an opinion or anything."

"The people at the shelter do their best, but they always have more rabbits than they can find homes for."

Abby's lips flattened with something that looked an awful lot like pity. "You're going to hate me for saying this, but if there are too many of them…"

"They didn't ask to be born." Her throat tightened at the thought of all the death she'd seen all too recently, and her voice became rough. "The least we can do is try to give them a good life."

Abby slid the roll of duct tape off Gwynne's wrist and taped a flyer to the next lifeguard stand. "You're a good person."

I'm not, Gwynne wanted to say, but then Abby would ask why, and it was better if she didn't. And hadn't they been over this already? Abby thought Gwynne was a good person for not hating her ex, Megan thought she was a good person because Megan saw the best in everyone, and Dara thought she was a good person because Dara was blind—a judgment that proved right there that Gwynne was no Mother Teresa.

They walked some more in silence, the distant sounds of partying from the remaining wedding guests lost in the crash of waves. Abby drifted closer, seemingly drawn like a magnet to Gwynne's hastily erected force field that should, if this were *Star Trek*, have kept her at bay. Couldn't she tell Gwynne was poor company? Didn't she care? Or maybe she simply wasn't aware that she was standing in Gwynne's space, dangling her high heels by their skimpy straps an inch from Gwynne's thigh, swinging her arm with a motion that would have been hypnotic if her footwear weren't so dangerously close to impaling a body part. Her face, after all, was turned away, toward the dark ocean. She could be completely oblivious.

Great, Gwynne. Walk a little closer to her, why don't you? And be sure to tell yourself that's not what you're doing.

"I wanted to ask you..." Abby's voice was hesitant, directed toward the horizon.

"Yes?" She'd almost forgotten that Abby invited her out here to talk.

"You can see auras, right?"

Gwynne groaned. Auras. Abby knew she didn't do energy healing anymore and ought to know she didn't like talking about this stuff. Except how could she know the topic was on Gwynne's do-not-discuss list when Gwynne went and opened her mouth about seeing the unseen? She'd never been particularly good at restraining her natural tendency to be a blabbermouth, and she hated hearing Abby question her own sanity, so it had slipped out.

"What do you want to know?"

"Is there anything unusual about my aura?"

"Like what?" she said carefully.

"So it's not obvious? Nothing jumps out at you?"

Besides how beautiful her aura was? Too many people's auras were muddy, but Abby's was bright and clear, the colors lit from within.

"Can't you see auras yourself?" If she could see angels…

"Sometimes," Abby said. "Not that well. Not well enough to know if my aura looks normal."

Normal. What was normal? "Everyone's aura is different. It's the same structure, but it's individual. Besides, it changes with your health and your emotions and your stress level." Gwynne sighed. There was something Abby wasn't telling her, some question she was building up to. She blocked Abby's path and faced her full-on. "What do you really want to know?"

Abby reluctantly met her gaze. "If you see anything weird about me on the energetic level."

Weird. Normal. Unusual. How many words was Abby going to come up with to ask her the same vague question?

"The information's not right there on the surface," Gwynne said. "I'd have to take a closer look to see anything." Like she wasn't tempted to take a closer look every time they were in the same room together. But she wasn't going to admit that she already knew exactly what her aura looked like. "You have to get into the right mindset. It's like figuring out what ingredients go into a morning glory muffin. You have to savor it to decide—is that apple I taste, or pear?"

Abby swept her hands in tumbling, impatient circles, motioning that she got the point and could they please get on with it. "Can you look at it?"

It wouldn't be hard to take another look and make her happy. Not hard at all. She stopped walking and stared at her, let her eyes lose focus. Abby's inner light blazed in the darkness. At her core was a thin strand of silver-white light, and looking into it was like falling into a bottomless well that fractured into a kaleidoscope of mesmerizing, ever-changing colors. Her aura *wasn't* normal, but she wouldn't call it weird. It was unique.

"You have more colors. Really beautiful ones that blend into all these amazing shades." She'd never noticed quite how many different colors Abby had. She'd never allowed herself to go this deep. The sheer complexity of it…the sheer beauty of it…"You have…so…many…colors." Her words slowed as she was drawn further in. "That must be why—" She didn't finish her sentence aloud. *Why I'm so fascinated by you.*

Abby's gaze was steady and serious, waiting for more. Gwynne stared back, lost in the swirling vortex of color.

"That must be why…" Abby prompted with a smile of encouragement.

That smile. It sparkled in her eyes with an intimacy that didn't belong there, a closeness they didn't have, a connection Gwynne had been hoping for even though it was too soon. Abby leaned toward her and Gwynne's chest warmed with the certainty that Abby was going to touch her. Brush her arm. Take her hand. Not let go. Her throat constricted. Abby's smile deepened, like she could tell that all rational-sounding responses had fled Gwynne's brain and found it adorable.

Gwynne swayed closer, only marginally aware of what her body was doing, feeling like she was going to…what? Kiss her? Could she? Could she really kiss her? She could. She had to. Abby's smile faded and her gaze fixated on Gwynne's mouth. Gwynne's lips felt heavy with need. She really was going to—

A flash of fluttering angel wings dive-bombed the space between them, momentarily blinding her before vanishing. The intrusion snapped her out of her trance and she pulled out of her collision course with Abby's mouth.

Abby gave a sharp shake of her head. Her chest lifted with a deep intake of breath. She looked rattled. "Remember that angel you saw talking to me earlier?"

Oh, no. Abby was going to pretend nothing happened. That time hadn't stood still before they were pointlessly interrupted. That their friendship hadn't been about to change. How could she do that? She must have felt *something*. Or had Gwynne imagined that moment of connection, that feeling of being on the verge of something important?

Abby shot a furtive glance at the spot where their dive-bombing guest had disappeared. "This is going to sound bizarre, but she claims I'm an angel born into human form."

"What?" Gwynne's throat clenched with irritation at the interfering ways of angelkind, all thoughts of kissing her—and of not kissing her—pushed aside. Of all the ridiculous, dangerous things to tell someone…

"I don't know whether to believe her," Abby continued. "How would I know if she's right?"

Now Abby's insistent curiosity about her aura made sense. If she *were* an ang—

Except she wasn't. But if she *were*, Gwynne might be able to detect it.

"You look like a human being to me," Gwynne said, making her voice as firm as possible. The angel's claim had to be a mistake. It had to be. "It's not an angel's aura."

As if to prove her point, Abby's aura fluctuated again, and in that moment it reminded her of her sister's very human aura, which used to be the bright vibrant green of young grass shoots, back before Heather messed with it.

Crap. Now she was thinking of Heather again, remembering how they had chased each other through the weedy lawn that thirteen-year-old Gwynne was supposed to be mowing with their impossibly heavy mower because her father had moved out. Gwynne had danced away from her sister, hiding behind a tree, doing a fake-out, then racing to the other end of the yard, slowing at the end to let Heather catch up, then slowing even more to let herself get tagged.

"Ha." Heather forced the word out with the last of the air in her little lungs before throwing herself on the ground to catch her breath. She eyed her big sister suspiciously. "Did you let me tag you?"

"Why would I do that?"

Heather got up from the grass and planted her hands on her hips. "You can't let me catch you," she commanded. "You have to try to get away."

Gwynne lifted one foot as high as her knee and then stretched her leg in Heather's direction, balancing dramatically on one leg and flashing monster claws. "I'll get you."

Heather giggled and scooted back a few steps. "It's not monster tag."

"It's not?"

"No."

Gwynne did her monster roar. Heather shrieked and Gwynne had chased after her…

"Do you see anything?" Abby asked, jarring her back to the present.

Abby's aura wasn't as green as Heather's used to be, and Heather's had never been as bright, but there was a youthfulness that was the same. If you took an angel's energy system and forced it into the frequencies of the human system, would it remain the bright, golden sunlight it was before? There was no way of knowing. Maybe it *would* sparkle in swirls of aquamarine, turquoise and teal shot through with streaks of yellow and pure white light, glowing in the dark like the aurora borealis. It was easy to imagine Abby as an angel soaring through the night sky, her freckle-covered shoulder blades rippling with movement, her bra a forgotten memory.

Somehow it always came down to the bra.

Or lack thereof.

"What do you see?" Abby prompted.

Nothing she could say aloud, that was for sure. "Nothing angelic."

Abby looked disappointed. "I asked Grams about it and she said she has some boxes in the attic I might want to take a look at. It's not like her. I'm going to take the bus down to Baltimore in a couple days to check it out."

"You're taking the bus?" Gwynne said, jumping on the safer topic. "What about your van? There's only, like, one bus a day."

"My license was suspended."

Gwynne burst out laughing. She hated when she did that—like her body was a malfunctioning pressure-release valve. It was so wrong to laugh at things that weren't funny—at things that called for condolences, or understanding, or a sad face at the very least. She clamped her hands over her mouth, but Abby didn't seem to have noticed. Maybe Abby thought it *was* funny, since apparently a suspended license was not enough to stop her from driving herself to work or giving Gwynne a ride to their evening's shindig.

"For what? Drunk driving?" It was the only thing she could think of that would get your license suspended.

"Speeding."

"Speeding," Gwynne echoed, letting that sink in. "How fast do you have to drive to get your license suspended for speeding?"

"Pretty fast." Abby winked conspiratorially.

God, she was cute. And crazy. Just the way she liked her women—cute and crazy.

What a coincidence.

"Sober," Gwynne confirmed. Because cute and crazy was one thing, and cute and crazy and drunk was another. Although the way hope seemed to spring eternal around her sequin-covered witch, maybe it didn't matter.

"I don't have a death wish," Abby said.

"You must have an incarceration wish if you drive to work on a suspended license."

"I'm not going to get pulled over when I'm only driving a few blocks."

"Not in that mom-mobile, anyway." The rusted, ancient, unreliable-looking minivan was so not what she imagined her driving. She understood why she owned it—because it was big enough to transport her harps—but it clearly wasn't the vehicle her illegally speeding heart would have preferred. "I'm shocked it's actually capable of breaking the speed limit."

"I have a good mechanic."

"If you ask me, you have a miracle worker."

"Wow, I thought the M-word was on your never-ever-cross-your-lips, do-not-pass-go, do-not-collect-two-hundred-dollars list."

How did she know that? It was a little scary, the stuff Abby knew about her.

"I'll drive you to Baltimore if you want," Gwynne said. "So you don't have to take the bus."

Abby hesitated.

"It'll be fun." Yeah, like she didn't have enough crazy in her life.

"Thanks." Abby's aura danced orange and deep, hazy blue, glowing like a breathtaking sunset. "Elle must be telling the truth, right? I mean, she's an angel."

"God, I don't know." Gwynne pressed her fingers to her forehead. Everyone thought she was an expert, and she really wasn't. She'd be happy if no one mentioned angels to her ever again.

"She has no reason to lie. Why would she lie? She must think I can help them, or she wouldn't have asked."

"Asked what?"

"Um…" A guilty look crossed her face. "She thinks I can help her with something."

Something Abby apparently didn't want to tell her about. Not that it was any of her business. She didn't want it to be her business. She didn't. Because whatever that angel had asked Abby to do, she was sure she wasn't going to like it.

Gwynne shrugged, telling herself she didn't care. "Keyword: think."

"You think she could be wrong?"

"I think anyone can make a mistake. Even an angel."

CHAPTER NINE

When Abby arrived at Dara's niece's house for the birthday party the next day, she found Gwynne wearing a top hat and tuxedo, flat on her stomach on the floor of the living room, participating in a nose-twitching competition with two rabbits. Gwynne was talking to them, egging them on, and for someone loud, she had an amazingly soft, gentle way of crooning to her pets. It was a voice that could pull you through your worst fears and make you want to be brave. A private, intimate voice that made Abby's insides tense with longing.

Gwynne rolled up from the floor and tossed her a second top hat, obviously remembering that Abby had said she wanted one. "Nimbus is the gray furball," she said, introducing the rabbits and switching to her normal voice, making Abby wish she'd approached more quietly so Gwynne wouldn't have noticed her right away and she could have enjoyed listening to that sexy voice a little longer. "The black one is Peter the Fifteenth."

"Don't tell me you've had fourteen other Peters."

"Yup. Peter was my first bunny. He was great at magic. Just an all-around great bunny." Gwynne covered Nimbus's ears like she didn't want him to hear and get jealous. He twitched her away. "But these guys are great too."

The rabbits weren't too skittish when Abby tried to pet them. Gwynne had her practice holding them, and then practice putting them in their carrier and taking them out. They did a quick run-through of what Gwynne needed her to do during the show, and then kids started arriving at the front door and were funneled to another part of the house for games, leaving Abby and Gwynne alone in the room with the rabbits, waiting for everyone to arrive so the kids could be led to the magic room as a group.

"Ready?" Gwynne asked.

"It's the rabbits I'm worried about. Are they going to panic?" Of course they were well-behaved when Gwynne was there supervising, but that was likely to change in front of two dozen excited children. Combine that with Abby's questionable rabbit wrangling skills, and there might not be anyone popping out of that magician's hat.

Gwynne scooped up Nimbus and scratched him under his chin. Peter watched morosely, then flopped onto his side for an insta-nap. "They probably will mess up, since this is their first magic show, but that's okay."

"Mine too." Good thing the kids would be more excited about seeing live bunnies than about whether the trick worked. She hoped.

While Gwynne had her hands full hugging Nimbus, Abby brushed pale gray rabbit hairs off Gwynne's official magician's black tuxedo jacket. It was an excuse to touch her—and not a very subtle one, judging from the way Gwynne met her gaze at the touch, making it clear she'd noticed.

She wished she'd kissed her the night before. Then she wouldn't be obsessing about it now, wondering when she'd get another opportunity, worrying that if she did, she'd once again be startled by someone not of this world whose blaze of speed made her impossible to identify, and lose her nerve. She shouldn't have pulled back. So what if an angel had warned her not to date Gwynne? She didn't fully trust Elle, and even if she did, her warning was too much like one of her grandmother's overprotective rules to take seriously. Yet somehow she'd been knocked too off-balance to try to recapture the mood. Now, though…

"It's okay if you mess up the trick too," Gwynne said. "Besides, I've got lots of other illusions planned that don't involve the bunnies."

"What about you? Are you any good at this?" Gwynne had talked her through the big trick, but she hadn't seen her perform it. She hoped Gwynne, at least, had rehearsed.

"Doubting me?"

"Um…no?" Abby laughed and fussed a bit more with Gwynne's jacket, plucking at a few stubborn hairs and straightening her collar.

Gwynne leaned into her, her shoulders subtly responding to her movements. But then she settled on the floor with the rabbits, and Abby pulled herself together and stopped touching her, and Gwynne stroked the rabbits' furry bodies with a technique that had them lolling on the carpet in ecstasy while Abby stood and watched.

Kiss her? Now? What was she thinking? They had a show to do.

"Don't worry. I've been doing this trick since I was a kid. I thought pulling a rabbit out of a hat was the coolest trick in the world. That's how I got the first Peter. It took me ages to convince my mother I couldn't be a real magician without a bunny, but my sister and I spent so much time practicing the trick and got so good at it that she finally gave in. On one condition—that there would be no sawing of holes into the kitchen table, the dining room table, the card table, or our desks."

"Your poor mother."

"She didn't need to worry, because by that point I didn't need a trick table—it was all sleight of hand. My sister Heather came up with all these off-the-wall ideas for distracting the audience, like twirling around dancing or telling knock-knock jokes, so they wouldn't see me sticking the bunny into the hat."

"Did it work?"

"Yeah, it worked great, since our audience was Heather's stuffed animals sitting in a row, all lined up on the dining room chairs. Great audience. They never saw it coming."

"Oh my God." Abby wished she could have seen Gwynne at that age. She must have been adorable, doggedly practicing her magic trick and conning her little sister into helping her.

"They loved it when I asked for a volunteer from the audience to be the rabbit in the hat. One of them really was a rabbit, so she got to volunteer a lot."

"The others must have been jealous."

Gwynne shook her head with a rueful smile. "Not if they heard me arguing with Heather that real magicians' rabbits were white, not pink. I thought it was a pretty convincing argument, but Heather wouldn't let me bleach her stuffed animal."

"I would think your *mother* wouldn't let you bleach your sister's stuffed animal."

"She knew I'd never go through with it."

"I'm not so sure about that."

Soon the kids trooped in and piled onto the floor in front of the makeshift stage. Gwynne got the show rolling with some knock-knock jokes and an impressive array of card tricks and other illusions.

When it was time for the rabbits' star appearance, Abby handed Gwynne's top hat to the birthday girl and asked her to look inside. The girls didn't quite grasp the concept of waiting their turn or passing the hat around; instead, they all had to get in on the action and huddle around it to confirm that yes, it was a normal, untricky, unsuspicious, empty hat. Abby returned the hat to Gwynne.

"And now, for my next trick, I will pull a rabbit out of this hat," Gwynne announced. "But first, the magic words. Abracadabra…" She reached into the hat. "Rabacadabra…" She fumbled inside the hat, like she knew the rabbit was in there but she couldn't find it. "Rabbitcadabra…" She pulled her hand out of the hat and raised her arm aloft in victory, showing off what she'd conjured—a faded pink plush rabbit. Its pale blue glass bead eyes were loose and its ears were worn and furless. "Yes! I knew I could do it!"

The kids giggled.

"No?" Looking puzzled, Gwynne lowered the stuffed animal.

The stuffed animal shook its head *no*.

"Let's try this again." Gwynne made the plush rabbit disappear underneath her table, which was covered by a floor-length drape, the better to hide the cuddly black rabbit who was snoozing in a black hammock hooked within easy reach. She placed the hat, brim down, on the table. "Abracadabra…"

Abby stepped behind the folding screen that was off to Gwynne's right. She crouched by the rabbit carrier and lifted the black rabbit's brother out and nudged him toward his favorite person. He hopped out from behind the screen.

"Look!" squealed the girls, wiggling with excitement.

Gwynne peered over the table and jumped in exaggerated surprise at the gray rabbit on the floor. The kids' squeals turned into giggles.

"What is that?" Gwynne said.

"A rabbit!"

The kids were having so much fun, and she could tell Gwynne was too, which was nice to see. She liked seeing her happy.

Gwynne looked at Nimbus suspiciously out the corner of her eye and then made a show of waving him away and ignoring him as she reminded the audience to join her in the magic words.

"Abracadabra, rabacadabra, rabbitcadabra…"

Only Abby, standing off to the side behind the screen, saw her scoop Peter the Fifteenth, hammock and all, into the hat as she swept the hat from the edge of the table and flipped it over. She was amazingly fast, moving in that eager, enthusiastic way of hers that could not be called graceful but was certainly not uncoordinated. Abby shivered. She was supposed to be distracting the audience by coming out from behind the screen and chasing Nimbus while Gwynne flipped the hat, but instead, she was the one who was distracted. She couldn't take her eyes off Nimbus's mom.

Gwynne reached inside the hat to free Peter the Fifteenth from the hammock and pulled him out with both hands. Half the kids gaped and the others didn't realize or didn't care that they'd missed her big trick because they were scrambling after Nimbus.

While the adults in the back of the room clapped, Abby took Peter so they could move on to the next trick, and as they transferred the rabbit, her bare forearm brushed against Gwynne's sleeve. She stilled. Goose bumps rose on her arm. She stared at Gwynne's sleeve, at the spot where they'd touched, and realized just how close they were standing, with their heads close together, breathing the same air. Why hadn't they practiced this move before the show? She liked this move. She took her time, making sure she had a secure hold on the rabbit. No other reason.

Right. She was going to have to do something about this attraction. Soon.

* * *

Gwynne couldn't remember the last time she'd done laundry, and the only clean T-shirt she had left was the one that said *Cats are Angels with Fur*. Her mother had given it to her—that was the only reason she owned it. Not that she ever wore it. She did have standards.

Or maybe she didn't have standards, because she'd broken down and worn the shirt a few weeks ago, even though she was beyond pissed at the angels and didn't owe them free advertising on her chest.

As if she didn't think about her mother often enough already.

Today, however, she was not in the mood for kittens with cheesy cartoon halos. Not even if those halos were hidden under a sweater, because she wouldn't last ten minutes at work wearing a sweater or even a chamois shirt—with or without anything on underneath—since she and the massage therapists liked to crank up the heat for the clients. Still, there must be something she could wear.

But there wasn't. Not a single clean T-shirt in sight. Even her *Holy Cow!* T-shirt was in the laundry basket. It too featured an animal with a halo, and was another gift she was never going to have the heart to get rid of because it was from—who else?—her misguided but always supportive mother. She rummaged through the rest of her drawers. Oh, wait. A rumpled long-sleeved silk blouse that should have been hung in the closet. Perfect.

Her phone rang and she snatched if off the bedside table as she tried semi-one-handedly to button her sleeves' cuffs.

It was Megan. "Kira has a friend in town visiting from New York and we're all going down to the beach after lunch. Want to join us? Catch some rays?"

"What rays?"

"In case you haven't rolled out of bed yet, it's a beautiful spring day."

Gwynne pulled on her favorite chamois shirt over her blouse, juggling the phone to get her arms into the sleeves. The chamois probably clashed, but she didn't have a lot of choices, and she'd need something warm later, when she left work. "Spring, yes. Beautiful, no. Are you trying to set me up with this friend?"

"Of course not." Megan's earnest Minnie Mouse squeak was unconvincing.

"You totally are."

"She's nice. And she's a dancer. Not to be shallow, but she has a great—"

"No," Gwynne said, cutting her off. "What's gotten into you? You never say stuff like that. I'm the crass one, remember?"

"Too feminine?" Megan persisted. "I never did figure out what your type was."

"And you never will." She wasn't about to tell her she might have finally figured it out herself. "Set her up with someone else."

"Like who? Hank?"

"What?" Hank was taken. Or at least she was the last time she saw her, which, besides third-party gossip, was the only way to know anything about Hank, because she wasn't the type to broadcast her personal life online. "Don't tell me Hank and Aisha broke up."

"They broke up."

Crap. "When?"

"Last week," Megan said.

She'd had high hopes for those two, but very few of their friends could see past Hank and Aisha's constant clashes to agree with her. Now it seemed her friends were right and she was wrong. "Hank must be devastated."

"Devastated enough to sleep with a stranger from New York and turn on the rebound to the loving arms of her dear friend Gwynne?"

That would never happen, and Megan knew it.

"Knock it off."

"I'm worried about you, that's all."

Megan was worried. Great. She'd have to make it a point to act happier next time she saw her.

"I don't need a woman to make it better." Not that she hadn't tried that approach in the past, but she liked to think she'd learned something from the experience.

"Of course you don't," Megan said. "I just thought…"

"I'm working this morning."

"I know. That's why I said we're going after lunch."

"I already have plans for after lunch. Abby and I are driving to Baltimore."

"Really." Megan sounded instantly suspicious. This was the problem with being friends with women who were smart. "What are you doing in Baltimore?"

"I'm helping her go through some boxes in her grandmother's attic."

"You'd rather go through musty old boxes than walk on the beach?"

"I can walk on the beach anytime," Gwynne said, ignoring Megan's unspoken question.

It didn't remain unspoken for long. Like, two seconds, really. "Why would Abby ask you to help?"

Megan was going to love this. "I offered."

"Typical," Megan said, and she was right.

Gwynne didn't need to help. She didn't want to help. But somehow she always found herself opening her mouth and volunteering. She should start her own chapter of Butting-Into-Other-People's-Business Anonymous. The thing was, though, she didn't trust Abby not to decide at the last minute to drive despite her suspended license. And besides, she was curious. She'd asked the angels what the deal was with Abby—what they needed her help with, why they thought she was an angel—and they'd refused to answer.

When Megan spoke again, she'd turned serious. "Is everything okay with her?"

Damn it. Did Megan sense something she should know about? Had Abby been asking Megan about her aura too?

"Uh…why?"

"I know I shouldn't have peeked in the windows of her van, but the backseats are missing and it looks like she has a mattress in there. I was concerned she might be sleeping in there. She's not homeless, is she?"

Gwynne felt a rush of relief. "She's not sleeping in her van. The mattress is in there to protect her harp."

"Oh. Good. Her harp." Megan sounded undecided about whether that made sense.

Well, it made sense to Gwynne. Maybe a pile of blankets would look less odd, but a mattress provided more padding, and considering the dilapidated appearance of Abby's minivan, she wouldn't be surprised if its suspension was subpar.

As she mumbled something about how there wasn't anything wrong with being slightly eccentric, Nimbus dashed into the room with Peter the Fifteenth at his heels, their nails scrabbling on the hardwood floor. They raced around her feet, circling and skidding at top speed, stopping on a dime to reverse direction and circle again. And again. Gwynne spun in place in her own version of rabbit dancing, and Nimbus got so excited that he jumped straight up and flicked his head spastically in midair while he tossed his hindquarters in the opposite direction.

Gwynne flicked her head over one shoulder but made sure she remained on the ground. The last time she'd attempted to add the full-body twist in midair, she'd crashed into the dresser, and she'd just as soon not repeat that fiasco while Megan was on the phone.

"So tell me again why you're driving with her to Baltimore?"

Nimbus sat back on his hindquarters between Gwynne's feet, his front paws lifting off the floor, and flicked his ears at Peter, who pounced on him.

Gwynne stepped over and around the fuzzy obstacle. "I'm doing her a favor, okay?"

"Int-er-est-ing." Megan dragged the word out.

"It's not interesting. We're friends."

"*Friends* is such a vague word. It can mean so many things."

True. So true.

Which made it the perfect word.

CHAPTER TEN

Gwynne was running late. The spa had been unusually busy that morning, and by the time Abby was supposed to show up for Gwynne to play chauffeur, she was still dealing with customers and desperate for a bite of the provolone, avocado and roasted red bell pepper sandwich that called to her from her desk drawer. What she was really desperate for was to spend time with Abby. Well, no, not *desperate*. Feeling a tingle of anticipation at the thought of spending the afternoon together didn't mean she was desperate. Not necessarily.

The phone rang. "Abby?"

"I'm here," Abby said. "Where are you?"

"Inside. I'm sorry, I'm not quite done here."

"No problem. I'll wait for you outside."

Gwynne finished up with a customer while half listening to Yolanda, who was taking the afternoon shift for her, tell a long-winded story about her cat's visit to the vet, which would normally have interested her, but not today. She finally extricated herself and left through the hotel's side door rather than the front to cut her walk to the parking lot by a few seconds. While she walked, she got her arms into her coat sleeves and pulled out her phone. "Where are you?"

"Out front," Abby said. "By the benches."

Oops, wrong way. Holding the phone to her ear, Gwynne headed in that direction, around the side of the building and toward the main entrance where several marble benches nestled among tall ornamental grasses the landscaping crew hadn't yet sheared to the ground for spring. "Looking forward to visiting your grandparents?"

"Yeah, I haven't seen them in a while. How about you? You get an afternoon off and you decide to spend it stuck in a car with me?"

"I'll live."

Gwynne came within sight of the benches and spotted Abby lying flat on her back in a shaft of sunlight, one boot-clad leg sprawled over the front of the bench, the other leg dangling off the end, the inseams of her jeans stretched tight. She had one arm folded behind her head, which made her fisherman's sweater ride up; with the other she pressed her phone to her ear. She was the sexiest thing she had ever seen.

"You haven't seen my backseat driving," Abby said into the phone as a gust of wind rustled the ornamental grasses. "I can be pretty distracting."

"Now you tell me."

Abby's back arched—just a bit—in a discreet yet incredibly sensual and open way. Gwynne sucked in her breath, on the edge of arousal. Tension coiled in her thighs. Abby was attracted to her. She was moving like that because she was thinking about her, talking to her.

Gwynne gripped the phone more tightly and stopped walking, afraid to startle her from the bench. She wanted to climb onto her. Her hips wanted to grind into hers—wanted it badly. The contact would be electric. Devastating. She became dizzy thinking of that broad expanse of bare skin she'd come so close to touching in her bedroom, that bra she wanted to unhook, the toned arms that Abby hid under long sleeves when she played the harp.

Abby swiveled and sat up. "Where are you? Are you still inside?"

"I'm here." Gwynne put her phone away and closed the distance between them with quick, shaky strides. "Ready to go?"

Abby started to get up, but then with a sharp, abrupt movement pressed one hand to the side of her face and sank back down, rubbing her jaw, clearly in pain. Her aura turned muddy.

"Is your ear infected again?" Gwynne sat next to her on the bench, her hands burning with the need to help. "Did you see a doctor? You didn't, did you?"

"I didn't have time."

"You need antibiotics." Gwynne peered into her ear. "It's completely swollen."

"The antibiotics never work for long. The infection always comes back."

"There must be something they can do."

"Yes, doctor."

"Sorry." Abby wasn't a client. She didn't need her to tell her what to do. She certainly didn't need to push her away with her usual I-don't-see-clients-anymore, go-see-a-doctor attitude. The last thing in the world she wanted to do was push her away.

What she wanted to do was take away her pain. She *could* take away her pain. She'd never had a problem easing her clients' suffering. She couldn't save their lives, but at least she could make people more comfortable. And with all the light that bubbled up in her heart in Abby's presence—with all the love—the healing would be effortless.

She wasn't talking about platonic love, either. No, that effervescent weightlessness coursing through her body was not the least bit platonic.

"I can get rid of the swelling," Gwynne offered, trying to keep the emotion out of her voice. "That should help."

"With your energy?"

"Yeah." Without waiting for a response, Gwynne opened her heart and threw her consciousness out into the void, letting herself disintegrate into vast, exhilarating nothingness. After a breathless eternity, the void began to vibrate. The vibration was quiet at first, barely audible, but soon it became louder and louder until the void became filled with it, became a universe of countless sparks that sang and pulsed and swirled into eddies and currents.

Another healer might have tried to pull that swirling energy through her body and channel it. But she didn't draw energy from the universe, she *was* the energy of the universe. With a thought, she burned out Abby's infection, chased down the microbes that evaded her, and, acting on instinct grounded in years of experience, found the biofilm where they hid and broke it down so they wouldn't return.

"I already feel a difference," Abby said. "There's less pressure now."

"You don't feel dizzy?"

"No, I feel great."

"You sure?"

"Yeah, thanks."

Abby skipped to the parking lot and surprised Gwynne by ending up at the right car. Gwynne followed more slowly, part of her still out there in the seductive void, reluctant to return to earth. Abby hopped onto the hood of Gwynne's car and waited for her to catch up, sitting there with her ankles crossed and swinging her legs.

"What did you do to me?" Abby said when Gwynne arrived and unlocked the doors. "I mean, energy healing. What is that, really?"

"Basically? It's faith healing without the religious bullshit."

Abby slid off her perch and leaned back, pressing her hands behind her against the car.

"I like you, Gwynnosaurus. You're not afraid to have an opinion."

Abby *liked* her. Jesus.

Gwynne stared at her. "Usually people feel dizzy afterward." The energy was a lot to handle, and her clients *always* felt dizzy as a result. Sometimes they even…"You're not going to throw up, are you?"

"Do I look like I'm going to throw up?"

Abby's aura looked strong, but also fiery and chaotic, which gave her pause. "You look like I need to do a bit more to finish this."

"Okay."

"I could try to hold back," she said doubtfully.

"Don't hold back. I can handle it."

"Such an optimist." At least they were outdoors if she did upchuck. With her mind, she touched the essence of Abby's immune system and energized it, giving it the strength to overpower what was left of the infection on its own, then soothed the ear with a final pulse of compassion.

Abby prodded her ear, testing it. "It's like magic. No wonder your clients don't want to let you go."

Make that her *ex*-clients. Gwynne's mood instantly soured. "They'll survive without me."

* * *

The drive to the leafy Baltimore suburb where Abby grew up took an hour longer than it would have taken Abby to drive herself, but after an eternity of watching Gwynne keep to the speed limit, they arrived at her grandparents' familiar split-level. Finally she could stop thinking about Gwynne, about how her healing energy had swept through her, warm and overpowering, charging her up, making her weak in the knees.

When Gwynne had asked if she felt dizzy, she'd lied, because she seriously doubted she was having the usual reaction. Dizzy? Sure, she could believe other people got dizzy. But did they also get warm and turned on? Probably not. She hoped not.

She pushed those thoughts aside and traipsed up the buckled walkway to the front door. Gwynne was right behind her, which made it difficult not to think about her, but the irritating whine of a chain saw coming from somewhere nearby and the sound of barking dogs helped. Anything that distracted her was good. There was a note stuck to the screen door telling them to go around back, so they circled to the backyard.

Grams, in purple flowered gardening gloves, was wielding a chain saw against a fallen maple tree, turning it into firewood. Grams spotted them and stopped the saw.

"How are you even lifting that?" Abby surged forward to try to take the chain saw away before Grams hurt her back or dropped the thing on her toe. Just four weeks ago, she had broken her foot under vague, unexplained circumstances and ended up in the hospital. "Don't you think you should let somebody else—"

"Do you know how much people charge for tree work? It's outrageous." Grams revved the engine and swung the saw to prove she had it under control, even as she struggled with her footing.

Abby placed a restraining arm in front of Gwynne, who wasn't hanging back, to keep her well out of range. Where was Gramps? He shouldn't let Grams do stuff like this, but then again, he never could stand up to her, so why start now? When Grams decided something needed to be done, she did whatever it took to get it done.

Grams pointed her chain saw in Gwynne's direction. "Who are you? Do you live with my granddaughter?"

"We work together, Mrs. Vogel," Gwynne said.

"Is that what they're calling it these days?"

"I suspect you know exactly what we call it these days." Gwynne flashed her a smile that would charm anyone's socks off.

Grams eyed her suspiciously. "Oh, nonsense."

Gwynne winked at her.

Grams beamed.

Oh, God. Gwynne was flirting with Grams.

"Grams, this is Gwynne Abernathy," said Abby, belatedly making the introductions. "She works at the spa where I play."

"How nice. Would you girls be interested in homemade gingerbread cookies? I was just about to pop some in the oven."

"That sounds great," Abby said as Gwynne simultaneously agreed, clearly onboard with anything that got Grams to relinquish the chain saw.

"I made gingerbread girls just for you, Abby," Grams said as they followed her into the kitchen. The oven was already on, a tray of shaped raw cookie dough waiting. "I know you like them better than the gingerbread boys."

Abby kissed her on the cheek. Grams gave her a tight squeeze and shooed her into the living room. Gwynne stuck close beside her as everyone settled into chairs around a coffee table that was usually buried under several inches of her grandfather's newspapers but today was clear.

"Are you a musician too?" Grams asked Gwynne.

"I'm the spa manager," Gwynne said.

"She supervises the staff," Abby explained. "She used to be a massage therapist."

Grams nodded approvingly. "How wonderful to be able to help people in pain."

A mask fell over Gwynne's face, but she smiled politely. "I try."

"When Abby was a child she was always curious about others' injuries. I'd have a scratch on my arm and she would want to put a bandage on it. Once, she stopped a stranger on crutches in the street, went right up to him and asked him how he got hurt. He told her he fell, and she looked up at him, absolutely puzzled. 'You fell?' she asked him in that tiny voice, and you could see plain as day that she didn't understand. So she deliberately tripped herself. Over and over. I had to take her hand and tell her to stop because I was afraid she was going to hurt herself. She knew something was wrong and she was simply determined to figure out what happened to that poor man."

"You never told me that," Abby said. It seemed like it was always the embarrassing stories that were deemed worthy of being repeated, not the nice ones.

"Your grandfather and I were convinced you were going to become a nurse. You had such empathy at such a young age."

"Where *is* Gramps?" Abby asked.

"He's puttering in the basement like he always is. He removes his hearing aid so he has an excuse to ignore me when I call down the stairs, but the smell of cookies in the oven will lure him up here eventually. Cookies and anything in a skirt—that's all he notices."

Abby glanced at Gwynne, but she appeared to be listening with amused interest, not thrown by Grams at all. Maybe she had lots of experience meeting girlfriends' parents.

What a depressing thought.

When the cookies were baked and they'd all eaten a few and Gramps had made a brief appearance before retreating to the basement, the three of them trooped upstairs to the trapdoor to the attic. Abby pulled down the squeaky wooden ladder and unfolded it, then tested her weight on the rungs as Gwynne and her grandmother looked on, both of them ready to grab her by the waist and steady her.

"No one's been up there in years," said Grams. "I sure hope you don't see any rodents."

"Me too." Wasn't that the truth. Not that she'd scream or anything—rats and cockroaches had never bothered her—she'd just rather not have anything interfere with her search, especially not a critter known to chew paper. She crawled through the opening and made her way to the middle of the attic where the sloped roof was high enough for her to stand. Her hands were covered in dust.

"Is that the smell of rodent pee?" Gwynne asked, emerging from the trapdoor behind her.

"God, I hope not."

"What type of rodent was she talking about, anyway?"

"Squirrels," Abby said firmly. She didn't know if Gwynne was squeamish about rats, but if she was, ignorance would be bliss, and she would try to prolong her bliss as long as possible.

Gwynne winked. "If you say so."

"Holler if you need anything," her grandmother called from below.

"Sure thing," Abby called back, positive she wouldn't. The last thing she wanted was for her elderly grandmother to get it into her head that she should be climbing rickety ladders, although why she bothered to worry about a ladder when Grams was out there with a chain saw, she didn't know.

* * *

The way Abby was bouncing on the balls of her feet, Gwynne expected her to attack the boxes immediately. Instead, she spun around to look at them all.

"I can't decide where to start," Abby said.

Gwynne helped her out by picking a large cardboard box at random and dragging it to an open spot. "How about here."

Abby humored her and opened the flaps, which were tucked corner over corner. "I hope it was okay that I told Grams you used to be a massage therapist. I don't know how to explain what you really do."

"I did used to be a massage therapist. It's close enough."

"But that's not really what you do. Like with my ear—it doesn't hurt anymore. And all those people who come to you for help. What do you do, exactly?"

"I don't do anything."

"Obviously you do something."

"I used to think so." Gwynne opened her own box and discovered it was full of toys. She closed it and put it back.

"What changed?"

Gwynne opened another box and pulled out a kindergarten scribble on orange construction paper. "Hey, look at this." She held it out so Abby could see. "I think this one's supposed to be an angel."

Abby took the sheet from her and reached over her to lift the next one out of the box. "This one too."

One after another, she pulled them out—pipe-cleaner angels glued to paper, fuzzy felt angels sprinkled with glitter, angels drawn on construction paper in pencil, in colored markers, in every single color that came in a sixty-four-crayon box.

"I had no idea I did all this. No idea." Abby spread the artwork out on the floor. "And I can't believe Grams saved all this stuff. I can't tell you how uncomfortable she was when I asked her if there was anything unusual about my childhood, like, oh, let's say, a connection to the Angelic Realm."

"You couldn't finesse the question any better than that?"

"I finessed my way to this box, didn't I?" Abby unfolded a chain of paper dolls that were joined wing to wing instead of hand to hand and laid it carefully on top of the drawings. "This is amazing."

"Did she say anything else?"

Abby grimaced. "She said she hoped I'd forgotten my childish fantasies."

Abby seemed annoyed. But she was lucky. She was lucky someone had tried to talk her out of the angel stuff.

If only Gwynne had done the same for her sister.

Like the time she was eight or nine years old and climbed onto Heather's bed, which was the one under the window. She balanced on her tiptoes, clutching the window ledge to peek out, and was riveted by the zillions of bright yellow lights blinking in the darkness. She stared as hard as she could, fixing on a light and watching it blink out, waiting for it to reappear in the same spot. It was so beautiful she hardly breathed.

Heather jumped up and down, trying to reach the window. "Let me see!"

The bouncing mattress made it hard to balance. Gwynne picked up her little sister, hauled her against her body, and lifted her as high as she could. Her back arched from the effort.

"Up," Heather demanded.

"You *are* up," Gwynne said, but then she realized Heather had her nose to the wall and the window ledge remained above her head. She tried to boost her higher, but she stumbled on the wobbly mattress under her sister's weight and they both fell.

She tried another couple times, then thought of another approach. She gathered their pillows and books and all of Heather's stuffed animals from around the room, piled them under the window, and shoved Heather to the top. Heather clung to the window ledge for dear life.

"Fireflies," Heather said.

"And fairies," Gwynne pointed out. "And angels. The big lights are angels."

"Big lights."

"See them?"

"I want to see big lights."

"They're right there, see? Dancing in a circle with the fireflies."

"I want to see big lights!"

"Can't you see them?" *She* could see them. They were right there.

Heather looked at her reproachfully with those big eyes and promptly toppled off her tower of stuffed animals and onto the bed.

And never gave up trying to see what her big sister could see.

Gwynne wished with all her heart she had never mentioned those damn angels.

Abby was a different story. She had psychic perception, same as Gwynne. They saw the world in the same way, and she had to admit there was something very attractive about that.

Attractive? Try enchanting. Seductive. Tempting.

That didn't mean she should pursue her, though.

Abby was the good-girl type. She had class. She didn't survive by flirting with anything in a skirt, as Abby's grandmother put it, or, as Gwynne preferred to think of it, anything in a bra. Or out of one. Abby was approachable without flashing her sexuality. She wandered the halls of a hospital with her harp or disappeared into the corner at weddings instead of being onstage being a star, begging people to notice her.

She was pure. And Gwynne wasn't.

Gwynne was a fraud. Women were always purring around her and she didn't deserve any of it, but she'd been oozing charm for so long, she didn't know how to turn it off. Not that turning it off would make any difference—even when she was grumpy, women were still drawn to her, and for all the wrong reasons.

If only things had been like that in high school. Back then, she couldn't wait to grow up and find a magical land where girls didn't giggle and primp around the gawky, boastful enemy. Back then, she would have worshipped any girl who noticed her.

And that was the problem. Once they did start to notice her, she'd been so afraid no one else would ever go out with her that she threw herself into relationships with girls she wasn't particularly in love with, girl after girl, ever hopeful, stupidly picking the ones she was the least compatible with and trying as hard as she could to prove she was worth keeping. Not surprisingly, the relationships never lasted long.

Offering to drive Abby—that fit her pattern. The difference was, she really did have some solid reasons for liking her that had nothing to do with their physical attraction. That was unfortunate, really, because she liked her too much to subject her to the Gwynne-capades.

Which didn't stop her from watching for a glimpse of cleavage as Abby dragged out another box labeled with her name.

"Resting?" Abby asked, setting the box in front of her.

"Distracted."

Abby gave her a quizzical look, but didn't ask. She rocked the box onto its side and pulled out the contents—all paper. "Come on, Gwynnosaurus. Let's get cracking." She divided the stack and dropped half of it in Gwynne's lap.

It was an effective distraction from her don't-go-there thoughts. With Abby sitting on the rough wooden floor across from her, Gwynne flipped through and discovered report cards and letters home from school and medical records providing proof of vaccination and all sorts of other things in torn envelopes. One of the report cards had several sheets attached.

> *Abby received an incomplete for the first quarter because she was not in class for a significant portion of the marking period and has not caught up on the work she missed while receiving inpatient psychiatric care.*

"What is this?" Gwynne thrust the packet at Abby.

Abby glanced at it without touching it, then looked at her hands in her lap. "Nothing."

"Nothing. Right." Gwynne tossed the report card onto the floor. "You were in a psych ward?"

"Not for long."

God, she was only in elementary school. She remembered Abby mentioning something like this, but this was so much worse than she realized. Had Abby even been old enough to understand what was happening to her?

"When you told me you went through psychiatric testing, I imagined a doctor asking you a few questions and sending you home. I didn't think it was *this*."

Abby clasped her hands together and cracked her knuckles like she needed something to keep her hands busy. "Yeah, I don't like to talk about it. I *don't* talk about it, actually. Only with you, I guess."

"Was there anything wrong with you at all besides the angel sightings?"

"They never said. All I knew was I couldn't go home until my friends left. They meant the friends in my head."

Gwynne mentally thanked her own mother for being sane and not panicking about invisible winged playmates. Not that every parent could enjoy playing pretend as much as her mother did, but no defenseless child should be hospitalized for speaking her truth.

"I learned to give the doctors the answers they wanted to hear so they wouldn't put me on antipsychotics."

Gwynne's heart burned with a possessive need to travel back in time and take Abby home with her so her mother could adopt her. Her mother would have taken her in and loved her and told her she wasn't crazy. "I can't believe they would do that to a kid."

"They were worried about me. The doctors thought I might be early-onset schizophrenic and need to be put on medication, and my grandparents were afraid the doctors were right—that I inherited the voices in my head from my mother. At some point my mother had told them the reason she started drinking and doing drugs was to drown out the voices. They reminded me of that constantly, trying to scare me out of following in her footsteps, arguing with each other over whose fault it was that she destroyed herself." Abby lowered her voice, probably so her grandmother below wouldn't overhear. "Gramps accused Grams of bad parenting, and Grams insisted there had to be something wrong with his genes, because there was nothing wrong with *her* side of the family, and it was his bad seed that put her through all those miscarriages and gave them a daughter who wasn't right in the head and maybe a granddaughter who wasn't, either."

"Fun childhood."

Abby twisted her hands. "Maybe my mother would have taken the doctors' drugs to quiet her voices, if she'd had the chance."

"Maybe *her* voices weren't real."

Abby closed her eyes and sighed. "What my grandparents really were worried about was brain damage. Grams says my mother told her she was clean during the pregnancy, but I don't blame them for not believing her."

"Brain damage does not cause hallucinations." Gwynne didn't know if that was actually true, but it didn't matter, because Abby was not hallucinating.

"They were worried about me. They were trying to do the right thing."

"Hospitalization doesn't seem like overkill to you?"

"Grams lost her daughter. She wasn't going to lose her granddaughter."

"Yeah, but—"

"It wasn't that bad. The nurses were nice to me. They played games with me and stuff. It was okay. And they didn't threaten to put me in foster care if I didn't behave, the way my grandparents did."

Abby didn't even seem angry. She accepted what happened to her like it was all perfectly okay that the adults in her life had treated her like there was something terribly wrong with her when she was surely just a normal, sweet little kid. It was a miracle she'd survived with her innate goodness intact.

"You're amazing, you know that?"

"Not that amazing."

"You are."

Abby shrugged dismissively. She turned to her pile of papers and continued working her way to the bottom, muttering as she leafed through. "SAT scores. Birth certificate. Adoption. Adoption. More adoption." She paused. "Police report. There was a police report?" Her voice rose in surprise.

Gwynne held her breath, wondering what the next bomb was going to be.

"Listen to this." Abby peered at the yellowed report in the poor lighting, bringing it close to her face and then standing to hold it under the bare lightbulb overhead. "Toddler found wandering on the sidewalk unattended," she read aloud. "Mother found dead from suspected drug overdose." She lowered her arm. "I can't believe Grams never told me the police found me on the street. She told me about my mother's screw-ups often enough. Why didn't she tell me this?" She bent down to hand the thin sheet of paper to Gwynne, as if she needed her to confirm what it said.

Gwynne ignored the report and pushed to her feet and put her arms around her. She didn't know what else to do, and physically touching people in pain was such an ingrained response that she didn't think twice. Abby tightened her arms around her before it could turn into an awkward dance of oh, wait…okay…I guess I could…hug. It was a real hug, with Abby's head at her shoulder and her chest pressed close. Thank God.

"What else didn't they tell me?" Abby said near her ear.

"Why don't you ask them?"

"I can tell you what they'll say. Gramps will say 'Ask your grandmother' and Grams will say she doesn't remember, that's what they'll say. I should ask the officer who wrote up this report—maybe she remembers what happened."

Abby was still clinging to her, and her body heat felt way better than it had any right to. This hug was supposed to be for Abby's sake, not her own. Gwynne pulled away before she gave in to the temptation to close the miniscule gap between their lower bodies, but as they pulled apart, she trailed her fingers down Abby's arms, tracing her forearms and lingering at her wrists, not sure she was willing to let her go.

The police report fluttered from Abby's fingers to the ground. There was desire in Abby's flushed face, and her nipples were hard. They hadn't been…visible…before, had they? She was pretty damn sure she would have noticed.

* * *

Abby reached for her again. Gwynne's hug had been…too polite. She wanted to press into her with the full length of her body. Needed it. She pulled her close and her curves felt exactly the way she knew they would, warm and yielding and irresistible.

She had to kiss her. She wanted to kiss her. She wanted…

And one more thing. Don't go out with Gwynne. I don't want any other complications. Elle's bizarre warning flitted through her brain and made her pause. Besides, her grandmother was downstairs. She let her arms drop. "I'd better not."

"Better not what?" Gwynne asked softly, but it was clear from the gruffness of her voice and the invitation in her lips that she knew exactly what Abby meant.

Abby shivered. "Kiss you."

"Kiss me. Is that what you were planning to do?"

Gwynne had a great voice. They were standing so close she could feel it thrum through her body.

Abby strained closer, as close as she could get without touching. "Couldn't you tell?"

"Of course I could tell. I thought *I* was going to kiss *you*."

"Only because I was going to kiss you first." And God, she still really wanted to.

Gwynne brushed her thumb over her cheek. "Are you always this verbal? Usually people don't talk about this, they just do it."

Abby closed what distance was left. Their lips touched, and a spark of static electricity zapped her with an audible pop. They jumped apart. Abby banged her heel into a packed cardboard box.

"Ow!" they both said simultaneously.

Gwynne rubbed her mouth and laughed with what sounded like disbelief. "Why are you so staticky?"

"Me? Maybe it was you!"

"I'm not staticky."

"Not anymore, you're not, not after that."

Gwynne traced the outline of Abby's body, her hands an inch away from her skin the way she'd seen her do during her healings. There was no touching, but watching her pay such careful attention to her shape—even if it was to avoid accidental contact—heated her skin. She wasn't sure what Gwynne was doing—maybe checking her for static?—but whatever it was, it felt intimate and caring and not as bizarre as she would have thought.

Gwynne pulled away, apparently finished with whatever she'd done. "I'm guessing that's not what people mean when they say they met someone and sparks were flying."

"Probably not." Abby rubbed her arms, soothing her frazzled nerves, and suddenly she wondered how natural the shock's natural causes had been. If it was Elle interfering, she was *not* going to help her with her pesky little engineering problem. But there was no sign of any angel.

"Elle warned me not to date you," Abby said.

"Don't listen to her."

In general, Abby agreed with her on that. Still, as much as she wanted Gwynne, there was a part of her that couldn't shake the feeling that if Elle had told her not to date Gwynne, there might be a good reason for it. Sapphire always gave her good advice. She told her which patients to play for, gave her job ideas like Candace's successful open house, and helped her avoid car accidents. If she trusted Sapphire, maybe she should trust Elle too. No angel had ever betrayed her.

"You think she caused the static?" Gwynne said.

"I don't know."

"I don't think she's here."

"I don't either," Abby said.

"So that leaves—"

"A natural repulsive force?"

Gwynne ran her hands through her hair and fluffed it into fresh spikiness. "So much for my attempts at seduction. Making you recoil from my touch has to be a new low."

"It wasn't that bad."

"Yes it was."

"Okay, it was pretty bad," Abby admitted. Who'd want to kiss again after an electric shock? She certainly didn't. Except it could have been so good. She moistened her lips. Maybe if their lips weren't dry…"Want to try again?"

Gwynne's expression softened. "You're fearless." She smiled, angling her head. "I like that about you."

Abby went for it. Gwynne moaned, and Abby decided that kissing her again was a really, really good idea. She smelled like sunshine and kissed like a goddess and being with her made her feel less alien than with anyone else. Their bodies strained against each other, joining everywhere, and her nerves lit up from the contact, dancing with sensory overload.

Gwynne tugged on Abby's sweater and pushed it up like she had every intention of undressing her, mere moments into their first kiss. Second kiss. Whatever.

"Not here." Hazy with desire but still able to remember where she was, Abby grabbed her hands. Her grandmother had probably returned to the kitchen, but the attic's floorboards were squeaky and the trapdoor was wide open. "Grams might hear us."

She twined their fingers together and raised their arms overhead, safely away from the hem of her clothing, creating a gap between their bodies that Gwynne immediately closed.

"Gwynne!"

"I'm no good with rules."

"Neither am I, but—"

"Perfect." Gwynne leaned forward so their foreheads touched, too charming for her own good.

Abby's heart thumped. This was how Gwynne would sound when she made love, like she was laughing inside and having fun, right up until the point where her breathing would become erratic and her voice would drop and that sexy voice would crack with a harsh cry. Abby desperately wanted to hear that.

Gwynne's gaze heated as if she sensed what she was thinking, and she kissed her, sweetly and not particularly apologetically. Abby melted into her and kissed her back because it was too wonderful a kiss not to. And it was no longer just her heart that ached, but lower, everywhere, because Gwynne's desire threw sparks that lodged in her core and burned inward and upward through to the filaments of her unprotected soul. She wasn't going to be able to walk away from this unscathed, and she didn't want to.

But Grams would never recover if she heard her granddaughter groaning and figured out it was not from lifting heavy boxes, so she reluctantly drew back an inch and tried to catch her breath. "Grams still has her hearing."

Gwynne lowered their joined hands and brought her elbows behind her own back, drawing Abby's arms forward to wrap around her waist. "We're being quiet."

"Not really."

Gwynne kissed her again. "Yes, really," she mumbled against her mouth between kisses, gentle but determined. "Unless you're planning to have sex with me up here. That might get loud." She pressed her lips to hers in another brief, addictive kiss. "I tend to scream."

Abby's mouth opened wider at Gwynne's confidence and Gwynne pressed her advantage, meeting her lips mid-gasp and deepening the kiss.

Abby finally came up for air to say, "That's very optimistic of you."

"You don't think you'd make me scream?" Gwynne said seriously. "You totally would."

Abby flushed. "What I *meant* was, it's very optimistic of you to think we might, you know…" She lowered her voice and hissed, because her grandmother taught her to be a good girl and she could barely say the words out loud, especially in this house, "…*have sex*…"—she returned to her normal volume—"…in the attic."

"You're right. That was more like wishful thinking."

"Be serious."

"I am." She curled her fingers around Abby's triceps and caressed her with a gentle but persuasive touch.

Abby's legs weakened. She wasn't that good a girl. "We have to stop."

Gwynne's fingers trailed down her arms and clasped her hands. "Because of Grams?"

"Yes."

Gwynne squeezed her hands and let go. "I can wait."

Abby shook her head. She'd been the one insisting they stop, but…Gwynne didn't have to sound so calm and reasonable about it.

Gwynne could wait? Good thing one of them could.

* * *

The icy clouds below were thin and wispy, as if the winds at this nosebleed altitude high above Baltimore had screamed through and torn the clouds apart in their wake.

Don't look down, Elle admonished herself as she unfurled her wings and soared higher. Not that she could see Abby from this height anyway, so there was no point in looking—logic that ought to work but somehow didn't.

One of the other angels swept in on the wind and joined her. "Why did you tell her not to date Gwynne?" asked the angel.

"You know why," Elle said.

"She's not going to listen to you."

"Probably not. Does she listen to me about anything?"

"She used to."

"Did she?" Elle's heart ached for the friendship she and Abigail had put on hold thirty-one years earlier. Abigail never listened to her, but Elle loved her anyway. It was the acting like they'd never met that hurt, even though it was unavoidable.

And Gwynne…

Not unexpected. Abigail had a weakness for smart, psychic women. Always had. Once Gwynne showed her her heart, it would be impossible for Abigail to resist her.

She'd be happy for them except, well…Gwynne saw too much. Which was also not unexpected.

Elle let the wind carry her higher, away from the city and the two women searching through boxes in the attic. Leave it to those two to have found each other.

CHAPTER ELEVEN

It turned out the police officer who rescued Abby when she was a baby was still on the force, and when Abby told her she was planning to visit the apartment building where she'd spent the first three years of her life, Officer Mawson offered to meet her there. Then Gwynne insisted on driving, and now here she was, standing on a glass-strewn sidewalk next to Gwynne as the smell of sewage wafted their way, and saying screw it to the socially-appropriate-for-outdoors amount of space between them and holding hands, leaning into her, staring up at a pair of eight-story buildings fronted by a circular driveway and an anemic holly tree.

She didn't recognize the building. Somehow she'd thought that seeing it again would help her remember.

Gwynne pushed back Abby's sleeve to check her watch. "When did she say she was coming?"

"She's coming," Abby said.

She let go of Gwynne and ventured onto the dirt inside the circular driveway, keeping a careful eye out for dog poop, catching herself just in time before she stepped on a tiny green luminescent fairy dancing in a patch of weeds.

And then she remembered.

There'd been more of them when she lived here—hundreds of them—and angels too. A shiny neighbor in a long, white nightgown had led her out of her apartment and out the front door of the building to play tag with her friends and race around the holly tree. It couldn't be the same tree, could it? Maybe. She had followed the lady, leaving her mother sprawled on the bathroom floor.

"I played here the day my mother died," she told Gwynne, disgusted with herself. She'd been so callous. She should have sat and cried about her mother, not abandoned her and let Sapphire and the others distract her with a game.

At the sound of a car slowing, she turned. A police cruiser pulled up to the entrance and parked under a "No Parking" sign. As the uniformed officer got out, Abby rushed toward her, running from what she didn't want to see. The officer's hand went to her gun.

"Abby!" Gwynne said sharply, but Abby had seen her movement too, and pulled up short.

"Abigail Vogel?"

"That's me."

"Look at you, you're all grown up." The officer let go of her gun and shook her hand with a motherly grip. "Jackie Mawson."

"I'm surprised you remember me. It was a long time ago."

"I'll never forget it."

"Really? Why?" With all the crime she must deal with, an unsupervised little girl didn't seem memorable.

Officer Mawson clasped her hands together and looked past her, into the distance. "It was the darnedest thing. I'm driving around, patrolling the neighborhood, when all of a sudden I see this female in a white nightgown jump in front of my cruiser and put her hands up for me to stop. I stop, all right. I thought I was going to flatten her." She looked away, then down at her feet. "I did smash into her. I slammed my foot on the brake, but the way she darted into the road, there was no way I could stop in time. I'm telling you, I hit her. But the weird thing was, when I get out of my cruiser, she's standing there like everything's fine."

"She must have jumped out of the way at the last minute," Abby said.

"No, I swear I hit something. I'm telling you, I felt the impact. I couldn't understand it until I noticed her feet weren't touching the ground."

Gwynne drew in a sharp breath.

"The female was floating a few inches off the pavement." Officer Mawson cleared her throat. "I ask her if she's okay, and she doesn't say anything, just points to this toddler who's about to walk into traffic. I run after the kid and grab her, and the lady disappears. I never saw her leave. She was just…gone."

An angel. Of course there was an angel involved. Abby felt like she'd known the angels were involved even before she started searching. And her grandparents, if they knew about this, had for twenty-eight years very carefully said nothing to her.

Officer Mawson shifted her weight from one foot to the other. "You probably think I'm delusional, but you deserve to know what happened. If it weren't for her, I never would've spotted you."

"I don't think you're delusional," Abby said.

"No need to sugarcoat it. Believe me, you wouldn't be the first person to say it. I tell lots of people this story. I know how it sounds. But I know what I saw." She nodded, emphasizing her certainty. "An angel. Never seen one before, never seen once since, but that day, I saw an angel. She saved your life."

"You saved my life as much as she did." It was Officer Mawson who deserved the credit, not just the angel who materialized against her windshield, not Elle, who could have stopped that angel back then and saved herself a lot of trouble all these years later. "Thank you for stopping me from running into traffic."

"It was lucky for you that you figured out how to get out of the apartment. I guess you were old enough to know how to open a door, but if that door had had a deadbolt or a chain you couldn't reach, you never would have been able to get out on your own. The neighbors might've heard you crying eventually, if you were lucky. Or you'd have starved to death in there."

Abby didn't tell her that she hadn't left on her own. That she was leaning over her mother's body on the tile floor, begging her to wake up, pushing open one eyelid—behavior that usually got her in trouble—when the shiny lady appeared and led her away. "How long do you think I was in the apartment with… you know…with…my mother…after she died?"

"Not long at all. It was like you knew right away that you needed to get out of there. That she wasn't taking a nap. Seems to me the angels were looking out for you."

* * *

After Officer Mawson left, Abby propped herself up against the passenger-side door of Gwynne's car and kicked at a crumpled hamburger wrapper on the sidewalk. She cracked her knuckles, one finger at a time, going through the sequence from pinky finger to thumb and then back again, seeing if she could get any more pops out of them, while Gwynne, saint that she was, waited patiently for her to spit out what was bothering her. Being around someone she didn't have to pretend with, who didn't think it was weird she saw angels, was such a relief, but she was so used to dodging the topic that it was hard to switch gears.

"You know when I said at Penelope's wedding that an angel asked me for help?"

"Yeah?"

"She wants me to help repair the bridge that connects earth with the Angelic Realm."

"There's a bridge?"

"But the catch is, the only way I can help is if I kill myself."

Gwynne leaned next to her against the car. She looked surprisingly calm, like Abby had presented her with a complicated math problem to solve instead of a shocking, real-life demand. "That makes no sense. How helpful can you be if you're dead?"

"Um, well, the thing is, she said I'd turn into an angel."

Gwynne shook her head like she could shake the thought out of her mind. "And you believe her?"

"I don't know."

"You'd still be dead."

"Not if she's right."

Gwynne's eyes widened. "Please tell me you're not seriously considering this."

"Of course not." She couldn't deny there was something appealing about the idea, but she'd never do it. She wasn't crazy.

"Good." Gwynne didn't look completely convinced.

"Do you think I'm hallucinating?" That was the million-dollar question, and she hated to ask it, but if she was going to bring this up with anyone, it had to be Gwynne. Anyone else would tell her she was hearing imaginary voices.

Gwynne hesitated, and Abby braced herself for a suggestion to seek professional help. But that would mean Gwynne needed help too, wouldn't it?

"Relax." Gwynne bumped her shoulder with a reassuring playfulness. Leave it to Gwynne to be goofy even when she was serious. "I have no doubt the angel is real. But—"

"But?"

"But that doesn't mean you should listen to her. She has no right to ask for your life."

"I'm not planning on giving it to her. But I do want to help if there's some other way."

"I'm all for being helpful, but why?"

"I followed that angel out of the apartment. She saved my life. Maybe I owe them."

"You don't owe them your life."

"I do if they saved me," Abby argued, not sure which side she was on. "A life for a life."

"That's not how it works. If they wanted you dead they shouldn't have saved you when you were three. I don't understand why they bothered."

"Thanks for caring," Abby huffed.

"Besides, that's what they want you to think. They want you to think you owe them, and should therefore do whatever they ask."

Gwynne was being unreasonable. "They saved me because they believe I'm one of them."

"You don't know that."

"I thought they were your friends."

Gwynne's face hardened. "I don't trust them."

"Why not?"

Gwynne kept her gaze fixed straight ahead, not looking at her. "You saw them at the hospital, didn't you? In my mother's room? You must have seen them."

"Yes," Abby said cautiously. Ever since Megan McLaren had pulled her aside one day and warned her that Gwynne was having a rough time because her sister and her mother were dead, Abby had avoided asking her about it, but she'd love to know why she'd sent those angels away.

"The angels could have done something to save my mother," Gwynne told her, seething. "But they didn't. They didn't save my sister, either."

"It's okay to be angry," Abby said.

She pulled Gwynne into her arms, but Gwynne pushed away and escaped into the car. Abby followed her to the driver's side and Gwynne actually scooted to the passenger's side to get away from her. Abby clambered in after her, expecting Gwynne to order her out of the driver's seat, but Gwynne only looked out the window.

"It's okay to be angry at them," Abby repeated.

"I'm not angry at them," Gwynne said. "I am angry at myself."

"For not being able to save your family yourself?"

"For deluding myself into thinking any of this was real. Angels and energy and fixing things with my so-called abilities."

"For failing."

"For wasting my life on this stuff."

The crazy thing was, Gwynne still talked to angels, still believed healing could happen through faith alone, still wanted to help the people who visited her at the spa. She could have left the healing profession completely, but she chose not to. She chose to take a job where she was surrounded by people who believed angelic healing was normal. Sure, she said she took the job as a favor for Megan, but if she'd really wanted to, she could have said no.

"I know you wanted to save their lives," Abby said, "but psychic powers don't make you God. You did your best."

"The one time I really needed the angels' help, they didn't do a damn thing."

"So you're mad at them."

"I am angry," Gwynne ground out word by word, "at myself."

"For believing in angels."

The bitterness in Gwynne's eyes was hard to watch. "Yes."

Abby touched her shoulder. Gwynne stiffened, and Abby dropped her hand to her side. But she wanted so much to reassure her that without even thinking about it, she reached for her again.

It was a stupid move. Gwynne took her hand and peeled it off her shoulder and placed it on the steering wheel. She was gentle about it, but the rebuff was clear.

"I don't want to do this right now," Gwynne said.

"Okay." Abby clenched the wheel and stared straight ahead, wishing she could disappear the way angels did. Such a great way to get out of uncomfortable situations, especially when they were caused by your own crummy timing.

Gwynne slapped her keys on the dashboard. Abby glanced at the keys but didn't take them. She wanted Gwynne to want her to drive because she trusted her, not because she was too upset to trust herself.

"I still want to be friends," Gwynne said.

Oh, no. No, no, no. Not that. "You're breaking up with me already?"

"It's not going to work out. And the sooner we realize that..."

Gwynne didn't mean it. She was upset. They'd talk later and they'd kiss and make up. They'd...

"I'm sorry," Gwynne said.

"Okay." Abby took the keys and started the ignition, wondering if she'd be able to pull out of their parallel parking space without jerky, telltale movements.

"You okay?"

"Dandy," Abby spat out. "You?"

Gwynne made an indecipherable noise that sounded vaguely like assent, but could easily have meant just about anything.

Abby maneuvered the car onto the road and blew through a stop sign as she peeled away. They weren't going to kiss and make up. And it was going to be a long drive home.

CHAPTER TWELVE

Abby followed a trail of solar lights along a well-groomed path through the trees on the grounds of Sea Salt in search of the hot tubs Gwynne had grumpily suggested. Abby had been stretching her back and massaging her shoulders after a long afternoon of playing music at the spa when Gwynne had thrust a fluffy towel into her arms and sent her in this direction. She wished Gwynne had offered to rub her shoulders instead, but apparently she was serious about them not touching. Probably serious about the breakup too.

Before she got very far, she ran into Dara Sullivan, who was holding a tree branch in front of her like it was a dowsing rod and taking stiff, awkward steps.

Dara spotted her and let the branch drop to her side. "Are you here for the energy?"

Abby had no idea what she was talking about. "I heard there were hot tubs." She held up her towel in explanation.

"Just follow the path," Dara said. "You'll find them."

"Thanks."

"This your first time here?"

"Yeah."

"I'm surprised Gwynne's not with you. I thought she'd want to show you Angel Rock herself. Isn't she off work yet?"

The last thing she wanted to talk about with Dara was Gwynne Abernathy—Dara had a crush on Gwynne, after all—and angels came in a close second. But she was curious. "What's Angel Rock?"

"This." Dara pointed to a large, upright boulder covered in lichen. "Gwynne thinks there's some kind of portal here that the angels use to travel back and forth between their world and ours. Megan agrees with her. So I was thinking, if I hang out here enough, eventually I'll see an angel, right? But no luck so far."

"Can't hurt to try," Abby said, flabbergasted. Where were all these people who believed in angels when she was growing up? This was certainly a conversation she never thought she'd have.

"Gwynne says it's one of those things where either you can see them or you can't. She has such a negative attitude. I think she just doesn't *want* me to try, and I have no idea why."

Abby bit her tongue.

Dara kept going. "Megan thinks I can learn. She says this place is a hot spot for healing energy and it can help me, and I'll take all the help I can get because my hands are in so much pain I don't know how much longer I can work as a massage therapist. I need to learn hands-off healing skills. I already do Reiki, which is kind of like what Gwynne does, but I need to get better at it. I need to learn to heal physical problems like Gwynne can. She's amazing. She could make millions if she opened a sunburn clinic by the beach, but she'd rather spend her time healing more serious problems. At least she used to. Which is important, I mean, of course she should be healing serious diseases if she can. But me, I'd be happy if I could get good enough to heal sunburn. It may seem minor to her, but it would be a real accomplishment for me. Or toenail fungus."

Abby couldn't help glancing at Dara's flip-flopped feet. They looked healthy enough. From a distance.

"Don't laugh. Do you have any idea how many people are embarrassed to go barefoot because they have toenail fungus that won't go away? If I could kill toenail fungus, I'd make millions." When Abby didn't respond, she shrugged. "Or at least make a living, that's all I need."

"Or you could become a podiatrist," Abby suggested.

"Sounds like something Gwynne would say." Dara dismissed the idea with a flick of her dowsing rod. "But it would never work. Megan understands. She's been coming here with me to help me practice my ability to sense subtle energies and work on a psychic level."

Dara was certainly committed. If this was the direction she wanted to take her career in, Abby didn't see why Gwynne wouldn't want her to succeed. "How's the practicing going?"

"Great!" Dara said. "Great." Her shoulders slumped. "Not so great," she admitted. "But it beats sitting at home in front of the TV worrying about my career and wishing I wasn't single."

But Gwynne had said…"I thought you were seeing someone."

"What? Oh." Her face fell. "That's just something I tell Gwynne. I don't want her to think I'm pining for her, you know? I don't want her to think I'm a loser."

"I'm sure she doesn't think that."

Dara fiddled with the giant quartz crystal she wore on a leather cord around her neck. "Yeah, because of my fake girlfriend."

"No, because she's not like that."

Dara looked at her blankly. "Not that I would say no if she ever did ask me out, but I know that's never going to happen. I know she doesn't want me."

If Dara only knew how much time Abby and Gwynne spent together—if she knew they'd kissed—she wouldn't be telling her all this. Of course, after the kiss, Gwynne had rejected her. She sounded like she meant it too, but that didn't mean… Because how could she kiss her and then turn around and say she didn't want her to touch her?

"Don't feel sorry for me," Dara said, reading only one facet of the expression on Abby's face. "I've moved on. I'm open to dating other people." She used her branch to scratch circles and zigzags in the dirt. "Besides, Gwynne has her eye on someone else."

Abby felt a flash of embarrassment. Dara knew? Dara didn't know. She didn't want Dara to know, because she didn't want to make her feel bad—if Abby and Gwynne had a salvageable relationship—or, if they didn't, to bond over both being rejected by the same woman. She didn't know what was up with Gwynne, and if she didn't know, there was no way an outside observer could know, no matter what Dara thought she saw.

"I wish she'd help me with my energy healing, though," Dara said. "Has she ever done any healing on you? She's amazing. It's like she opens up this space where you can breathe…and then the power of her energy slams you to the ground."

No, Abby hadn't felt any slamming when Gwynne healed her ear infection. The slamming came later, when Gwynne told her she didn't want her touching her—which was not a particularly healing experience. So yes, her ear didn't hurt anymore. Now it was the inside of her chest that hurt.

* * *

Gwynne pulled off the side of the road not far from the house where she grew up and tramped through pale winter weeds down to the river that flowed unnoticed under the white noise of the busy road. The water moved peacefully, relentlessly on its way. There was no sign that anyone had died here.

She picked her way down the steep, muddy bank, holding her arms out for balance, trying not to slip and land on her ass. This was the spot. Under the bridge. From here, she couldn't see the railing overhead anymore, only chattering sparrows who flew around the support beams building a nest.

The river was deceptively deep. Not that that mattered when the water was as cold as it had been in January. Her mother should have had more sense than to run onto the ice and try to save Heather on her own. She should have known the ice wouldn't hold. She was just like Abby, wanting to rush in and help without worrying whether it was safe.

No, not like Abby. Her mother was caught up in a frenzy of panic and wasn't thinking straight. Maternal instinct had taken over. She must have been terrified.

Abby didn't have the excuse of impulse or panic. She was calm, she was not terrified, she was trying to be logical—and letting logic lose badly to rationalization.

What Elle was asking her to do was dangerous. Irresponsible. Crazy. Not that angelic thought processes always made sense, but this was outrageous even for them. Couldn't Abby see that? How could she even consider doing what they asked?

Gwynne kicked the heel of her sneaker into the mud. This was why she couldn't date her. She needed to be with someone grounded and down-to-earth. Someone who wouldn't make her feel like *she* was the practical one. Someone who didn't talk to angels.

Unfortunately those down-to-earth types quickly lost patience with her once they figured out she spent most of her time, when she wasn't hanging out with angels or helping sick people go into spontaneous remission, staring off into space getting sidetracked by luminescent grids and vortexes of color that no one else could see. But that didn't mean she couldn't make it work. She'd try again. She'd meet someone, she'd be so charming that they'd overlook her habit of talking to invisible beings, and she'd forget all about Abby Vogel and live happily ever after.

Because she was not going to stand by and watch Abby self-destruct.

CHAPTER THIRTEEN

There was something to be said for not letting people know what you were capable of. Look at Abby sitting there behind her harp, wisely saying nothing—no one pestered *her* for tips on how to sense angels. No, they pestered Gwynne.

Gwynne planted her elbows on the spa's appointment desk and cupped her chin in her hands and glared at Dara. She was glaring at everyone today, wishing she didn't work in the same space as Abby.

"Don't try so hard," she told Dara, trying to think of something helpful to say. How did you teach someone to do something that came naturally? But Dara wanted it so badly. "Allow the angels to reveal themselves. It's the same with healings. Don't reach for the energy. Surrender into it. You strip away the noise and what's left is…nothing. That's when the energy starts to flow. Beyond that, I don't know what to tell you."

Dara keyed that bit of dubious wisdom into her notes. "But…"

"I don't know how to explain it any better."

"But…"

"And what I do is pointless, anyway." Her so-called abilities weren't as exciting as Dara seemed to think. "Why is this so important to you?"

"I need a new career. I can't keep doing massage forever."

"It doesn't have to be energy healing," Gwynne said with what she thought was extreme reasonableness. There were a million other jobs Dara could be trained to do.

"I wouldn't mind having your job, if you ever decide to go back to being a healer."

"I'm not going back to being a healer."

"How can you say that?" Dara protested. "You're so good."

Fortunately, she was spared from having to answer because Hank lumbered in with a stack of glossy brochures and wavered between handing them to Gwynne and clutching them uncertainly. Finally she settled on placing them on the edge of the desk and sliding them forward.

"Aisha wants to know if you'll display these for her."

Gwynne scanned the image of Aisha, standing out with her smoothly shaved head and her camouflage-print bikini, flanked by students doing pushups. Looked like she was offering her beach boot camp again this year. Aisha already had a successful career as a dentist, but had decided she liked to unwind from her day by yelling at students to haul ass. Supposedly she was friendly and gentle as a dentist, though. Go figure.

"I heard you guys broke up," Gwynne said. "Is that just a vicious rumor, or is it true?"

"It's true."

"I'm so sorry." Gwynne came around from behind her desk and gave her a hug, which was nothing like hugging Abby.

No. No thinking about hugging Abby. No thinking about kissing Abby. No thinking about…

"Want me to say mean things about her?" Gwynne said. "Like Aisha really, really, really doesn't deserve you?"

Hank shook her head mutely.

"How about like why is she making you run her errands for her? Dropping off these brochures?"

"It's okay, Gwynne."

"What's your favorite bra of hers?"

Hank choked. "You are not calling her the black satin bra, you hear?"

"Okay, but only because I don't want to confuse people and make them think she's *my* ex. I have enough exes around here."

Gwynne glanced guiltily in Abby's direction, but Abby was tuning a harp string, tightening the pin with her special wrench, and didn't look up. They may not have slept together, but after all the fantasizing she'd done, it almost felt like they had. She'd never felt that way after just one kiss.

Gwynne realized she still had her arms around Hank and released her. Hank plopped down on the nearest sofa and nearly landed in Dara Sullivan's lap.

"Excuse me," Hank said, mustering the energy to move only a few inches away before collapsing on the sofa cushions.

"I'm Dara, by the way," Dara told Hank's slumped form. "Would you like me to do some energy healing on you?"

Hank grunted. "You believe in that psychic crap Gwynne does?"

Dara leaned over her. "It's not crap."

Was that her hand on Hank's thigh? Okay, yeah, now it was on her shin. This should be interesting.

"You should try it," Dara said.

"Will it get my ex-girlfriend back?"

Dara jerked away. "No," she said stiffly.

"Then what good is it?"

"I'm just trying to help."

"Sorry." Hank sat up abruptly, showing more life than she had since she'd walked in. "I'm sure you're amazing. I'm probably missing out, right?"

Dara didn't bite. "Actually, I'm not that good. At psychic healing, I mean. I'm trying to get Gwynne to teach me."

Gwynne snatched the brochures from her desk in the vain hope that might keep her from being dragged into the conversation. She shuffled a few things on the display rack of local attractions to make room, then shuffled them a different way. Bored, she took a closer look at the beach boot camp brochure and noticed Hank was one of the students in the picture. Turning around, she made the mistake of glancing in Abby's direction and saw her smirk. Like Abby knew exactly what she was doing, messing around with the display rack when it did not need help.

"Why would you want to be psychic?" Hank was asking Dara.

"Who wouldn't?" Dara said.

"It's a waste of time."

"It's part of my spiritual path," Dara said. "I don't consider that to be a waste of time."

"If you want to be spiritual, just be a decent person," Hank said.

"I am a decent person," Dara said. "Thanks for the unhelpful advice."

"You don't need to be psychic to be spiritual," Hank insisted. "It's a distraction. Like…" She trailed off, like she couldn't decide on the perfect disparaging analogy. "Like…like having a hot body. You work and train and push yourself to get a great body—or in your case, ESP—and then what? So you have a great body. Or you see angels or ghosts or whatever. So what? All those hours of work, and on the inside you're still the same old sorry excuse for a human being."

Dara cleared her throat and Gwynne held her breath. Not thinking about hot-body beach boot camp babe Aisha, now were we?

Hank seemed to realize what she'd implied about Dara because she cleared her throat too. "Not that you're a…you know. No offense."

"I've heard worse," Dara sniffed.

"What I'm trying to say—badly—is do the work where it counts. You don't need to drink Gwynne's Kool-Aid like a girly girl and chase the shiny glitter."

"Psychic abilities are not glitter," Dara said. "They bring you closer to the nature of reality."

"Not in my book. You think Gwynne here understands the nature of reality?"

"Hey," Gwynne protested weakly. "I do you a favor and let you display your ex's brochures, and this is the thanks I get?"

She'd have to talk to Hank later, not because she couldn't handle the insults, but because she'd appreciate it if she watched her cracks about girly girls and glitter when Abby was within earshot. Hank didn't know how sparkly Abby's costumes could be, and she didn't want Abby to be hurt.

But hey, if Hank could convince Dara that her obsession with all things psychic was unhealthy, she'd tell her to knock it off with the glitter analogies and afterward she'd buy her dinner. Heck, she'd buy her flowers.

When Hank left, Dara rose from her seat and made a beeline for Aisha's brochure. She fished it from the rack and turned her back to Gwynne to stare at it, slouching over it like she needed privacy. "Her name is Hank?" she asked, not looking up.

"Yeah, I think it's really Henrietta," Gwynne said. "But she refuses to confirm or deny."

"Hank could be her real name," Dara said.

"Could be."

"It's cute. Is she on a spiritual path, do you think?"

"I'm sure you could find out," Gwynne said.

"She's single," Abby volunteered. She winked at Gwynne.

Gwynne's throat tightened. Abby was so beautiful. And so not for her.

It was sweet of her to try to steer Dara away from her and toward someone new, but wasn't Dara already involved with someone? Not that *that* relationship was working if Dara could still proposition Gwynne on a regular basis. Sure, she was joking, but underneath the flip attitude she was dead serious, and she made it obvious it wouldn't take much for her to break up with her mystery woman. Maybe Abby was right to push her into Hank's rebounding arms. She couldn't quite see the two of them hitting it off, but she'd be happy to be proven wrong. Thrilled. She'd buy *both* of them flowers.

* * *

In the spa's lounge the next afternoon, Gwynne watched Kira crouch in front of her rabbits' pet carrier and make an awkward attempt to talk to them through their jail bars. Kira really was trying. Which was sweet, because it was clear from her stilted words that animals were not her thing. Gwynne squatted next to her to coach her on the fine points of rabbit conversation, but instead of keeping an eye on the rabbits or on Kira—who was, after all, her boss—she caught herself glancing in Abby's direction again and again.

Abby looked so intent as she leaned over her harp playing scales, her hands reaching for the strings. Gwynne shivered, remembering how it felt to be in her arms. Was she always like that when she embraced a woman she liked? Focused and sure, giving you her full attention?

Giving *them* her full attention, Gwynne corrected herself. Someone else. Not her. Because Abby might possibly, maybe, be an angel, and another frickin' angel was the last thing she needed right now.

"They look so desperate chewing on the bars of their cage," Kira observed. "Should we let them out?"

Kira. She needed to focus on Kira. She opened the carrier and picked up Nimbus, who was occasionally better behaved with strangers than his brother was, and deposited him in Kira's arms. "He likes it if you pet him on the forehead."

Kira was hesitant at first. While she worked on getting the hang of it, Gwynne got Peter the Fifteenth out of the carrier and scratched his chin so he wouldn't get jealous.

"That's it," Gwynne encouraged her, congratulating herself because she had managed not to glance in Abby's direction for at least thirty seconds.

"He's soft," Kira said.

After a few strokes she'd had enough and put him on the floor in front of the open door of his carrier. Nimbus stared inside, nose quivering with interest.

"He'll go in on his own, right?" Kira didn't look like she wanted to touch him again to give him a boost.

"Maybe," Gwynne said. The boys were trained, but only to a point.

Nimbus turned his head, his nose picking up speed. If she didn't have Peter in her arms, she'd—

Too late. Nimbus zigzagged away from the safety of his carrier toward the treatment rooms.

Megan chose that moment to emerge from her massage room. She froze in the doorway, caught in a stare-down with the rabbit, then swiftly shut the door behind her. Nimbus rammed his head at the crack under her door, optimistic as always that he could squeeze himself into any space he wanted to, no matter how small. Megan double-checked that the door to her room was securely closed, the latch engaged.

"Somebunny wants to be your friend," Gwynne said cheerfully, hoping to avert a meltdown.

Megan rolled her eyes. "You are so weird."

"But you love me anyway."

Megan glanced down at Nimbus, who had given up on the door and moved on to her shoelace. She calmly watched him chew, then looked pointedly at her girlfriend. "You let her bring her rabbits here? You don't have to let her do everything she wants."

"They have a cage," Kira said. "And they're litter-trained."

Megan leaned down and freed her shoelace from Nimbus's teeth. "Not a good source of fiber, buddy."

"I'll get him," Gwynne said.

Holding Peter the Fifteenth in her arms, she approached nonthreateningly. Nimbus took off in a gray blur. The little stinker. She stalked him around the room. Too bad it wasn't Peter, who was older and not as fast, and generally easier to catch.

Abby got up from her harp and tried to help by chasing Nimbus toward Gwynne. He hopped onto the sofa, jumped off, dashed underneath. Peter jumped out of her arms and started to follow, but Gwynne nabbed him just in time. Once she had Peter in the carrier and secured the latch, she went to the sofa and stretched out on the floor to look for her troublemaker. Nimbus was on the side farthest away from her, of course, staying very, very still in the mistaken belief that this made him invisible. Gwynne circled to the other end of the sofa to grab him, and once again, Nimbus was out of reach, watchful and motionless. But at least he wasn't chewing on the furniture.

"Can someone help me and get on the other side of the sofa?" Gwynne asked. "This is a two-person job." She wedged her shoulder under the sofa and reached as far as she could.

Abby ducked her head near the floor at the opposite end and Nimbus sidled away from her to the sweet spot in the center where neither of them could reach.

"Come here, my little spazz," Gwynne pleaded. "Let's get you back in the carrier with the spazzette."

Nimbus went nowhere.

"Peter the Fifteenth is a girl?" Abby said.

"Pete's such a flamer, he doesn't mind what I call him."

Abby stood and lifted her end of the sofa and Nimbus raced across the room and out into the hallway.

"Crap." Gwynne scrambled up.

"I'll staff the desk," Kira said, not that anyone was listening to her.

Gwynne and Abby were already halfway down the hall. They caught up with Nimbus in the lobby just in time to see him dart out the front door as a guest entered. Not good.

Gwynne ran after him and Nimbus headed straight for the street. Gwynne stopped, horrified, but Abby sped after him, straight into traffic, waving her hands at the cars and yelling at them to stop over the sound of squealing brakes.

Gwynne followed more safely. When she reached her, Abby was crouched at the curb, trying to grab Nimbus and missing each time. He wasn't even running, just sidestepping her, conserving his energy for the ideal moment to make another mad dash. Wordlessly, Gwynne helped her corner the rabbit against the brick wall of the closest building. She bent to scoop him up, but he dodged her. Then Abby tried. His round eyes went wide and he froze and allowed her to pick him up, the traitor. He did look squirmy in her hands, though, as if he wasn't sure what he'd gotten himself into.

"You silly, silly, sweet little boy," Gwynne whispered, trying to calm him. She hoped Abby had an escape-proof grip on him. "Don't do that again."

Abby straightened and they returned to the other side of the street, with Abby this time mercifully looking both ways before she crossed.

"You nearly gave me a heart attack," Gwynne growled when they reached the sidewalk.

Abby pouted. "You love that rabbit."

Did she actually think she should be thanking her for this stunt? "You didn't even look before you ran into the street."

"I looked."

"You call that looking? Those cars were headed straight for you."

"They were headed straight for Nimbus too." Which was why she did it, of course. "I cut it close, but I did look. I'm not completely irresponsible."

"You could have been hit," Gwynne said.

"Nobody hit me. And Nimbus is okay too, right, Nimbus?" Abby rubbed the lucky rabbit behind the ears. He leaned into Abby's caress and gazed calmly at Gwynne, lapping up the attention, not acting guilty in the least for the scare he'd given her.

Abby held out the rabbit to pass him to her, but Gwynne couldn't handle the possibility of brushing against Abby's arms or, God forbid, her chest, if they did a transfer, so she turned her back on her and the spazz-case and marched back toward the hotel, even though everything inside her screamed at her to stop being rude. Abby followed silently.

The silence gnawed at her. She wanted to turn around and kiss her until Abby melted in her arms and forgave her, jerk that she was, but that was not a good idea. Definitely not. Knowing that wasn't an option made her grouchy.

"Are you trying to kill yourself?"

"Of course not."

"You are. That angel asked you to and you're going to do it."

"I saw the cars, okay?" Abby sounded pissed.

"Then you shouldn't have run in front of them."

Abby caught up with her, passed her, and turned around. She looked like she was planning to yell at her. But then their eyes met, and something shifted, and what came out was a soft voice devoid of anger. "Are you shaking?"

She wasn't, was she? Gwynne glanced down at herself to check. Her arms were covered in goose bumps, and she rubbed at them impatiently. Abby led her to a stone bench in front of the hotel and they both sat down.

"My sister almost got hit by a car," Gwynne said. "A friend was with her and saw her run into the street."

"But she didn't get hit," Abby said, making it both a statement and a question.

Gwynne rubbed her arms again. "She made it across the road."

"But…?"

"Her friend said that she thought something was chasing her, something that scared her enough that she ran through traffic. She managed not to get hit. But the road had a bridge, and instead of stopping, she climbed over a guardrail and jumped. She landed in the frozen river below. Crashed through the ice."

"That's terrible."

"She was hallucinating. She was caught in a fucked-up drug-induced hallucination."

Abby placed Nimbus on Gwynne's lap and rubbed his nose. "Your mom's upset, Nimbus. Make her feel better." Nimbus flopped onto his side, looking relaxed and adorable.

Gwynne hardly noticed. "Her friend said Heather thought she could fly."

"And your mother…" Abby sounded like she was trying to fit the pieces together with what she'd heard through the grapevine.

Gwynne was surprised she hadn't heard all the messy details, not that the messiest ones were common knowledge. Maybe someone—probably Megan, or by extension, Kira—had been trying to spare Gwynne the awkwardness of being whispered about.

"They weren't far from the house," Gwynne said. "Heather had moved back home because she couldn't hold down a job. When the friend saw what happened and called the house, my mother ran out there to try to save her. She fell through the ice too."

"I'm sorry." Abby started to put her hand on her shoulder, then jerked back, apparently remembering Gwynne's reaction the last time she touched her, and changed course to pet Nimbus instead. Except Gwynne was already petting him too, and their fingers ran into each other and made them both jump.

She hated that Abby was afraid to touch her, but what did she expect? She had pushed her away. Of course Abby was going to flinch at her touch.

That didn't make it easier to deal with, though. She wanted to reach for her and give her a hug and apologize for what she'd said in Baltimore, but she didn't know if she could do that without leading her on. She didn't know if Abby still wanted her, but either way, it was better if Abby thought she wasn't interested.

"I told Heather the drugs were screwing up her aura. She said no, they were *changing* her, helping her see things she'd never been able to see before. I asked her if she could even see her aura, and she gave me that you-are-not-my-mother look and told me she could feel how clear it was."

"It wasn't clear?" Abby said.

"Oh, it was clear all right, as clear as the water in a pond when acid mine drainage kills off all signs of life and you can see right down to the bottom. Maybe she could see it. I don't know. Maybe she thought poisoning herself was worth it."

"It's not your fault," Abby said.

Sure it wasn't. "I could see what she was doing to herself. I should have tried harder to stop her."

"She was an adult."

"It started a long time ago, long before she was an adult. She wanted to see what I saw. If I had never told her about angels, she would never have gone looking for them."

"You don't know that's what she was trying to do."

"Yeah, I do. She told me. She said I wasn't the only one with special powers anymore, that now she had them too. She could finally see the angelic beings I was always talking about when we were kids. She was so happy that she could see them. Other times, she sounded scared. The angels were turning into monsters, and there was this vast nothingness she didn't know how to handle. There must have been something off about it, because for me, the emptiness isn't anything to be afraid of. But for her…she panicked."

"You can't blame yourself," Abby said. "It was your sister's choice to do what she did."

Nimbus squeaked, and Gwynne realized she'd petted him too hard. She lifted the rabbit from her lap and hugged him to her chest. Abby could tell her it wasn't her fault until she was hoarse and she still wouldn't believe her. "I should get this guy back to his carrier."

They headed inside and found the spa's appointment desk unattended. So much for Kira keeping an eye on things. Gwynne heard a noise in the far corner and turned.

Kira held Megan by the waist and had her pressed up against the wall, and Gwynne was pretty sure Megan had her hands up Kira's shirt. She could tell, even from across the room, that Megan's face was flushed.

Kira twisted to look over her shoulder. She frowned. "That was quick."

Gwynne put her hand over her eyes. "Not in front of the children."

She retrieved the carrier and deposited Nimbus next to—and partly on top of—Peter.

"Go away, Gwynne. Abby."

"We're trying." Gwynne picked up the carrier and she and Abby skedaddled.

* * *

"I thought Abigail would be one of the easy ones," Artemisia said, hovering beside Elle above the mountains of New Mexico, two fireballs floating in the thin, dry air. "It's strange that she can't remember who she is."

"You agreed to be recalled," Elle said. "So will she." Angels who volunteered to incarnate tended to be fearless. Reckless, even. You'd have to be to sacrifice the beauty of the Angelic Realm and trade it for human separation consciousness. An invitation to return to the Realm, even if you couldn't remember where you came from, should be irresistible to someone like that. It was the adventure of a temporary lifetime.

Elle drifted closer to earth. It looked like another hapless hiker had ventured off the faintly worn trail trampled by elk who were smart enough to stay clear of certain areas. Oh, joy—a second hiker. They shouldn't be here. It wasn't safe.

She plunged at the two hikers to scare them away. Artemisia zipped around her in circles to enhance the effect.

The hikers looked at each other and inched back. "Is that a UFO?"

"It's an optical illusion," said the other hiker.

"An optical—?" Artemisia sputtered and zapped furiously around their heads. Static electricity sparked in her wake.

Elle glanced heavenward. "I cannot believe…"

"Maybe Gwynne could help us convince Abigail," Artemisia said as she darted aggressively at the hikers. "If you would stop hiding from her…"

"No. She sees too much."

"Abigail trusts her."

"She's supposed to trust *me*." Bringing Gwynne Abernathy into the situation was too risky. Gwynne was an aberration. Everyone loved her because she could see them and hear them, but no one knew for sure what she was capable of. It figured Artemisia would want to risk it, though.

"Why did I incarnate if you're not going to listen to me when I tell you how humans think? Abigail could stall forever."

"I'm not showing myself to Gwynne. And neither are you." Elle grew larger and larger. She advanced menacingly on the hikers like a tumbleweed on fire, rolling closer and closer until they got scared and ran. Worked every time.

"Fine." Artemisia stared after the retreating hikers. "But we need to step up our efforts to convince Abigail. Look how long it took us last time to get everyone back."

"I know." That was fun—everyone dying of the plague and the incarnated angels turn out to be immune.

"We can't afford to wait another sixty years for her to die of natural causes," Artemisia said as they drifted away from the mountain and morphed into winged form. They caught an updraft and floated on the warm air, letting it take them where it wanted them to go.

"The bridge hasn't collapsed yet and we have only one holdout," Elle said calmly. "We're in a much better position than we ever were before."

"All it takes is one."

"Deep down inside she knows she's an angel. Part of her knows that although her circumstances appear to have changed, reality persists. She'll come around."

"What if she doesn't?"

"She will."

CHAPTER FOURTEEN

Abby woke at four in the morning and lay on her back with her eyes open. She wondered if Gwynne's rabbits were awake. Were rabbits nocturnal? She had no idea.

She gave up on trying to go back to sleep and padded out to the living room and stopped next to one of her harps. She ran her hand over its curved neck, smoothing off dust that wasn't there. Her fingers itched to play, but her neighbors were only a thin wall away and would be furious if she did. They were understanding about her practicing during the day, but waking them before sunrise was not part of the deal. That didn't mean she couldn't play somewhere else, though. She returned to her bedroom and pulled on a pair of jeans, dug out the hurricane lamp she kept for emergencies, and packed one of her smaller harps in its padded case. She knew just the place.

She checked that she had the right tuning wrench stashed in the zippered pocket of the harp's carrying case and headed out to the woods at Sea Salt, to the boulder Dara had shown her, the one she called Angel Rock. Dara had said Gwynne thought angels liked to gather there, that it was a doorway for them, an accessway to their dimension. Was that why it called to her? Because she wanted to feel close to the angels? Or to feel close to Gwynne?

No, it was because it was a nice, isolated spot where she could play her harp and not bother anyone. Besides, she didn't see any angels around, glowing in the dark. And Gwynne…Something was going on with Gwynne and she didn't understand what it was, but she needed to give her some space.

Even if she couldn't stop thinking about her.

She settled on the sandy ground, one leg bent and one leg stretched to the side. She set the hurricane lamp where it would shine on the harp strings and not in her eyes, and warmed up with a series of scales. She plucked out a few bars of a new tune she was learning and noodled around, experimenting with the arrangement as she committed it to memory, repeating it, gradually picking up speed, training herself to smooth out the timing.

Playing the harp always calmed her when she was stressed. Focusing on getting the notes right blocked out everything else.

Except…it wasn't blocking everything out. She was worried about what Elle had told her. Was the reason the harp had captured her heart all those years ago because it resonated with who she really was and tapped into a soul memory she didn't know she had?

It made a nice story. But there were other possible reasons why the sound of the harp had enchanted her for as long as she could remember and tugged so possessively at her heart.

Besides, angels didn't play harps, not that she'd ever seen. They sang, yes. But there were no harps, no heraldic trumpets, no nothing.

But if she had to pick one instrument for them to play, she'd follow the path of countless others before her and choose the harp. Because if the theoretical physicists were right about string theory, then the universe itself was a kind of harp with billions of gajillions of unseen, rubber band-like strings, vibrating at different frequencies in complex, multidimensional patterns, creating an unimaginably elaborate tune.

In the beginning...In the beginning, God sang the universe into existence.

If the voice of God resonated through the stuff of creation, singing atoms, singing stars, singing gravity, singing light…

If we are the echo of that song…

If all life, and all matter, and all energy are the echo of a song that never stopped…

Then yes, the harp was the right instrument.

An angel the size of a wispy dandelion seed shining against the night sky floated down from above and wafted between the strings of Abby's harp and out the other side. The angel's song tinkled like a wind chime.

Elle.

Abby stilled her hands, unsurprised to see her. To be honest, she'd been subconsciously waiting for her.

"Have you changed your mind yet?" Elle asked.

Abby stared, praying for the right answer to pop into her head. She still didn't know what to do. She'd been hoping for insight, but it hadn't come.

She wanted to help. If there was any other way, she would do it in an instant. Working at the hospital, she'd seen patients miraculously improve after a visit by angels, or find peace with impending death. Angels comforted those in anguish and eased their suffering, whether the person was aware of their presence or not. They lightened fear and restored faith. They made the world a more relaxed, hope-filled place. If the bridge collapsed and they could no longer visit earth, the human race would have a harder time remembering the light that shone inside its own darkness.

"Can't I help repair the bridge in human form?" Elle would likely shoot the idea down, but it was the logical win-win solution.

"You retain very little of your angelic power when you take on human form." Elle grew to human size and came so close that if her body had had physical substance, one of her enormous, luminous wings would have brushed her face. "This is absurd. Are you sure you don't remember being an angel?"

"I'm sure."

"You're supposed to remember."

"I thought you said I *wasn't* supposed to remember. That my memories were suppressed."

"They were suppressed, but I can restore them by touching your forehead with my wing. It usually works." That must have been what she'd been trying to do with that blinding light at Penelope's wedding. "I don't know why it won't work with you."

"Then how do you know I'll turn into an angel when I die? What if that doesn't work, either?"

"It'll work."

"How do you know?" Abby insisted.

"Because you're an angel. It's the nature of who you are."

"But the wing thing didn't work." Not that it made any difference. Whether she was transformed into an angel or not, her life here would be over.

"It doesn't work with everyone," Elle backpedaled. "But not to worry. Once you're in your true form, you'll be able to help us repair the bridge, and after that there'll be plenty of time to—"

"Wait a minute—"

"We can worry about your memories later. But I don't see why they wouldn't eventually return."

"How reassuring." Knowing that Gwynne could see angels and even Officer Mawson had seen one—once—was enough to convince her angels were real, but that didn't mean she believed everything Elle told her, especially when Elle sounded like she was making stuff up on the fly. How could she believe her? What she was telling her was insane.

"When did you get so stubborn?" Elle said. "You were always so helpful before you became human."

Abby's mouth fell open. "I'm trying to be helpful. Maybe if you understood your own technology…"

Elle fluttered her wings agitatedly. "I don't know why it didn't work. We're not perfect, okay? You were supposed to regain your memories, and the bridge wasn't supposed to crack."

Abby took a deep breath. She'd always known angels to be lighthearted and full of love. She'd never seen one so stressed, and that worried her. "I can't trust you. You don't know how any of this works. If something goes wrong, you don't know how to fix it."

Elle glowed brighter. "When you play the harp for someone who's dying and they don't die, you don't know how that works, either. That doesn't stop you from doing it."

"At least I know my music won't make anything worse. If your plan doesn't work, I end up dead."

"If your music doesn't work, that patient ends up dead too."

"They would have died anyway!"

"As will you, eventually."

"And when I do," Abby said calmly, "it's not going to be because I did something stupid." Elle couldn't be as cold as she sounded. She couldn't be. "I can see why you need to send us down here to help you understand humanity."

"So you do believe part of what I've told you. You do believe you're an incarnated angel."

The note of hope in Elle's voice made her sad. An angel. Shouldn't they know everything? Weren't they watching from heaven?

"I believe you, just…not completely. I'd feel pretty stupid if it turned out you were just a hallucination."

"A hallucination?" Elle screeched. "Come with me. I want to show you something."

"Okay…" Abby fumbled for her harp case. She didn't want to travel too far with her instrument, but she also was not going to leave it here in the woods. "Where are we going?"

"Home."

Abby froze. "You mean…"

"Look up. Do you see the bridge?"

"You said you wouldn't kill me." And Abby had been gullible enough to believe her.

"I'm not going to kill you. I just want to show you something."

Against her better judgment, Abby craned her neck back to look. All she could see in the night sky was murky cloud cover.

Elle took her hands and for the first time she could feel physical contact with her. The feel of her hands was both solid and electric, amplifying the buzzing she already felt in her fingertips from plucking harp strings. She didn't understand how it was possible for Elle to take physical form, but it made sense, really, because if they did deflect asteroids headed for impact with earth, how else were they supposed to do that? Officer Mawson had felt a physical jolt when she crashed into her white lady. And how else could that angel have unlocked the door to allow Abby's toddler self to escape the apartment?

Elle squeezed her hands in a death grip that left no doubt about her ability to assume solid form and pulled her to her feet. A whirlwind rushed by and whisked them off the ground, leaving her harp behind. Wind roared past Abby's ears at incomprehensible, exhilarating speed. A sound like harp strings resonating with unheard laughter filled the air. She caught a glimpse of distant mountains, great swaths of clouds swirling above the ocean which receded far below, the bright curve of the planet's horizon.

Unexpectedly, her feet landed on something. Dizzying kaleidoscopes of shifting color made it impossible to see what she might be standing on. The air, if there was air, was so thin it hurt to breathe. Then she was flung again through space, past the fiery, erupting surface of star after star, her head spinning with vertigo.

It took her a moment to realize they'd stopped. "Where are we?"

"On the bridge, of course."

"And I'm not dead?"

"Sadly, no."

Elle released her hands and Abby patted her own arms and legs to make sure she was still alive, still in her body. She couldn't see much in the dazzlingly bright light, but she felt solid enough. As her eyes adjusted, she realized she was on some kind of superhighway through space, with angels zipping by in both directions in a haphazard jumble of fast-moving traffic.

"How did we get here?" Abby asked, entranced.

"Remember that boulder?"

She nodded. So Dara and Megan and Gwynne were right about it.

"Anchored to the ground beneath that boulder is a shortcut to the bridge, a chute we can slide up or down, like a two-way zip line. Humans can't use it, but as an incarnated angel, you can. If you were truly human I wouldn't be able to bring you here. Setting foot on the bridge would kill you."

"Nice of you to warn me about that." Somehow the news didn't concern her as much as it probably should.

"You're in no danger. The Angelic Realm is your home. It's why you've always felt cut off, abandoned. Because you left the Angelic Realm to live a human life."

She had a feeling that if she felt abandoned, it might have more to do with her mother dying when she was three years old than with any forgotten angelic past, but that didn't seem important right now. None of her life on earth seemed important. "I don't remember leaving the Realm."

"It is your home. It is where you belong. You'll see. I stopped us here so you could try navigating on your own. You have the ability."

Abby tried it and found it effortless, like standing on a conveyor belt. All she had to do was think how fast she wanted to go, and the bridge responded. Other angels moved by at different speeds, passing them or falling behind.

"This is incredible," she said. "How come astronomers don't know about this?"

"Their instruments can't detect it. The bridge exists in a dimension that lies beyond your four-dimensional universe, although it intersects it too, just as it intersects the dimension where the Angelic Realm lies. It has to, otherwise it couldn't connect the two. That's also why you can travel on the bridge in human form."

"What happens when I enter the Angelic Realm? Can I do that?"

"You can," Elle said. "I think."

"You *think*?"

"We'll find out. We're almost there."

The angel who was ahead of them jerked to a stop, and as they caught up, a gaping fissure opened up beneath the angel's feet, knocking her off-balance. The angel instinctively extended her wings and flapped furiously against the pull of the interdimensional vacuum, fighting to escape, but despite her struggle she spiraled slowly, inexorably down, trapped by the overwhelming force.

Elle seemed to be frozen in place. “Sidonie…” Her voice was a strangled whisper.

Without thinking, Abby jumped forward and grabbed at the struggling angel. Their fingertips touched and she tried for her wrists but the angel was already out of reach, falling…falling… falling into the void, screaming, disintegrating, lost between dimensions. Gone.

Abby looked down into the fissure in shock. She swayed as the edge cracked and started to give way beneath her feet. She stumbled and pitched sideways, scrambling for purchase, and wished desperately for a guardrail, for something—*anything*—to grab and use to save herself, but there was nothing but the crumbling surface of the bridge itself, too slippery to gain purchase.

CHAPTER FIFTEEN

Arms like steel snatched her from the edge.

It was Elle, yanking her to safety. Abby sucked in lungfuls of too-thin air that burned all the way down.

"We need to return to earth." Elle held both her hands in a safety lock. They were already speeding away from the widening gash. "The bridge is too dangerous right now. It's unstable."

Elle could have let her die.

All the angels in existence—according to Elle, that's what they needed to repair the bridge. If she hadn't saved her from obliteration in the interdimensional void, their bridge problems would have been over. She was probably kicking herself right now. Instead, she was taking her back to earth because the bridge wasn't safe.

Almost as if she cared about her.

It didn't make sense. Elle wanted her to die—she'd said so repeatedly. She had no business saving her. For the second time in her not very long lifespan, an angel had saved her.

Abby scanned with hyper-alert awareness for cracks and potholes as she watched the surface of the bridge glide by under her feet. Elle could have let her die. But she didn't. Abby owed her, and more than that, she *wanted* to help. What if that had been Sapphire on the bridge when that hole opened up? If she could prevent more angels from dying, she wanted to. And protecting them meant protecting the earth too, making it possible for angelkind to continue to help humankind.

When they reached earth's solar system, Elle slowed their descent, and Abby saw her home planet, small and fragile and precious. Beneath its violent surface of cyclones and earthquakes and volcanic upheaval and the equal violence of life-forms competing for survival, she saw pure light emerging. The vegetation, the rocks, the rivers, the oceans, the atmosphere—even the concrete and steel cities—were alive with an energy and a light that was uniquely earth, but mixed with a spark of angelic light, a spark that was bubbling laughter and bliss, undimmed by human darkness. Earth would survive on its own, but it wouldn't be the same. It wouldn't have that angelic presence. And that was a loss she didn't want to live to see.

* * *

Elle skimmed the surface of the ocean, weaving among ice floes as she and a few friends trailed a pod of humpback whales who rose and fell like dark shadows in the Antarctic twilight.

"I was hoping that putting Abigail on the bridge would zap some sense into her," Elle told the others, "but no such luck."

"It was a good idea," Artemisia reassured her.

Tatiana, who rarely voiced an opinion, spoke up. "We need to recall her. Now."

"We should check the bridge first," Sapphire said. "We should count the nodes. With Sidonie and Hortense dead, we're two angels short now. Even if we recall Abby, if the bridge didn't adapt, we'll never be able to position one angel at each node. There'll be two empty nodes."

And if they didn't have the right number of nodes, they were stuck. What a sickening thought.

"Of course the bridge adapted," said Artemisia.

"We don't know that," Sapphire said.

"It wouldn't hurt to check," Elle said. "I don't trust that alien technology."

"We could never have built this bridge without it," Artemisia said.

Elle sighed. "I know. I just wish we understood how it worked." The bridge was a perpetual nuisance. It had never been completely stable. They knew how to use it and how to fix it, but even eons ago, when it was originally built, they'd never understood its inner workings. That was what came of using leftover parts left behind by a vanished alien race.

She called out to all the other angels through their mental link. Thousands of them responded and they all went out and canvassed the bridge to count the nodes. The number of nodes matched the number of angels, including Abigail Vogel as well as all the other incarnated angels who had already made it back to the Realm. At least that part of the bridge was functioning as expected. As long as the number of nodes matched the number of angels, they could fix it.

* * *

After what she'd seen, Abby doubted everyday earthbound existence was ever going to feel the same. Her body felt heavy, like gravity was pulling on her too hard, and the spa's lounge made her claustrophobic. It felt strange to be at work. She wanted to escape the spa and get back out there, into the sky, into the colors and the wind and the speed. She wanted the excitement of it. She wanted the sheer sense of awe. She just… wanted.

She told Gwynne she was taking a break, then hiked through the parking lot and into the woods to Angel Rock in search of Elle.

She didn't have to wait long. Elle materialized as a ball of light high in the clouds and tumbled from the sky, slowing only at the last split second before she crashed into the rock. She morphed into winged shape, unhurt.

"Are you ready to help?" Elle sounded impatient.

"I was thinking—" Abby began.

"The bridge didn't kill you on contact. What further proof do you need?"

"You said the bridge intersects this dimension, and obviously I was able to travel on it even though I'm human. So why can't I fix it now? You know, without killing myself?"

"You can't."

"Why not?"

"Because it doesn't work that way."

"Will you at least try it my way?" Gwynne would probably be mad that she was considering helping at all, but this way had to be safe. She'd been on the bridge. This would be no different. And she had to try. She couldn't live with herself if she didn't at least try.

"All the other incarnated angels have already reverted to angel form," Elle informed her.

Abby shifted uncomfortably. So she was the only one left. That explained the pressure. "I think this is a good compromise."

"You can't help in human form. You won't resonate with us."

"You don't know that for sure. All you know is what worked before."

Elle spun slowly around the boulder. "This is not a good idea. There's no telling how the bridge will react. Or how your body might react. It could be dangerous for you, for all of us."

"Would it really hurt anyone else?" She didn't want to harm them. They were her friends. And if Elle and Sapphire were right, they were more than her friends—they were once her family, her community, her world.

"I don't know. Perhaps not." Elle paused. "To be honest, it's highly unlikely."

"I'm willing to risk it if you are," Abby said.

"I still don't think this is a good idea."

"But you want me to die. And the bridge is already damaged. What's the harm in trying?"

Elle spun around herself, throwing off a flurry of sparks, then stopped. "Fine. If this is how you choose to kill yourself, fine. Just try not to make the bridge any worse while you're at it, okay?"

Abby was besieged by second thoughts. She'd assumed Elle would be happy if the bridge killed her, considering her death seemed to be Elle's main goal. But she wasn't. Was there something Elle wasn't telling her?

"You really think this will kill me?"

Elle seemed to deflate. "Nothing's going to happen. We'll link up, your body won't have the right angelic frequency, nothing will happen. It'll all be a big waste of time."

"But you don't know for sure."

"I don't know for sure," Elle agreed.

She should call Gwynne, tell her what she'd decided to do. But she couldn't, because she was mesmerized by the warm breeze that blew around her, ruffling her hair, and by a song that hovered at the edge of her awareness, a song of incredible longing. The breeze whisked her off the ground and into the sky, and she was caught in a dizzying, familiar whirlwind.

Gwynne. She didn't get a chance to tell her, to say goodbye, just in case this didn't work.

But it would work. She wasn't going to die, and if she had told her what she was up to, Gwynne would have tried to stop her. And if she didn't make it back—which she wasn't going to think about because that wasn't going to happen—Gwynne would figure out what she'd done. Heck, Gwynne could ask the angels. They'd tell her.

And her grandparents, they would miss her. They'd never understand the truth, though. She hoped Gwynne would make up some explanation for her disappearance that would make sense to them. Not that they needed one. They'd assume she'd followed in her mother's irresponsible footsteps, just like they always warned her not to. Just one more irresponsible choice in a long history of skipping class and driving too fast and being friends with troubled classmates and donating the boring, fugly, age-appropriate dresses her grandmother spent good money on to the church's homeless without permission. Not to mention dropping out of college and failing to get a real job with health benefits.

They wouldn't understand that this time, she really was trying to do the responsible thing.

CHAPTER SIXTEEN

They stood in the void in complete darkness. It was silent, so profoundly silent and empty that Abby couldn't feel where her body's edges were. She had no edges—her awareness seemed to stretch out toward infinity.

After a time—once she remembered she had feet, had a body—she realized her feet were on a surface. She was standing on the bridge.

Out of the darkness, angels appeared like points of light, lining up along the bridge span as far as she could see in either direction, lighting up the void. They took each other's hands, linking up, and as energy currents began to flow from one angel to the next, the angels became brighter, shining like pure, transparent crystals, each a slightly different shade along the spectrum—yellow sapphire, citrine quartz, topaz, amber, copper, gold—each one a dazzling, brilliant complement to the whole.

"Each angel stands at a node," Elle explained in a hushed voice. "The number of nodes evolves over time, always one per angel, always attuned to our exact number. When all of us are linked, our combined energy forms a wave that returns the bridge to its normal state."

Elle and Sapphire had volunteered to take the most dangerous positions, standing on either side of Abby. She was the weak link in the chain, and no one knew what would happen with a weak link. They'd never had one before.

Sapphire took her hand, and then Elle. And then…nothing.

"I told you this wasn't going to work." Elle started to pull her hand away.

But before she broke contact, for a fraction of an instant, the link flickered through Abby, connecting her to all the other angels. In that instant, she felt their emotions flow through her and knew they loved her with a love beyond all reason. They missed her. They wanted her to be with them. They were her family, the family she never felt her grandparents, although they loved her too, quite gave, because there was always that undercurrent of disapproval, that unspoken reminder that she was unstable and her mother was irresponsible and her father was scum.

In that instant, her heart filled with love for all these countless trillions of light-filled beings whose capacity for love outstripped anything human. The immense power of it was overwhelming. Her heart felt like it couldn't expand to hold it all. Time stretched out and that fraction of an instant lasted an eternity.

She clutched Elle's hand and reached for the link with all her heart, desperate not to let it go. It called to her, pulled at her, made it hard to think. She wanted to join the angels right now, for real. She could do it. She could cut the lifeline that kept her away from them. This was where she belonged, inside this supernova where love was pure and fearless and unconditional.

She gripped Sapphire's and Elle's hands, but they released her, and the fragile link flickered away.

Her nerves screamed in shock and her heart seized up in agony at being cut off from her glimpse of who she was meant to be, at losing that beautiful connection, at being deprived of that light. She doubled over and fell into Sapphire's arms.

* * *

Gwynne padded to her kitchen in her pajamas to wash some breakfast lettuce and carrots for the vegetarians in the house. The kitten rubbed against her ankles to remind her the carnivores needed to eat too, nearly tripping her in her enthusiasm. Gwynne filled the kitten's bowl and took the veggies to the living room where the guinea pig and rabbit cages sat on tall tables out of the kitten's reach, far from any feline launching pad. She stopped.

Crap. She crept closer to the guinea pig's cage.

"Pigness!" she gasped, cooing and covering her mouth.

Apple, who had not looked pregnant when she took her in, but had recently developed quite the suspicious don't-look-at-me, I-swallowed-a-couple-of-golf-balls bulge, was cuddled in a corner of her previously solitary cage with three furry, bright-eyed babies.

* * *

No one knew what she'd done. No one knew how close Abby had come to doing something they wouldn't understand. Something they'd condemn. As she tuned her harp, she glanced up every once in a while past Gwynne's unstaffed desk to scan the handful of clients waiting in the lounge, but no one was paying any attention to her. She was sure someone would sense her brush with angelkind just by looking at her, and yet, no one said anything. Because no one could tell.

Gwynne rushed in, late for work, and didn't say a word. Because even Gwynne couldn't tell. Of course, Gwynne was probably trying her best to ignore her.

Gwynne tossed her bag on the floor under her desk and switched on her two digital picture frames and fiddled with them before returning them to their usual position, back-to-back, one facing her and the other facing out for the guests to see, with a small card positioned in front inviting people to Ask

About Adopting a Rabbit. As usual, a slideshow played of her menagerie.

Abby came over to check them out, acting casual. "More rabbit shots? No," she corrected herself, realizing she'd seen these before. "These are your old ones."

"Keep watching. The new ones are coming," Gwynne said. "They're fun. My guinea pig had babies."

Abby leaned over the desk and cocked her head upside down to see the photos that faced Gwynne. A family photo was next—a gawky Gwynne in her early teens, curled on a sofa with two white rabbits in her lap next to her sister and her mother. Then came the picture of her garden, with the sun shining on purple asters and a rabbit at the edge of the shot. Then came another rabbit.

"When are the guinea pig pig-tures coming up? These are all rabbits."

"That's my sister," Gwynne bristled.

Oo…kay. Abby refrained from pointing out that her sister had a rabbit on her shoulder. She thought Gwynne knew about this *Where's Waldo?* rabbit thing.

Maybe not.

The new photos were next. Gwynne paused the slideshow to point out her newest additions. "Here's Apple, the mom, and the babies—Nittany, Fuji and Apple Jack."

She expected them to look like naked rats, but instead they were tiny little bundles of fur, all redheads like their mother, each with its own unique pattern of white patches. Their huge brown baby eyes stared right into the camera. "They are so cute."

Abby shifted so her hair, hanging upside down, didn't block Gwynne's view. As she did, her hair swept against Gwynne's extended forearm. They both froze.

Gwynne wanted to be *friends*, and maybe for being friends, leaning over the desk was too flirtatious, but it was hard to keep her distance when it felt so comfortable not to. Gwynne had been pretty clear, though, that she didn't want her to touch her.

Abby straightened and pretended nothing had happened. "Hoping someone here will want to adopt them?"

"They're not ready to leave their mother yet. But when they are…I don't know. I'm thinking I might keep them myself."

"You can't save them all, Gwynnosaurus." She was a hypocrite for saying it, but she said it anyway. Compared to what she'd risked her safety to do for the angels, caring for a few more critters was nothing.

Gwynne looked at her like she could see into her hypocritical soul and wondered what it would take to make her fall in love with her. She blinked, and the look was gone.

"That doesn't mean I can't save some of them."

A customer came in, so Abby returned to her harp. She watched Gwynne out of the corner of her eye while she meandered from one Irish ballad to another.

"I'm a friend of Kira's," the woman was saying. "I'm visiting from out of town and she sent me down here for a free massage."

"Rae, right? She told me." Gwynne checked the computer. "I have you on the schedule. If you'd like to make yourself comfortable, it'll just be a few minutes."

The visitor leaned forward to check out Gwynne's photos—in the outward-facing frame, like a proper guest should. "That kitten is adorable! Oh, the rabbits too. Which ones are up for adoption?" She kneeled gracefully on her impossibly long legs to get a closer look. "They're so cute. I wish I could adopt one."

Gwynne perked up. "You can."

"I really can't. I'm a dancer and we go on tour. I'd have to leave them with someone else for months." She rose and backed away, probably worried that Gwynne was going to pester her if she didn't make it clear she wasn't interested. "Maybe someday."

At least Gwynne wasn't flirting with her. Listening to them talk was bad enough. Abby transitioned to a lively Scottish reel she thought a dancer might appreciate and played it as loudly as she could. If it distracted her from Gwynne, so much the better.

As Rae turned away from the desk and chose a sofa, Gwynne glanced in Abby's direction. Their eyes met and Abby fumbled her tune. She looked away immediately, shaken by her reaction. There was something in Gwynne's eyes, something in the set of her jaw, something that said:

I see you.

I am aware of you.

I could be making love to you right now if we weren't both pretending to do our jobs.

Her link with the angels had been like this, except far, far less sexual. How a single human being could fill her with as much yearning as the light of a trillion angels, she didn't know, but gazing at Gwynne made her realize she belonged on earth as much as in the Angelic Realm. She loved playing music for her sick patients at the hospital and she loved…her. Did angels fall in love? Or was that something you had to be human to experience? Was she in love with Gwynne?

Angelic love was searingly pure and absolute. Human love was less simple. What she felt for Gwynne was both.

She switched to an even trickier, faster-paced reel that required her full concentration. She barely noticed when Dara Sullivan arrived for her weekly appointment with Megan McLaren. What she did notice was Gwynne tapping something into the computer.

"Your appointment's not for another hour," Gwynne told Dara. "Did I mess up the schedule?"

"No, I'm early," Dara said.

"Would you like to relax in the whirlpool while you wait?"

"I like it here. I like listening to the harp music."

Abby smiled up at her in thanks.

Dara gave her a flicker of a smile in return, but it was Gwynne she addressed her next comment to. "I also like watching you count down the nanoseconds until the clients are gone and you and Abby can jump each other."

Abby ended her tune midway, rolling a finishing chord in a feeble attempt to pretend she'd reached the tune's real end. She had never seen Gwynne turn red.

Gwynne ran a nervous hand through her hair. "We don't—"

Dara nonchalantly picked up a magazine and flipped it open. "Megan says she doesn't know what's going on between the two of you, but I think she's just being tactful."

Gwynne met Abby's gaze again. There was vulnerability exposed beneath the raw desire that had been there earlier, and it made her want her even more.

Gwynne closed her eyes. "I have work to do in the back," she said. "Come get me if anyone needs me." She disappeared into the storeroom.

Abby rocked her harp onto its base. Gwynne couldn't look at her like that and then walk away. What a chicken.

She marched across the room and poked her head into the storeroom. Gwynne was pouring massage oil from a gallon jug into small squirt bottles using a funnel that she transferred from one bottle to the next.

Gwynne looked up from her work. Her eyes were bleak. "Is there a customer at the desk already?"

"No." Abby stepped into the room and pulled the door shut behind her. "Do you need help with that?"

"Abby. I don't know if it's such a good idea for you to be in here."

Chicken.

"Because I might steal some of the inventory?" Abby approached the worktable and screwed the tops onto the squirt bottles Gwynne had just filled. "These could be worth a lot on the black market."

Gwynne continued to pour oil into more bottles. Abby was standing right next to her, in her personal space, helping her when she asked her not to, and she wasn't backing away. This was good.

Except the next words out of Gwynne's mouth were, "I don't want to lead you on."

Abby tightened the lid in her hand too hard. Gwynnosaurus wasn't chicken at all.

It made her want to kiss her even more.

"You think *this* is leading me on? What about the way you were looking at me out there?"

"I know. I'm sorry." Gwynne put the jug down and sidestepped Abby and opened the door. "Dara?" she called out. "Come get me if a customer shows up, okay?"

"Like I want to walk in on you two making out?"

Gwynne flushed. "We're not—"

"Don't worry about the desk," Dara said. "You think I don't know how to do customer service? I am the personification of customer service."

"I want you to come get me," Gwynne said.

"You want me to disturb you." Dara clearly didn't believe her. "When I am offering to help."

Gwynne stepped out and strode to her desk. "You must really want my job."

She leaned over and fiddled with the mouse. Dara slid into her unoccupied seat like she belonged there and Gwynne showed her what to do.

"You should be healing people," Dara said. "Not filling out spreadsheets recording payments."

Gwynne straightened from the computer. "Leave the billing program to me, please. All you need to worry about is the appointment schedule."

"Relax." Dara waved her away.

Gwynne started to leave, then stopped and looked over her shoulder at Dara. Abby watched from the doorway, half afraid Gwynne would not return to the storeroom, but she didn't disappoint. Gwynne closed the door and once again they were alone in the small room.

* * *

Gwynne had no idea why Dara was so gung ho to take her job except that it was yet one more way to worship the ground she walked on, something she dearly wished she would stop doing. If Dara and Hank would just hurry up and sleep together…

If it wasn't imperative that she hash it out with Abby, she wouldn't have let Dara take over her desk. Not because she didn't trust her to handle it, but because she didn't like knowing Dara was on the other side of the door assuming she and Abby were getting in each other's pants. Especially since now all she could think about was getting in Abby's pants.

Why *was* she here?

Um…yeah. She wanted to apologize for earlier.

If only Abby wouldn't stare at her mouth.

"You know what would really be leading me on?" Abby stepped closer and angled her head.

Gwynne swallowed. Abby was going to kiss her. She could see it coming. This was not a drive-by assault by a woman intent on making contact before she could react. This was calm and deliberate. Abby knew perfectly well that she might be rebuffed, yet she was confident enough not to care. Abby would give her all the time in the world to reject her, and still get what she wanted. It was hypnotizing.

She loved that about her, that she wasn't afraid.

Her blood thrummed. She swayed toward her and met her halfway, and for the first time in her life, she understood what it meant to swoon. Her body buzzed with crazy pleasure and she knew denying herself this happiness was a terrible mistake she would never make again. Abby kissed her and kissed her and Gwynne clung to her and drank her in. Abby clutched the front of her shirt to bring her closer, and when that wasn't enough, got underneath it and wrapped her small, gentle fingers around her bra straps with a fierceness that made Gwynne want to pass out from oxygen deprivation. She wouldn't have minded. But it didn't happen, because Abby broke the kiss.

"I want to be with you, Gwynnosaurus. I know I should have more pride and not put that out there, but what the hell. If I'm going to off myself, I might as well."

Gwynne sucked in some air. "You are not going to kill yourself, damn you."

"Yeah, that's not the point."

She didn't think Abby really meant her death threat, but really, how *was* she supposed to respond? And anyway it was easier than figuring out what to say to *I want to be with you.* The only response she could think of was to kiss her again. Abby welcomed her and pressed her curves into her with intoxicating surrender until they came to their senses and broke it off. They separated and she immediately felt the aching loss of not having her in her arms. She snatched her back.

Abby's chest rose and fell with quick, shallow breaths. She smoothed a lock of Gwynne's choppy hair. "Don't kiss me like that and then tell me you want to be friends."

"I don't want to be friends."

"You'd better not be saying that just because you're turned on."

Harsh. She deserved it, though. It wasn't fair to kiss her, or even to flirt with her the way she had, and then run away. She wouldn't do that anymore. She should have known she couldn't stay away.

An angel fluttered in and immediately winked back out, giving them privacy. Good. They needed privacy.

"I haven't been fair," Gwynne said, "and I'm sorry."

"You weren't being unfair on purpose," Abby said, giving her the benefit of the doubt, which made her feel even guiltier. "You were confused."

"I was…conflicted."

"And now you're not?"

"I'd be happier if you forgot about Elle and her scheme, but…"

Abby's hand slid from her hair and landed on her shoulder. Her fingers tightened on her shirt. "I tried to fix their bridge," she blurted out.

Gwynne became very still. "Without killing yourself, I take it."

Abby's grip tightened on the shirt and Gwynne felt the fabric pull across her back. "I wanted to see if there was another way. It didn't work."

"What did you do?"

"I…I was on the bridge. And it was beautiful, Gwynne, you can't imagine. It was the most beautiful thing I've ever seen."

A knock sounded at the door.

"Gwynne?" Dara turned the knob and cracked the unlocked door but didn't push it open. "You're needed."

"I'll be right there." Gwynne kept her eyes fixed on Abby and spoke over her shoulder in the direction of the door. Without waiting for Dara to leave, she gently brushed Abby's arm, trying to convey everything she was feeling through that one, simple gesture.

"We'll talk later," she told Abby. "Don't go home without talking to me, okay?"

* * *

It was hard to spend the rest of the day listening to Gwynne chat with clients and be reminded each time of how easy it was for Gwynne's unmistakable voice to kick-start her imagination. Even playing complicated tunes that she didn't have completely memorized—which should have forced her to concentrate—didn't stop her vivid, enthusiastic, depraved imagination. It felt like the end of the day would never come.

When it finally was time to leave, they walked to the dark parking lot together and Gwynne helped her slide her harp into the back of her ancient minivan. Abby made sure her harp was secure, then closed the hatch.

"You should ask me to drive you to work. I'd be happy to do it," Gwynne said.

"Thanks," Abby said, even though she had no intention of taking her up on the offer. She knew she shouldn't be driving, but she didn't want to impose on Gwynne for a ride in her own vehicle, and her harp was too big to fit in a taxi or on the useless bus that didn't go anywhere but up and down the shore to shuttle tourists.

Gwynne ground the heel of her hand into her forehead as if she could hear the excuses churning in Abby's head. "I mean it."

"I appreciate it."

"Now about what happened on the bridge…"

What Abby really wanted to discuss was that thing about not wanting to be just friends, but it seemed Gwynne had other priorities and that conversation was going to have to wait. This was what she got for letting those words—*I tried to fix their bridge*—fly out of her mouth unchecked. But she could live with that, because she couldn't *not* tell her. Especially if Gwynne was serious about a relationship.

Gwynne plowed ahead. "Now that you did what they wanted, are they going to leave you alone?"

Probably not. And Abby didn't want them to. She knew how deeply the angels loved her—she'd felt it in that momentary link, and felt an answering love in her own heart—and she couldn't let them die falling off an unsafe bridge. Elle was right—Abby was one of them. She couldn't abandon them.

"I didn't fix the bridge," Abby said. "It didn't work."

"They're going to keep after you."

She understood why Gwynne was unhappy, but the truth was, she wasn't angry at Elle anymore. "Elle saved my life up there. She caught me when I almost fell off."

"You *what?*"

"Forget I said that."

"Okay," Gwynne said, humoring her for one-point-five seconds. "She did *what?*"

"She caught me."

Gwynne made a noise that sounded like a laugh, but wasn't. "She knew it wasn't safe. If she hadn't taken you there in the first place, she wouldn't have had to save you."

"Did you ever try to fly when you were a little kid?" Abby said, hoping the question wouldn't remind her of her sister's fatal jump. "Leap off the furniture and flap your arms like crazy?"

Gwynne's hand was again on her forehead, like this was just one more thing to add to her headache. "A lot of kids do that."

"Did you?"

"No, but—"

Abby felt a twinge of disappointment. "I loved that game. *Loved* it. I thought I really was flying, even if it was only for a few seconds."

"I see where this is going, and—"

"When I got older, I figured it appealed to me because I had so many angel friends, and I wanted to be like them. I wanted to fly. But now, thinking back on it, there was always this feeling of rightness about it. A cellular memory. Like I knew I had done it before. Even though I could never flap my arms hard enough to stay in the air for as long as I expected, and the shock of my feet hitting the ground surprised me every time, something inside me always said *This feels right*. If I really am an angel, that explains that feeling. My body remembers being an angel."

"You were a child. You were playing. It doesn't mean anything. It doesn't mean—"

"I think I should listen to that feeling."

"Abby…"

"It's my decision."

"It's a bad decision."

"If I were you, I would probably tell you the same thing." Abby took a deep breath. "I'm not one of those people who's ever considered…you know…escaping. I'm kind of shocked that I'd consider it at all, but I want to help them, and…I think…I think I might do it."

CHAPTER SEVENTEEN

"Please don't."

It wasn't the presence of hotel guests under a lamppost on the far side of the parking lot that prevented Gwynne from yelling at her, it was the vise around her throat. Abby was going to do something stupid, and Gwynne couldn't stop her, and the hollowness in her heart and in her lungs and in the pit of her stomach hurt more than she thought possible.

"I think I should do it," Abby said.

"No! Please no..." It was Heather all over again, chasing the angels' treacherous lure.

"I'm not positive, but—"

"At least when Heather jumped off the road onto that frozen river she was high. She didn't know what she was doing. If you can honestly consider doing something like that when you're sober, you're..."

"I'm not insane," Abby whispered, supplying the word Gwynne couldn't bring herself to use.

The metallic taste in her mouth was not pleasant. "I can't believe you would do this!"

"They need help. Elle wants me to do it, and she's an angel, and they've always been good to me. It's a big step, but…I see people pass away at the hospital all the time."

She sounded so logical. So calm. How could she be so calm?

Gwynne tried to be calm and logical too, even though all she wanted to do was scream. Abby trusted her enough to confide in her; Gwynne's job was to keep herself under control before she made her wish she'd never said anything.

"I want to do this," Abby said. "For the good of mankind and angelkind."

"Which is admirable. But you don't know what Elle's goals are. You don't know if she knows what she's doing." Gwynne sucked in a deep breath through her teeth but felt no calmer. "Are you willing to trust your life to someone who admits she has no idea how the bridge really works? What if you die and it doesn't even work?"

Gently, she placed her hands on Abby's shoulders, unsure of her reception, and thank God Abby leaned into her touch because she had to touch her, had to reassure herself she was still here and safe and solid and warm and not dead. She pulled her into her arms and rubbed her hands up and down her back, tracing the shape of her body the way she'd been aching to ever since the last time they'd touched. Mere hours ago, yes, but those few hours had felt like an eternity.

Why, why, why did she have to go and fall in love with someone who was always going to want to save the world? Why couldn't she have ended up with someone selfish? Someone who wouldn't scare the shit out of her?

She hated that Abby wanted to help the angels with their cockamamie plan. Hated it. But that was who Abby was—she wanted to help. Her empathy and her optimism were going to get her killed one of these days—either on this bridge project or on some other undeniably worthy cause—but those qualities were what made her who she was.

"No one's going to thank you for this," Gwynne said.

"Thank me? I'll be happy if people even believe me when I tell them what I've done, but they won't. They'll think I live in a fantasy world. They'll decide I'm weird, and they'll back away. They won't know they were ever in danger of losing their connection with angels, and if I tell them, they won't care. But I'm going to do it anyway."

Gwynne couldn't help but love her for that. But she still had to stop her. "Please don't rush into this. Take more time to think about it."

"I always wanted to be an angel," Abby said.

"Not like this," Gwynne said. "It's not worth it."

"It might be."

A flock of angels appeared out of nowhere and swarmed them, making it difficult to say anything more above the cacophony of their singing. The timing of their sudden appearance combined with their deafening volume made Gwynne suspect this was not an innocent outburst of high spirits, but an attempt to prevent them from talking. To prevent *her* from talking. Maybe that meant she was close to talking Abby out of her suicidal plan.

She climbed into the driver's seat of Abby's minivan and spoke through the open door. "Let's get going. If we can outrun them, it'll be quieter."

Abby stayed put. "If they want to follow us, they'll follow us."

"Then I'll help you get your harp home and we'll take it from there, find somewhere they'll leave us alone."

"Like where?"

Abby was right, of course; there was no place an angel wouldn't follow. Their only hope was to wait for their singing friends to get distracted or bored. But that didn't mean she and Abby had to sit in the parking lot all night. Gwynne reached across the seat and opened the passenger door so Abby would get the hint and get in.

"Come on."

Abby approached the driver's side and leaned against the open door. She dangled her keys within Gwynne's reach and snatched them back. "Move over," Abby ordered.

"I don't mind driving."

"It's not far."

Gwynne sighed and moved to the passenger seat as Abby got behind the wheel. "Why am I in the van if I'm not driving? I thought I was here to help you not get pulled over by the cops."

Abby swiveled in her seat and looked over her shoulder as she backed out of her parking space. She caught Gwynne's eye and winked. "Is that what you thought?"

No, she knew why she was in the van. They were going to talk, and in order to do that they were going to find a place where the angelic choir would give them some privacy, if that was possible. They drove out of the parking lot with the engine rattling. The angels followed. Big surprise. Even if there was no angelic agenda at play, Gwynne had always been popular with them and so had Abby. With the two of them spending so much time together, their odds of being mobbed by an angelic crowd doubled. And angels loved to sing.

"The Sanctus," Abby said. "I love this one."

"You know it?" Gwynne said.

"Of course. Bach's Mass in B Minor. All those different voices overlapping, individual but coming together like they're all part of a single organism, guided by a single thought…when they do it right, it gives me chills."

"It's okay." She was too annoyed with the singers to buff their egos by acknowledging that the weaving of hundreds of angelic voices was unforgettably haunting.

"It's *okay*?" Abby's voice choked with disbelief. "It's the most beautiful piece of music ever written for voice."

"For *human* voice," Gwynne clarified. "I know my mother said Bach wrote it to sound like angels, like heaven on earth—"

"It *is* heaven on earth—"

"If he had any idea what angel song was really like—"

"He would have loved it," Abby insisted.

"I don't think he meant it to sound like your head was cracking open."

Abby pulled up to a red light. "The only reason your head's cracking is because you're fighting it. You have to relax into the unbearable beauty of it." She sang a few notes and sighed with happiness.

The light turned green and Gwynne studied the look of bliss that lingered on Abby's face even as she drove, making turn after turn through the maze of residential streets without ever really looking where she was going. Gwynne ignored whatever danger they were narrowly avoiding in the streets and kept her gaze fixed on the outline of Abby's features in the shifting shadows, memorizing the shape of her eyebrows and her nose and her cheekbones and her lips and the fine creases that deepened at the corners of her eyes when she smiled, every line precious and perfect.

She was going to lose Abby to the angels, wasn't she? Abby was already half in their world. Just look at how she felt about their music. Gwynne's stomach formed a hard knot. She hadn't even had a chance to make love to her yet.

* * *

Still singing at ridiculously high volume, the angels followed Gwynne and Abby into Abby's apartment, shrinking to perch on the curtain rods like sparrows on a roofline while Abby unpacked her harp from its protective case. When the curtain rods got too crowded, the overflow took over the windowsills, and after that, they fluttered in the folds of the double-layered drapes—airy red lace overlapping a second, more substantial fabric in subtle lemon.

Their choir of angels didn't want to leave them alone? Too bad, because Gwynne knew how to make them disappear.

She cupped Abby's face and brushed her thumb along her jaw. "They leave when we kiss," she whispered, trusting Abby would hear her despite the singing. Angels were known to stand guard over people while they slept, but when it came to anything that hinted of sexual behavior, their sense of propriety suddenly kicked in. Well, not that one time when she and Abby got dive-bombed on the beach when they were about to kiss, but every other time she could think of. And she had no qualms about taking advantage of it. Really, she should have thought of this detail sooner. "Want to try?"

Abby nudged at her hand, encouraging her caress. Glints of silver sparkled in her pale blue-gray eyes. Looking into them was like staring into the depths of an endless, star-filled universe. Lightly, worshipfully, she touched the beautiful crinkles at the corners of her smiling eyes, then traced her cheekbones, her jaw.

"You think I got you into my van and drove you here to talk?" Abby asked.

"You didn't get me into your van. I got myself in."

"And why did you do that, Gwynnosaurus?"

"For this," Gwynne admitted, leaning in to kiss her. Shooing away their angelic choir was just an excuse—she would have done this anyway. Their lips and tongues met like they belonged together and Abby kissed her back, meeting her stroke for stroke. Gwynne slipped one hand between them to cup Abby's ample breast and Abby pressed her body into her even harder, bumping into her with a rhythm that had nothing to do with the angels' song, which, come to think of it, had stopped.

She had other things on her mind, mainly the underside of Abby's breast, which was soft and full, and which felt even better when she slid her hand underneath her clothes. Thank God Abby was wearing a light sweater and blouse over a skirt rather than one of her impenetrable dresses, although she'd find her way through one of those too, if need be. She'd find her way under anything.

She adjusted Abby's collar to bare her shoulder, felt Abby's hair sweep against her face, and pressed her lips to her smooth skin. She couldn't get enough of her. God, this was why she'd snapped at her in the car for touching her, because the slightest touch, even when she didn't want her…the slightest contact made her insane with need.

Not wanting her had been a lie.

She wanted to kiss her everywhere, touch her everywhere, breathe her in. She wanted to pull her to the floor and imprint herself on her before she escaped to join the angels and it was too late.

* * *

Abby wanted to pull Gwynne to the floor before the woman had the chance to change her mind. She didn't think she could take it if Gwynne got scared and decided, once again, that they couldn't be together.

She wasn't sure how to get her to the floor, though, so she tugged her into her bedroom instead and onto her bed. That worked okay. She yanked open Gwynne's belt and undid her jeans and Gwynne helped her with the rest, and the shock of finally seeing her beautiful bare body made her heart race.

Abby hitched up her skirt and straddled her, in too much of a hurry to be on top of her to deal with her own clothes. She crawled forward and kissed her on the mouth and tasted butterscotch.

Gwynne pushed Abby's skirt out of the way and curled her hand around the waistband of her underwear and gave it a tug. "Off," she demanded, breaking their kiss. Her breath came loud and ragged.

"But that would mean getting off of you," Abby argued. "I like it here."

If she scrambled off, Gwynne would move, and she liked her right where she was. She sat back so her lace underwear made contact with Gwynne's pelvis and she rocked into her. Gwynne angled to meet her, heat against heat, rubbing against her with a friction that spread sparks through her body and made her want to slide her legs farther apart.

Gwynne reached up to touch her breasts through her layers of sweater and blouse and bra, doing half a sit-up to get close enough to lift her sweater. Abby rose involuntarily to her knees to help, and Gwynne took advantage of the gap that opened between them to snag her underwear by the crotch.

Gwynne fell back to the mattress and tugged on the lace bunched in her hand. "Get this off."

Abby tensed her thighs, resisting, but Gwynne held firm against the tension on the elastic and caressed what she could reach in the space between her and the lace. Oh, God, that was good. Abby sank back down, her thighs shaking, her pelvis tilting of its own accord, angling to let her in. Her innermost muscles pulsed hard, wanting it, wanting her, wanting to come.

"You're first," Abby protested.

"Says who?"

"Says the one who's on top. The one with all her clothes on?"

"Like that's going to stop me." Gwynne's voice was deeper than she'd ever heard it, laced with arousal and amusement.

Abby's skirt shifted and Gwynne pushed it out of the way again as she continued to stroke between Abby's legs. Abby trembled. She rubbed her hands up and down Gwynne's body and Gwynne's pelvis lifted her off the bed, thrusting beneath her. Her legs clamped around Gwynne's hips. She wanted her so much, she was shaking with it. Her thighs squeezed harder and Gwynne groaned—which turned her on even more.

And more. And more…

"*Oh.*"

Abby's orgasm overtook her. She reached blindly for Gwynne, needing to take her with her. Gwynne's cries got faster and louder and more urgent and then Gwynne was coming and coming and coming, her fingers spasmodically clutching her skirt.

Abby collapsed on top of her and held her, her head tucked against her chest, riding the rise and fall of her ribs as Gwynne tried to catch her breath. Filled with tenderness, she skimmed her fingers across Gwynne's collarbone.

"We should do this again sometime," Abby murmured.

"We should." Gwynne tightened her arms around her.

Without warning, Gwynne rolled on top of her and almost knocked them both off the bed, catching her at the last second and pinning her to the edge of the mattress. Abby giggled hysterically. Maybe they would end up making love on the floor after all.

"You have the smallest bed I've ever seen," Gwynne complained.

"You love it," Abby scoffed. No way could she not love the site of their first time together. "Roll on top of me some more."

Gwynne wrestled her out of her clothes and Abby let her, and then Gwynne was touching her with a purposeful desperation that was so perfect she could hardly breathe.

"Oh my God, Gwynne. Gwendolyn. Gwynnosaurus."

Gwynne's relentless touch was the only thing in the world, the only thing in the anchorless sea where her consciousness—what pieces were left of it—surged with sharp, painful pulses of need, yearning for what was almost…almost…almost within reach. Mindless, she shifted into another dimension where she hovered on the brink of searing implosion, pushed further and further into oblivion, until release pounded through her in wave after wave of chaos.

* * *

Abby rose in the middle of the night, and Gwynne, attuned to her every movement, woke. She'd fallen asleep with Abby curled in her arms, and she never wanted to spend another moment of her life in any other position. Abby was only a few steps away and already she missed her.

Apparently coming countless times in one night made her clingy.

In the dim glow of the clock radio, she watched her disappear into the bathroom and wondered how she'd gotten herself into this mess, joined at the hip after half a night together like a novice who'd never had sex before, yet too deliriously happy to have the sense to worry about it.

And as clichéd as it sounded, it wasn't only about the sex. It was being with her. It was talking with her, laughing with her, seeing her at work, driving with her, feeling safe enough to fall asleep with her.

Wanting to have all the time in the world with her.

Abby returned and slipped into bed and snagged something from the top of her cluttered nightstand. It was the gold circlet she'd worn on her head at Penelope's wedding. She fingered it thoughtfully, turning it over in her hands, and grinned. Mischief glimmered in her eyes. "Let's see how this looks on you."

Gwynne glued herself to the pillow and folded her arms over her forehead, warding her off. "Let's not."

Abby came closer with the circlet, raising it overhead. Her heart was a blazing, whirling vortex of light.

"I don't do sparkly," Gwynne protested.

"You do now." Abby dragged her from the pillow until she was sitting up. She placed the circlet on her head like a crown and balanced it so it wouldn't slide off. Her mischievous grin turned hot.

Gwynne's world spun slowly upside down. She tossed her head and let the crown fall to the bed. Abby grabbed her and any thought of sleep vanished.

* * *

Dawn glowed pink through a gap in the curtains as a fiery ball of golden light whooshed into the room. An angel. Who else? They never left her alone for long.

Sleepily, Gwynne reached for Abby and curled her arm around her more securely. She pressed her ear to Abby's ribcage and closed her eyes and forgot about their visitor. She could feel Abby's heartbeat, feel the steady rise and fall of her breathing, and she waited for each breath and listened for each heartbeat, silently asking Abby's lungs and heart to stay strong and healthy and keep her alive, and, if they wouldn't mind, to please convince her brain she was needed and loved right here on earth.

She must have fallen asleep because the next thing she knew, she was jolted awake by a voice that registered at a non-human frequency.

"We need to talk." A ball of light floated at the foot of the bed. As it took angel shape, it grew to seven feet tall, wings emerging like a starburst of shattering glass.

Gwynne squinted against the intense light. "This is not the best time," she whispered under her breath. She didn't know how Abby could still be asleep after that noise, but if she was, she didn't want to wake her.

"In private."

Gwynne did not want to get up. She wanted to stay right where she was, with Abby in her arms, and go back to sleep. She hadn't gotten much sleep. The angel whooshed around the bed, around and around, over and under, passing an inch over her face. Gwynne tried squeezing her eyes shut, but it was no use. She knew she was there.

"All right, all right." She wasn't going to be able to enjoy lying peacefully in bed in her own personal heaven knowing this angel was watching, especially if she kept up with the ridiculous yet annoying whooshing, which Gwynne had no doubt she could easily keep up for days.

She gave Abby a kiss on her bare shoulder and slithered out of bed, doing her best not to wake her. She threw on her clothes from the day before and went to the kitchen to pour herself a glass of water. The angel followed silently. Gwynne trudged to the living room, threaded her way through the harps, and dropped onto the sofa in the corner. She was sitting on something—a discarded sweater or a throw. She pulled the thing out from under her and discovered it was a crocheted granny shawl, almost as hopelessly old-fashioned as Abby's harping outfits and not nearly as sexy. She draped it over her shoulders to stay warm and smoothed the fringe, wondering why she'd allowed this now-silent angel to talk her out of bed. She swiveled sideways and put her feet up.

"Private enough?" Gwynne asked.

"It will do." The angel hovered at the far end of the sofa. "I'm Elle."

Gwynne snapped her head toward the bedroom and started from the sofa. The last of her sleepiness was gone. Elle. What was Elle doing here? If she was here to kidnap Abby again…

"Is Abby still here?" Gwynne rushed to the bedroom and shoved open the door.

"Still trapped in human form," Elle said from behind her.

The relief of seeing Abby safe and asleep in bed made her light-headed. She shut the door as quietly as she could. "Thank God."

"You don't understand," Elle said. "It's imperative that she stop stalling."

Gwynne didn't consider herself to be a violent person, but she wouldn't have minded having a weapon handy to threaten her with. Not that anything could hurt a non-physical being, but it would express her feelings quite well. "In case you haven't noticed, things have changed here over the last few bazillion years. We don't do human sacrifice anymore."

"The bridge is getting worse. The longer we wait, the more chance there is that we'll lose more angels. It's not safe."

"I don't care."

"Furthermore," Elle continued as if Gwynne hadn't said a word, "we believe Abigail's refusal to join us is the reason it's getting worse."

"You're blaming Abby?" That was totally not fair. Abby was a beautiful human being and had nothing to do with their problems. Dragging her into their repair efforts was bad enough, but now they were blaming her?

"When our involvement with humankind leads us to venture too far into human patterns of separation consciousness, as Abigail has done, the bridge calls us back. It's a fail-safe mechanism. It's dangerous, but it's designed to protect us too."

"From what?" Gwynne demanded.

"From forgetting our true nature." Elle grew larger until her wings filled the entire room, leaving only a sliver of breathing space for Gwynne. "You could help me convince her."

The bright, angelic light that had always seemed so ethereal and easy to ignore now felt dangerous. Gwynne crossed her arms over her chest and stationed herself in front of Abby's bedroom door. "I have no intention of helping you."

Elle's light intensified. "Abigail must help us."

"She won't."

"She has to. She has to die."

"No. She doesn't." Gwynne wasn't about to tell her the angels were closer to succeeding than they thought. "You need to accept that."

"I'm sorry you see it that way," Elle said stiffly. "I thought that since you're able to see us and communicate with us, you'd want to help."

"Not at the cost of Abby's life."

Elle's screech reached the painful edge of the outer reaches of human hearing. "It's not a real life! She's only pretending to have a human life."

"It feels pretty real to her right now."

Elle threw her hands up and disappeared in a flash of light.

Gwynne had never seen an angel get frustrated. She didn't know if this was good or bad. Probably bad.

Elle reappeared. "We can't afford to continue waiting. If she refuses to be reasonable, I'm going to have to take matters into my own hands."

Oh, crap. Fear burst inside her, searing her gut and leaving behind bits of burning ash. "You told Abby angels don't kill." As if manipulating someone into committing suicide wasn't murder—although right now that was not the point.

Elle's light began to fade, her energy withdrawing as if she were no longer interested in talking. "When she dies, she reverts to angel form. I've decided that doesn't qualify as killing."

CHAPTER EIGHTEEN

Elle had almost finished disappearing into the ether when Gwynne heard the bedroom door open behind her. She spun around. Abby stood in the doorway, gloriously naked, the previous day's eyeliner smudged from sleep.

Abby looked wide awake—awake and pissed. It would be hard not to be after Elle's screech. Her eyes narrowed at the afterimage of the angel's wispy form. "You got tired of waiting."

"Don't," Gwynne warned, but it was too late. Elle was brightening now, no longer in retreat. "She wants to kill you."

"I heard." Abby kept her gaze fixed on the intruder.

"I thought you might," Elle said. If angels could be catty—and Gwynne hadn't thought that was possible—this was what it would sound like.

"Let me try to help again," Abby said. "In human form."

She appropriated the shawl from Gwynne's shoulders and wrapped it around her body under her arms like a towel. Not that it covered much. Later, when Gwynne could think about something besides Elle's threat, she would have to move crocheted shawls up from the bottom of her fashion list. After she made a fashion list. Abby could help.

Because there would be a later. She might be cracking under stress to even think about something so irrelevant, but Elle was not going to take Abby away from her.

Elle's glow intensified as she floated toward Abby. "You weren't convinced after one attempt?"

Abby tightened the shawl around her bust. "It almost worked."

"Nothing happened," Elle countered.

"I felt something," Abby said. "We almost had it."

Elle's angry blaze made the room brighter than day. "Your way doesn't work."

"Stay back," Gwynne ordered, knowing she was helpless against the approaching creature. She put her arm around Abby's waist and pulled her snug against her side. Elle wasn't going to kill her *now*, was she? Abby was so naked and loveable under that shawl, and all she wanted to do was keep her safe. "I can help fix the bridge." How she could help, she had no idea. And then it came to her. "I can use my field to boost Abby's. I know how to channel energy to do it. We'll have more power than you did last time."

Elle seemed to hesitate. "It's brave of you to offer," she said. "But what we need is Abigail's help—not yours."

"Abby's help isn't enough, not in human form. You said so yourself."

Abby fussed with her shawl and adjusted it at the side. "Gwynne. There's no need to get involved."

"I disagree." Abby was out of options, and Gwynne was going to change that.

Dodging harps, Elle twirled around Abby's living room. "It'll never work. We need an angel, not two humans. Not a million humans. You don't have the right energy frequency. Besides, it's not safe for you to touch the bridge."

The killer was worried about her safety. How nice.

"Not safe for me, or not safe for the bridge?"

"Not safe for you," Elle said. "Touching the bridge might kill you."

"What do you mean, *might*?" Abby demanded. "That's not what you said before. You said it *will* kill anyone human. Now you're going with *might*?"

Gwynne tightened her arm around her waist. The nubby texture of the shawl pressed against her side. "It didn't kill you, Abby."

"Because Abigail is an angel," Elle said. "As I've told her repeatedly. She looks human, her physical body is human, but her energy field and her soul are not human. She's an angel. You are not. She can safely interact with the bridge. You, as much as you might like to, cannot."

Gwynne stared at Elle thoughtfully. "So which is it? It *will* kill me? Or it *might* kill me? Which would imply it might not."

Elle morphed into a ball of light, spun around, then resumed more human shape. If Gwynne had to guess, she'd say the angel looked flustered.

Interesting.

"It might not," Elle admitted. "I can't be positive."

"Lovely," Abby said.

It *was* lovely. It was more than lovely—it was great.

"Here's the thing," Gwynne said. "Abby is not going to kill herself, so this is your only other option."

"What?" Abby turned on Gwynne. "What happened to not trusting her?"

"You don't have enough power," Elle told Gwynne.

"I don't have *any* power," Gwynne said. "That's not how it works." And Elle knew it. There was no way that members of the Angelic Realm had followed her around her whole life, and helped her heal her clients, and they didn't know this.

Elle looked heavenward. "Semantics. You pull your power from the earth's vital web."

Was that what she thought? This was not good. The idea that she pulled power from the earth was a common misperception, but Elle should know better. Pulling power was exhausting. And not that effective. And rude to the rocks and life-forms you might be pulling from.

"I don't *pull* power," she explained. "I access it. I locate the energy and throw myself into the current. It's not the same thing." By diving into the flow, she became part of the flow, and huge amounts of energy became available to her, much more than she'd ever get from "pulling." All she had to do was focus.

And she was about to develop a hell of a lot more focus.

But maybe to Elle, whose entire explanation of how the bridge worked was, *No one understands it, it's alien technology*, it really was semantics.

"It doesn't matter how much energy you can harness," Elle said, "because earth energy is not what we need. We need angel energy."

"That can't be true," Gwynne said, taking heart from the shift in Elle's explanation. Because if the *amount* of energy wasn't the issue, but instead it was the *type*…"Energy is energy, right?"

"Not in this case," Elle said.

"No, listen. Maybe I can't help on my own, but Abby's got both a human energy system and an angelic energy system. Her field already knows how to integrate them. She'll be able to link to me while she's linked to you, and I'll read the flow and I'll push her into alignment with you. I'll shift her into phase."

Abby leaned into her. "It's too dangerous."

Gwynne tightened her grip. "I'm not losing you. Do you hear me? I am not losing you." She might not have been able to save her mother or her sister, but she could save Abby. And the angels. She'd save them all.

"Your killing yourself on that bridge is not going to help," Abby said. "Elle, don't let her do this."

Elle shrugged. "If Gwynne wants to die, she can be my guest."

"What?" Abby shrieked.

"Actually," Elle said, "there's a slight chance it might work."

Gwynne perked up. "What does that slight chance depend on?"

"It depends on whether your energy field can handle the energy that flows through the bridge."

"I can handle it. It will work." It was going to have to.

"A minute ago you said it wouldn't work," Abby reminded Elle accusingly.

"The others have their doubts," Elle said. "I do too. But you never know."

"You never know?" Abby's voice rose with barely contained hysteria.

"Whatever gets our bridge fixed."

"I'll be fine," Gwynne said with more conviction than she felt.

"Possibly." Elle drifted toward the ceiling. "Your channels are clear enough, and your vibrational frequency is higher than most people's."

"No." Abby gripped Gwynne's arm.

"If not, I have a backup plan," Elle said breezily.

Yes, they all knew about Elle's charming little backup plan. Gwynne gritted her teeth. "We're going with my plan."

"She's not going to kill me," Abby said.

"That's optimistic of you," Gwynne said.

"Unless she thinks killing you off is going to make me suicidal."

Gwynne's stomach churned. What a thought, that they might be playing into some twisted angelic plan. "Would it?"

Abby bit her lip. "Of course not."

"I wouldn't do that," Elle breathed. Her voice cracked a little, as if she was hurt that they were both angry at her. "I wouldn't do anything to break your heart."

"Thanks," Abby said gently, sounding like she didn't want to hurt Elle, either.

"Which doesn't mean Gwynne won't die," Elle reminded her.

Not helping. Gwynne almost said it aloud, but caught herself in time. She rubbed Abby's side and glared at Elle. She needed Abby to not think about what she risked. Thinking would lead to dwelling, and dwelling on the danger to Gwynne's life would lead to her doing something rash like running off to save the world without her.

"You signed up for suffering when you volunteered to live as a human," Elle added.

Still not helping.

"And I'd have eternity to get over it?" Abby suggested.

"Don't think like that," Gwynne said.

Abby leaned her head against Gwynne's shoulder. "You're going to do this even if I say no, aren't you? You'll find a way to do it without me."

"Yeah." Gwynne buried her fingers in Abby's hair and held her close. She'd do anything for her.

"Then let's do it together."

* * *

"We can't let her do it. It's too dangerous," Artemisia said. She stretched her wings and banked right, circling Elle as they flew over the glittering lakes and hidden caves that dotted the landscape of the Angelic Realm.

They hit a cross breeze and Elle took an exhilarating breath of crisp, unpolluted air. She tacked into the wind, Artemisia at her side. "I know she's special to you, Artemisia, but she volunteered. Of her own free will."

She'd known Artemisia was going to be upset. They all were. Gwynne had a lot of friends among the angels. A lot of fans. When you spent most of eternity being invisible, it was fun to hang out with someone who could see you.

"You must have manipulated her."

"I didn't." Elle flew harder into the wind. "I tried to talk her out of it."

Artemisia sighed. Dropped back. Flapped her wings to catch up. "I believe you," she said. "Gwynne has a mind of her own. There's no talking to her."

Elle couldn't agree more. "I told Abigail not to date her because I knew Gwynne was going to end up being a problem. I knew she was going to interfere." Of course, if Elle hadn't made the bad decision to talk to her in a last-ditch effort to convince Abigail, they wouldn't be in this awkward situation. It really was not Gwynne's fault.

"Maybe I can stop her," Artemisia said.

"No," Elle said quickly. "We're going to have to use her. We need to fix the bridge before it kills anyone else."

"She doesn't understand what she's getting into. The bridge will kill her!"

Elle fell in beside her. "We don't know that for sure."

Artemisia crumpled. "My brave girl. I should be proud that she wants to help."

"It'll be dangerous for her, but it might work."

"And if it doesn't, she's dead." Artemisia shuddered and the wind swept her away.

CHAPTER NINETEEN

Gwynne stowed her suitcase in the trunk of their rental car at the Albuquerque airport and reached for Abby's carry-on.

"Did Elle tell you how far it is?" Abby asked.

"Would have been nice." All she knew was they were supposed to drive north to Santa Fe and then on toward Taos until someone bright and shiny showed up to navigate.

She'd assumed they would access the bridge from Piper Beach as Abby had, but Elle said Angel Rock was just a jumping-off spot, something that was safe to tether in populated areas because it didn't harm humans who accidentally came in contact with it. They couldn't use it in this case. For Gwynne to be involved, they had to travel to one of the four places on earth where the bridge was anchored so that Gwynne, who could not safely touch the bridge, could stand on the ground yet be within arm's length of it. That meant they were headed for New Mexico, which was far, far easier to reach than the Sahara or the singing sand dunes of China or the virtually impossible to get to anchor in Antarctica.

Leaning into the backseat, Abby strapped a seat belt around her harp, a small squat one that fit in the airplane's overhead luggage compartment. She'd insisted on bringing it, saying she'd feel naked without it.

"I'll drive," Abby said, her head inside the car and her backside wiggling flirtatiously.

"I don't think so." There was no way Abby had already forgotten her name was not on the rental agreement, or why it wasn't there. She liked the wiggle, though.

Abby emerged from the back and shut the door. "I only speed when it's safe. And I never go as fast as I really want to."

Gwynne was sure that was true, but what happened when a strung-out kid like her sister ran into the street without looking, or a woman broke a high heel and stood hopping on one leg in the middle of the road, or a deer leaped across the highway? Were angels going to pluck those pedestrians and randy deer out of the path of an oncoming car, just because Abby was driving? No, they were not.

"I'm driving," Gwynne said.

"I've never been in an accident," Abby protested. "I have excellent reflexes."

"Nice try, but no."

Abby gave up and climbed into the front passenger seat while Gwynne figured out the controls and started the car. She adjusted the rearview mirror and caught Elle's reflection. Ugh. Back to work. Wiggle appreciation time was over.

"I thought you were going to meet us later," Gwynne told Elle.

"Careful with the harp," Abby warned over her shoulder.

More angels popped in and crammed into the back and Elle scooted closer to the door to make room for them. One enthusiastic angel arrived out of nowhere and landed in Elle's lap shouting "Road trip!"

Gwynne exchanged a look with Abby. "I guess this means we're all riding together."

Abby leaned back in her seat. "You must be psychic."

Over the next few miles, more and more angels arrived until hundreds of them swarmed alongside the car—as well as behind the car, in front of the car, and presumably above the car.

"Could you please not crowd in front of the windshield?" Gwynne asked. She glanced at the speedometer and noted she was going ninety miles an hour. North of Santa Fe, they'd lost what little traffic there was, and with few landmarks and the vastness of the desert, it was easy to ignore how fast she was driving. Abby certainly wasn't going to ask her to slow down. "It's hard to see where I'm going with all that light shining in my eyes."

The swarms of happy angels continued to turn somersaults and narrowly avoid midair collisions, but the ones who had stationed themselves in front of the car did move off to the sides, which helped considerably with her vision problem.

Gwynne kept her foot on the pedal and did not slow down. She didn't want to be a hypocrite about the speeding thing, but the sooner they got where they were going, the sooner they could get this over with, and the sooner that damn angel would stop threatening her girlfriend.

"Never drive faster than your angel can fly," Elle said piously from the backseat.

Gwynne glanced again at the speedometer and then at the angel's reflection in the rearview mirror. "You have got to be kidding me."

"I never kid."

"Are we going to have to listen to cheesy bumper sticker quotations the whole way there?" As if pissing her off with the whole bridge thing wasn't bad enough, now Elle had to carpool.

"It's not cheesy. I like it," Elle said.

"Oh, for the love of God."

Elle began to sing, and one by one the others joined in. The Sanctus again.

Abby clicked off the radio and rested her head against the seatback. "It's so beautiful."

Gwynne started to make a negative comment about the angels' song choice but swallowed it when she saw Abby was completely enthralled, a blissful smile on her face. Besides, Abby was right. It *was* beautiful, in its own crazy, angelic way.

Abby added her voice to the others, following their ascent up the scale and hitting every note with her unexpectedly beautiful, sweet tone—didn't she say she couldn't sing?—until she breached the end of her range and her voice cracked. She filled her lungs with air, rejoined the flurry of voices as they chased an even higher note, and missed again. Instead of backing down, she cheerfully launched herself way beyond her range and hit a God-awful screech of an off-key note. She threw her head back and laughed with joy.

"You have a nice voice," Gwynne said. It was true, too, up until that last part.

She took one hand off the steering wheel and took Abby's hand in hers, pulling it into her lap and to heck with all the uninvited chaperones, who continued down the scale and back up again with an unceasing chorus of *holy, holy, holy*. Normally holding hands might have been enough to make them disappear, but not today. Either they were taking their road guide duties seriously or they were too caught up in timing their musical entrances just right to notice.

"This is why I don't hire myself out as a singer," Abby said. "My range sucks, and I have way too much fun. At least when I have fun on my harp I don't damage anyone's hearing."

Gwynne rubbed her thumb over the palm of Abby's hand. "It wasn't that bad."

"You don't have to lie."

Abby twisted in her seat like she wanted to check on her harp, and as she did, Gwynne loosened her grip on her, worried that Abby was moving because she was uncomfortable with the public hand-holding. Abby freed herself and even though Gwynne was expecting it, it still made her slump. But then Abby positioned her body so she blocked Gwynne's hand from returning to the steering wheel and proceeded to press against her thigh, her fingers digging into the fabric of her jeans in a private caress that would be barely perceptible to anyone watching, like oh, say, from the backseat. Which meant all of Abby's shifting in her seat *wasn't* because she was uncomfortable.

Gwynne's mood perked up. She reached up to smooth Abby's hair. Abby made a happy sound and then pretended to be jostled by the moving car and fell practically in her lap. And still the angels did not skedaddle. Abby moved her hand higher, sending licks of heat up her inner thigh.

Gwynne's heart hammered. "If you keep that up, we're going to get in an accident," she murmured.

Abby fingered the seam of her jeans and followed it upward. Gwynne stopped breathing. Her thighs tightened and her back pressed against the seat as her blood pulsed against the crotch of that seam, throbbing with anticipation, impatient for her fingers to reach her, squirming with worry that if Abby did ever get there—and she was damn close—she'd rise off the seat.

"I used to be able to hit that high note," Abby said matter-of-factly. "So I just go for it, because, you know, maybe one day I'll surprise myself."

Gwynne slammed her hand back onto the steering wheel to maintain control of the car.

"I love you," Abby murmured, brushing her lips close to her ear as she returned to her seat.

She loved her. Abby loved her.

Gwynne swallowed. She had to tell her this at ninety miles an hour?

Abby crossed her arms and settled in her seat as if nothing had happened. "Why are all you angels here, anyway? Couldn't you just give us directions to this mystery mountain and meet us there?"

Elle spoke up from the back, her broken-glass voice carrying over the singing. "We want to make sure you arrive safely."

"And doing a bang-up job of it too," Gwynne said, wishing she could be alone with Abby. Elle wasn't the major source of distraction here—she had Abby to thank for that—but Elle wasn't helping. Maybe once they fixed the bridge they'd get a break from all the angelic visitation. That would be nice. Privacy. Alone with Abby Vogel. Alone with her in a very private room. With a "Do Not Disturb" sign on the doorknob. What was that saying, *Angels are all around us*? This sign would say *Angels are NOT all around us. PLEASE.*

The brake lights on the cars ahead of them lit up simultaneously and she eased her foot off the accelerator.

"*Now* you slow down?" Elle sounded annoyed.

"Speed trap," Abby said before Gwynne could figure out why everyone was slowing, but several seconds later, she saw Abby was right.

"I did warn you," Elle said.

"This was why you wanted me not to drive faster than my angel can fly?" Gwynne held the car steady at five miles below the speed limit. "Could you have been a little less cryptic?"

If she couldn't be clear about something as innocuous as a speed trap, what else hadn't she told them?

* * *

Odina Fierro rang up two extra-large bottles of spring water, various snacks, and a bunch of postcards of one of the supposedly extinct volcanoes up the road to the north.

"You're buying postcards?" one of the two young ladies asked the other, as if there was something wrong with the merchandise.

Odina didn't see what the customer was so worked up about. Sure, personally, she thought the pictures of the Sangre de Cristo Mountains at sunset, when the mountains turned bloodred, were prettier. But these were nice too. The aerial views of the lone mound rising from the plains always sold well. Nothing wrong with any of her postcards.

The other girl fanned out the postcards to show her friend. "Elle says this is where we're going."

"When did she tell you that?"

"While you were outside digging through the trunk for your purse."

Odina hadn't noticed the girl talking to anyone. Had to be texting. "You girls planning to visit the mountain?"

"That's why we're here."

"Risk-takers, I see." They didn't seem like the type. Usually it was skinny testosterone junkies who hiked up that mountain, daring each other to do something stupid, trying to feel alive. Her neighbor's kid went up there last year and came back with an armload of thunderwood and carved it into souvenirs he wanted her to sell in her shop. No thank you, she told him. No sir-ee. Wood injured by the lightning spirit was bad luck. The kid said the tourists didn't know any better. They'd think it was traditional. But she told him no.

"Lots of other mountains around here you could hike," Odina told the girls. "Just as beautiful."

"What's wrong with this one?"

"You don't know?"

"What do you mean?" one of them asked.

Odina counted out their change and handed it to them. "We call it the Bermuda Triangle of New Mexico. Every year someone disappears up there. Or gets struck by lightning."

The two girls exchanged meaningful glances.

"No one ever proves it's lightning that kills 'em, of course. If it was just disappearances, I'd put my money on a mountain lion having them for lunch. A mountain lion could explain the fatal heart attacks too, if you ask me. But the dead bodies, no. Never heard of a mountain lion killing folks and not eating 'em."

"We'll watch out for mountain lions," said the one buying the postcards, tucking her change into her purse. She didn't look like she was taking her seriously—just humoring an old woman.

"And lightning," added the friend.

Odina hoped nothing happened to these girls. They were so young. Maybe if she told them about the mysterious lights and strange sounds…

"Then there's that hum they talk about. Folks that can hear it, they say it sounds like an engine gone bad, but it would have to be one hell of an engine to be heard for miles and miles. Could be coming from Los Alamos. Who knows what the government does up there. They sure don't want us knowing about it, that's for sure."

The girl nodded. "We'll listen for the hum."

You know, now that she thought about it, maybe they did believe her. The thing was, though, they were going to do whatever the hell it was they planned to do anyway. They weren't scared. What was wrong with kids these days, anyway?

CHAPTER TWENTY

Abby returned from the convenience store's restroom and hopped into the rental car where Gwynne waited for her in the driver's seat, pressing a postcard against the steering wheel and tapping her mouth with a pen.

"You could die this afternoon and you're writing postcards?" Abby pulled the door shut. "If you're writing a suicide note it would be easier to post it online."

"It's not the same. Didn't your grandmother teach you the olden ways? A handwritten note says you care." Gwynne scribbled something on the postcard. "Besides, I always send postcards when I travel. People expect it."

"What people?"

"Dara, Hank, Megan-and-Kira…"

A happy thought struck her. "If you want to write postcards, we could switch places and I could drive."

"Nice try."

It was, wasn't it? "You must be tired after all that driving," Abby said, antsy from too much time in the passenger seat and unable to resist needling her. "Especially with the angel light shining straight into your eyes. Wouldn't it be safer if I drove?" Not that driving safety was at the top of their priority list right now. If that clerk at the convenience store was right, Gwynne was going to die anyway as soon as she touched the angels' humming secret government property. Either that or get eaten by mountain lions.

"Relax."

Oh, sure, like that was going to help. Abby squirmed in her seat. "Are you writing about the hum?"

"There's no hum."

"Maybe we just can't hear it."

"I doubt it." Gwynne kept writing.

"All that stuff she was talking about—it must be the bridge."

"Of course it's the bridge." Gwynne tapped her pen on her stack of postcards. "I hope Dara's not having any problems running the appointment desk."

"You should tell Dara about the hum. She loves that stuff."

"There's no hum."

"Hmmmm," Abby said, anxiety making her act silly. She walked her fingers up Gwynne's arm. "Hmmmmmmmm."

Gwynne's eyes twinkled. She stashed her postcards in the door and started the car. "I don't hear a thing."

* * *

Half an hour later they were driving at Gwynne's idea of highway speeds when the car slowed and Gwynne started swearing. Abby glanced at the road, trying to spot what was wrong, but saw nothing. The cords in Gwynne's forearms visibly worked as she gripped the wheel.

"Hang on," Gwynne said tersely as she pulled the car off the road onto the dirt where the shoulder should have been.

They hit a bump and bounced farther from the road before coming to a stop beside a clump of what she guessed was sagebrush. Abby stared at Gwynne's hands—one held the gearshift that was now in Park, the other still gripped the wheel.

After the bumpiness and the gravel hitting the undercarriage, everything seemed oddly still.

"What happened?" Abby asked.

Gwynne stared straight ahead, motionless except for her ribcage moving up and down. She laughed, but she didn't sound amused. She turned the ignition and the engine didn't even try to start. But Abby hadn't seen her turn the engine off. Wait, did that mean…

"The engine stalled?" Abby asked.

"Yup."

"We drove off the road for that?"

"Sorry for not trying to restart the engine at seventy-five miles an hour."

Abby loosened her seat belt and refrained from telling her *she* could have done it. So Gwynne overshot the road by a few yards. No big deal. The important thing was no one got hurt.

Gwynne tried to start the car again.

Nothing.

Gwynne bent down to feel around the gas pedal. "Do you know anything about cars?"

"I know how to call a mechanic." Abby pulled out her phone and scanned for a signal. No signal. It figured. She got out of the car and held her phone up to the heavens. Still no signal. Staring at her phone, she walked several yards away, staying parallel to the road, then zigzagged away from the road, then back to the car.

"It's not looking so good," she said when she returned. "Not unless one of the angels wants to step in and do something."

All the angels in the vicinity promptly vanished.

"Right. You're not engineers," Abby said to empty air. She looked at Gwynne, who had popped the hood and was peering at the car's parts from enough of a distance that it was clear she had no idea what she was looking for. "What do you think the chances are they went to get help?"

"No idea."

"Craptastic."

"Yup."

Abby left Gwynne with the car and stationed herself at the side of the road to flag down help. It didn't take long for someone to pull over and agree to send a tow truck from the next town up the road. When she returned, she found Gwynne underneath the car, her feet sticking out.

"What are you doing?" Abby ducked her head to look under the car. Gwynne lay faceup in the dust, her arms outstretched like Jesus on the cross. She was petite enough that she had enough clearance, but…"Isn't the car hot under there? What if something sparks?" The last thing they needed was for Gwynne to get injured doing something stupid.

"I'm doing energy healing on the car."

On the *car*? Abby was glad Gwynne couldn't see her face. "Is it working?"

"I have no idea."

"Should we test it?" It seemed unlikely that anything Gwynne could do would have helped, but it was worth a shot. And it might get her out from underneath the car.

Gwynne wriggled out and scooted into the driver's seat. She turned the key in the ignition. Nothing.

"I'll do more healing on it."

"I don't think more healing's going to work," Abby said through the window. "Let's just sit and wait."

"Maybe I should try to flag down another driver for help," Gwynne said. "As backup, in case your Good Samaritan falls through."

"She said she would call a tow truck for us. She was very nice."

"I just want to be sure."

"Worrying is not going to help." Abby cracked her knuckles, which probably made her look worried. They could wait a few hours. If the tow truck didn't show up, they'd try again.

"Flagging down another motorist isn't worrying," Gwynne said. "It's doing something."

"So is waiting."

"What if she doesn't follow through? We're just going to sit here and wait for AWOL angels to save our asses?"

"They want us to get to the bridge. They'll make sure we get there."

"They want *you* to get to the bridge." Gwynne tried the ignition one more time. She slapped the keys in her palm and got out of the car and slammed the door shut behind her. "If we die out here in the desert, they get what they wanted all along."

Abby followed her away from the car. "They wouldn't do that."

"Elle wants to kill you, Abby. My coming along on this trip is her way of appeasing you."

"She said it might work."

"After I talked her into it," Gwynne pointed out. "How about we sit farther from the road, okay? I wouldn't put it past Elle to distract a driver and make him crash into us. She's bloodthirsty."

They found a spot a safe distance from the highway and settled down to wait. Gwynne sat on the ground with her forearms resting on her bent knees and stared out at the desert. She was gut-droppingly beautiful, the strong planes of her face outlined by the sun. Gwynne turned her head and met her eyes with her fathomless gaze, and the shock of it made Abby sway, made her feel like she was falling out of the sky.

Gwynne rose and sat closer, close enough to touch. "I love the gold streaks in your hair," she said. "You have so many colors. The blond, the brandy, the caramel—"

"The gray?"

"You don't have any gray." She lifted a strand of Abby's hair between her fingers and reverently tucked it back into place, smoothing it down.

"Flatterer."

"It will be beautiful gray too."

Gwynne stretched out on the ground beside her, the side of her thigh touching Abby's hip, one arm draped over her eyes to shield herself from the sun. Abby wanted to kiss her, wanted to roll on top of her, but she couldn't—not here. Anyone driving by could see them from the road.

She almost didn't care.

Instead, she got up and retrieved her harp from the car.

"Come back," Gwynne said.

An invisible thread of wanting stretched between them. Abby still wanted to kiss her. Seeing her flat on her back reminded her too much of making love to her. It was like a Pavlovian response, giving her ideas.

She returned with her harp and sat so her thigh pressed against Gwynne's while the harp rested in her lap. Back home, she'd loosened all the strings to protect them from snapping in the changing air pressure aboard the airplane, and now it took her a good ten, fifteen minutes to tighten each string and bring it back into tune, even though it was a small harp with only three octaves.

Gwynne moved her arm off her face and turned onto her side and propped herself up. "Maybe I should do some more healing on the car."

She was getting up? She shouldn't get up. She looked so sexy lying down. And touching her, even if it was only leg against leg through their clothes, felt too good to stop.

"It's an inanimate object, Gwynnosaurus. I don't think more energy's going to help."

"I need to prove to myself that I can fix it."

"Why?" Abby said. "It's not a good test. Your skills are designed to work on people, not cars. You can't expect a machine to behave like a living thing. If something's broken, no amount of energy is going to conjure up the replacement parts."

"The angels' bridge isn't alive, either. It's more like a car than like a person."

"It's not a car. It's not made of earth materials. And even if you *could* fix the car, we have no idea what the bridge will do. Even the angels don't understand how it works. They know how to use it, but if they had to build a new one, they'd have no idea how."

"That's exactly how I feel about that car."

"Gwendolyn…"

"I can fix inanimate objects."

"You don't have to prove anything." Gwynne's stubbornness was starting to worry her.

"Watch." Gwynne waved one hand over the harp, not quite touching it. "Try playing it now."

Indulging her, Abby played a few notes of the "Arran Boat Song," and the notes were more clear, more haunting than before. Was it the power of suggestion? Her fingers went up and down the octaves, testing it out, relieved that Gwynne's magic had worked and hopeful this meant Gwynne would stop worrying about the car.

"Better?" Gwynne asked.

Abby launched into an Irish slip jig. The difference in tone was amazing. She ran her hands over the frame of her harp. "What did you do?"

"It sounds better, right?"

"Noticeably so. You could get people to pay you for this."

"I'd rather be able to fix our car. My skills are so…minor. Useless when it comes to things like not getting stranded in the desert, or…" Gwynne plopped down in the sand. Her voice cracked. "Or saving my mother's life."

Abby's heart ached for her. "Your skills make people's lives better. You ease their pain. That's just as important as saving lives."

"Is it?" Gwynne's eyes looked pained. "If it's not enough to fix that damn bridge, I'm going to lose you too."

If something went wrong, it was far more likely that Gwynne would be the one to die and Abby would be left to take care of Gwynne's rabbits. Or, because they were linked, they'd both die. And if they both survived, what would happen after that? Would Gwynne decide she'd had enough angel craziness, and leave? There were many ways this could end badly.

Abby hugged her harp to her chest. "You don't have to save me."

Gwynne's expression didn't change. "Yes. I do."

* * *

Gwynne watched Abby's hands fly confidently over her newly improved harp strings, turning them into blurs of vibration. Her head was bent over her harp like a mother holding a baby, and a shaft of desert sunlight backlit her hair, making it glow like a shimmering, golden halo. She made an unbearably beautiful angel.

Gwynne dropped her head to her knees, torn between the overwhelming need to memorize every curve of Abby's body and her reflex to look away because it hurt too much to watch something that beautiful. She blinked away the moisture that blurred her vision.

She was going to lose her. They were going to fix this bridge and Abby was going to decide she wanted to stay in the Angelic Realm after all. Once she realized she really *was* an angel, what would stop her?

And it might not matter either way. Because once they had her, Elle and her bright, shining thugs were never going to let her go.

CHAPTER TWENTY-ONE

It was dark when the tow truck dropped them off at the auto repair shop. Abby checked out the touristy Native American dream catchers adorned with dangling pigeon feathers displayed above quarts of oil stacked against the wall while Gwynne explained to the mechanic what happened to their car.

"I can take a look at it tonight, but officially I'm already closed for the day," the mechanic told her, heedless of the stream of angels flying into the shop. Hundreds had returned en masse after having disappeared all afternoon.

"Didn't this happen the last time we rode in a car?" observed one of the angels.

"Coincidence," Elle said dismissively.

"What?" Abby said sharply.

"What do you think is wrong with it?" Gwynne asked the mechanic, covering for Abby's outburst.

Abby sent her a mental thank you for her quick reaction, because rude outbursts weren't going to get their car fixed any faster, and might leave them stranded instead.

The mechanic shrugged like it wasn't worth his time to explain stuff a city girl wouldn't understand. "Electrical, maybe."

"I wonder how *that* could have happened," Abby said, giving Elle a hard look.

"I felt something spark," volunteered one of the angels.

"Me too," said another one. "Right when I was trampled and fell through the engine."

Abby realized her mouth was hanging open and clamped it shut.

"It's not our fault cars these days have so many electronic controls," Elle said. "How about you call the rental company for a replacement car so we can get going?"

"Car won't be ready until tomorrow," said the mechanic, talking over Elle, clearly oblivious to the angels' commentary. "Any chance you're here for the yoga camp?"

"Just passing through," Gwynne said.

"No hotels here. You'll need a place to stay the night. My wife can drive you to the camp."

"We're fine sleeping in the car," Abby said. She'd never be able to pass herself off as a yoga enthusiast—she couldn't even touch her toes, let alone drape her leg over her head or whatever else it was they did.

"Replacement car," Elle said.

What was the big hurry? Was she afraid the longer they delayed, the more likely they were to change their minds and back out of the plan? Even if they did get a replacement car, it would take several hours to reach them. And surely Elle didn't mean for them to deal with the bridge in the dark. They might as well wait for morning and give themselves a few hours of sleep before they attempted to not get themselves killed.

"The yoga folks don't mind visitors," said the mechanic. "You'd be a lot more comfortable there than sleeping in my repair bay, but if that's what you really want…" He trailed off like he hoped what they really wanted was to get out of his garage and let him start on their repair.

Gwynne's elbow poked into Abby's side. "If I don't get some sleep, I'm going to be a grouchy-pants when we get to Elle's house."

Okay, so Gwynne didn't want to sleep in the car.

"They serve food," the mechanic said. "Vegetarian. Not exactly what I'd call food, but my wife likes it okay."

Elle flapped her wings open and closed. "Replacement. Car."

Abby distanced herself from Gwynne's elbow. As long as she didn't have to do any backbends…

Gwynne pulled her outside. "Yoga camp, here we come."

* * *

The sea of closely-packed tents glowed from within, and random laughter and muted conversations filled the night. A woman sipping from a mug the size of a soup bowl emerged from a wooden shed marked Office.

"Namaste," she said between sips that sent dozens of thin, gold bracelets tinkling as they slid up and down her forearms.

"Namaste." Abby brought her hands to prayer position, hoping she looked like she knew what she was doing. "We were told we might be able to stay here for the night?"

"Of course. Welcome. Our restroom facilities—toilets, sinks and showers—are located at the northern perimeter. Cold water only." She pointed to a corrugated aluminum shack strung with colored lights. "Did you bring a tent?"

"Uh…no." Abby tightened the strap that secured her harp to her back. "Our car broke down and…it's a long story."

"No worries." The woman led them into the office, which was jammed with stacks of shelving holding books, clothing, toilet paper, snacks and supplies. "We don't have any extra tents, but we do have blankets. Here." She piled several wool blankets onto their outstretched arms.

"Thank you so much." Abby adjusted her grip as the thick blankets slipped. "Will we need this many?"

"It gets cold at night, especially if you're not used to the altitude." Her bracelets clinked against each other as she added several more blankets and a flashlight. "If you'd like to join us for evening chants, we'll be meeting by the campfire in an hour."

"That sounds fun," Gwynne cut in, "but I think we need to turn in for the night."

The yoga chick didn't insist. They hiked into the desert, away from the tents, until the voices of the campers faded away and were replaced by the night sounds of the desert.

The moon was bright enough that Abby turned off their borrowed flashlight to conserve batteries. The city sky was nothing like this. The beach sky was nothing like this. It was almost like being out in space. She hugged her share of blankets against her hip to free one arm and slipped her hand into the crook of Gwynne's elbow, something she'd longed to do that night on the beach after Penelope's wedding. She wrapped her fingers around her arm and soaked in the warmth that seeped through her jacket. She watched the stars instead of her footing, and maybe Gwynne did too, because they stumbled over rocks and bumped into each other sort of on purpose for a long time until they found a spot that felt like a good place to stop.

"Are there scorpions out here?" Abby asked, trying to decipher the shadows as she unfurled the blankets and spread them on the ground, one on top of the other.

"I'm sure our angel friends will make sure no scorpion interferes with their plans," Gwynne said.

"That might be more reassuring if we knew what their plan really was."

"True."

Abby rolled one of the blankets into a long pillow they could both share. It was cold, so they removed only their shoes and sandwiched themselves between the blankets fully dressed. Gwynne tucked Abby under her arm and Abby stared up at the stars imagining atoms, with their random joy, birthing galaxies. The aliveness of creation was very close out here.

"I love sleeping outside," Abby said after a while.

"We flew two thousand miles to sleep on the sand? We could have done this on the beach back home."

"It's illegal to sleep on the beach." Abby tried not to laugh at how prissy she sounded.

Gwynne scoffed. "Tell me that's not what's stopping you."

"It *is* what's stopping me."

"Sure it is."

"It *is*." All right, so she was totally lying. "If you must know, I don't like getting sand in my clothes, okay?"

"We should do it when we get back."

"If we get back," Abby amended. If they got back, she would love to spend a night with Gwynne discovering whether the police patrolled the beach or not. If they got back, she'd let Gwynne rub sand in her clothes and make a whole list of fun, non-life-threatening things they could do together. "You touch that bridge, you could die."

"So could you. Who knows what my energy field will do. I could blow up the whole thing."

"Elle didn't seem to think so."

"Elle doesn't know. She's flying by the seat of her pants waiting for someone to bust her for not having a pilot's license."

"You don't have to do this," Abby said, even though it seemed futile to remind her. "You still have time to bail."

Gwynne squeezed her close. "I'm not abandoning you."

"It's okay if you change your mind."

"I'm not changing my mind."

She believed her, but she couldn't let it go. "If you want to later…"

"I won't."

Abby couldn't take it anymore. "Why are you doing this? There's no guarantee you'll be safe."

"Fools rush in where angels fear to tread?"

"I'm serious."

Gwynne clucked her tongue in mock disapproval. "You're not supposed to be so serious—you being an angel and all. You know angels can fly only because they take themselves lightly."

"Would you stop with the ridiculous angel quotations?"

"I'm kind of starting to like them."

"You are not." Was this what happened to Gwynne when she was nervous?

Gwynne's eyes twinkled. She kissed the top of her head. "We won't die. This is going to work."

Still locked in Gwynne's arms, Abby gave a push and rolled on top of her, because right now their relationship was the only thing that made sense. "You'd better be right."

* * *

Abby felt great on top of her. Her movement opened a gap in the blankets, though, letting in a whisper of cold air. Gwynne sat up, pulling Abby with her, and rearranged the blankets that had slipped. She shivered at the cold air at her back.

"Holy crap, it's freezing out here." Gwynne buried her face in Abby's shoulder and breathed in the familiar scent of her hair. It was a scent she dreamed about lately, a scent that made her whole body come alive. And on that note…

She dredged up the blandest tone she could get away with and met Abby nose-to-nose. "They say if someone has hypothermia you're supposed to get under their blanket with them. Naked."

Abby grinned like it was a worthy attempt, but it wasn't going to fly. "You don't have hypothermia."

What…She didn't want to get warm?

"Shouldn't you check?"

Abby stuck her cold hands under her shirt and grabbed her waist. Gwynne flinched.

"Better?" Abby asked innocently, the deepening laugh lines at the corners of her eyes the only thing giving her away.

Gwynne snorted and hugged her tight. It was her own fault, after all. She should have known Abby's hands would be cold.

Abby rubbed her hands vigorously against Gwynne's lower back, and her hands—although perhaps not Gwynne's back—did get a little warmer. Then she moved higher and found the back of Gwynne's bra. She traced the whole length of it and paused in the center. "Uh-oh. A bra that closes in front." She took a fun detour on her way to the front and found the clasp. "I'm not sure I know how these work."

"Want me to do it?"

"Absolutely not. How am I going to learn if I don't practice?"

"You don't need to learn," Gwynne said. "I can do it."

Abby traced the edge of the cotton cups. "I want to learn so I'll know what to do next time."

"You can practice another time," Gwynne suggested.

Abby fingered the clasp, feeling how the two pieces fit together. "Quiet. I'm concentrating. Pretend I'm being suave and I'm expertly undoing your bra. One-handed."

She crawled onto Gwynne's lap and pulled at the neckline of her sweater to look down it. Unfortunately she seemed to only want a visual to help her with the clasp. Or maybe that wasn't her only reason, since she doubted she could see much detail in the dark. The moon was bright, but it wasn't *that* bright. Her hands went up her shirt again, focused on her task.

"I've actually never taken off another woman's bra before," Abby said, fumbling with the mechanism.

"Never? How is that possible?"

"I guess it never came up."

"If I found myself in that situation, I'd make it come up."

"I'm sure you would." Abby wiggled against her, changing position to get a better angle. "I can do this, though. I just have to figure out how this clasp works."

Which at this rate was going to take until morning. Gwynne groaned, fighting the urge to help. The next time she was going bra-less. "In the interest of speeding this up, I'd like you to know there are no bonus points for doing this one-handed."

"That's what you think."

Abby demonstrated what she could do to Gwynne's breast if she had a free hand. Gwynne shivered, and this time it wasn't because she was cold.

"I'm sorry I'm not better at this," Abby said softly, her bravado finally slipping. "You probably didn't think I was a lesbian when you first met me, with the way I dress, and now I can't undo this clasp…"

"No, I did," Gwynne reassured her, straining toward her touch.

Abby abandoned the clasp and pressed her thumbs to the tips of Gwynne's nipples. Gwynne gasped as electricity lit a spot deep inside her. Abby pushed her sweater up and kissed her through her bra, licking at the peaks until there were two damp spots on the cotton. Gwynne arched her back. She reached for Abby's sweater, intending to yank it over her head, but Abby stopped her.

"Are you still focusing on my suaveness?"

"All this talking is making it hard for me to focus on how suave you are," Gwynne said, feeling a little light-headed.

"Then focus on how talented I am."

"Talented?" She shouldn't tease if Abby was worried about not living up to some mythical lesbian standard, but it was hard not to when she *was* so incredibly talented, even with her charming bra ineptitude. There was just something about even her awkward touches that made her want to lie back and see what she would do next that was guaranteed to turn her on.

"Fast?" Abby suggested, tugging again at her bra while her free hand continued to stroke her breast with a gentle insistence that made her tingle and tighten to the point of pain.

"This is fast?" A desperate sound escaped from the back of Gwynne's throat, half moan, half laugh. God, how did she end up under a blanket with someone who was so fun to be with? Who was weird, and optimistic, and genuinely nice? And crazy. Crazy in a good way. A very, very good…

Abby finally gave up on her attempt to undo the clasp one-handed and tried with both hands. "Aha! Got it." She stripped off Gwynne's sweater and the bra and captured one of Gwynne's breasts with her mouth.

Gwynne caught her breath in a sudden, involuntary inhale.

Abby had no problem getting the rest of Gwynne's clothes off, and Gwynne stayed remarkably warm as Abby crawled all over her, shoving a cushion of clothes between her and the blankets. She passed warm and was well into hot by the time Abby wedged herself between her knees and pushed her legs apart.

As Abby sank down and lowered her head, the ends of her long hair swept against her inner thighs. Gwynne tightened with anticipation. She knew what was coming, but still, the shock of Abby's warm, wet mouth made her jump.

Abby stayed with her and stroked her with a rhythm that made her absolutely crazed, made her writhe and moan and spread her legs farther apart and thrust her hips toward her, needing to get closer, so focused on the moment that she no longer knew where they were. She was burning up and all she saw was Abby, her eyes lowered and her hair hanging in her face and her aura swirling around her, aquamarine with sparks of rose, tangerine, and bright golden angel's light, the colors shifting as Abby hummed and moaned with pleasure. Gwynne's eyes closed and her neck arched. Her breath came harshly, frantically, out of control. When the scent of Abby's arousal reached her, she lost her mind.

Abby didn't wait for her to recover. She pushed her over the edge again, pushing her deeper this time, bringing her to where she was shrieking and gasping, pushing her beyond where she thought she could go. She was spent, but Abby went after her again and again, the colors of her aura spinning and swirling into a blur of searing white-hot infinity, waking surge after surge of power that left her quivering uncontrollably. She couldn't bear it anymore, and yet she craved her touch and clung to her with her inner muscles, begging for it, because dying at her hands was all she wanted to do.

* * *

Gwynne stirred, and Abby curled closer, unwilling to be separated from her by even an inch. It was warm in her arms, and perfect, and she didn't want to break the profound peacefulness of their sated energy.

"Are you in your clothes? Again?" Gwynne complained, apparently not onboard with spending the rest of the night doing the drowsy bonding thing if they could be naked instead. "I'm going to start thinking you don't want to take your clothes off for me."

Like she hadn't done just that an hour ago. Well, most of her clothes. Gwynne had gotten pleasantly distracted before she finished stripping everything off her, and by then Abby had come so hard they'd forgotten all thoughts of clothing.

Now the temperature had dropped and she didn't mind having on a sweater. "It's cold."

"Not that cold." Gwynne reached under Abby's sweater and unhooked her bra on the first try.

"Show-off."

Gwynne pushed Abby's straps over her shoulders in an attempt to take off her bra without removing her sweater. "Help me out here."

Abby completed the maneuver and handed her her turquoise lace bra as a reward for being thoughtful enough to leave her the warmth of her sweater. Gwynne took the bra and dangled it off one finger.

"Turquoise. I like this one," Gwynne said, swinging it back and forth. "It reminds me of the first time I got you naked."

"You remember which bra I wore?"

"You *don't*?" Gwynne stopped swinging the bra and opened her mouth.

"I do, but…I think you have a thing about bras."

"I think I have a thing about *you*."

Abby blushed. "I believe I heard mention of a red pushup bra in your past…"

"Ancient history."

Abby hunkered down inside her sweater. She didn't want to be another conquest. "Am I going to be known as the girl in the turquoise lace bra?"

Gwynne dropped the bra. She took her by the shoulders and kissed her with breathtaking tenderness, kissing away her insecurities. Abby's heart melted—a painful kind of melting. She molded herself to Gwynne's body, aching to be closer, frustrated by the physical barrier of their solid human bodies that didn't dissolve into ether.

"You don't get a bra nickname," Gwynne said, moving her lips against the corner of her mouth with little kisses.

"Why not?"

"Because I give bra nicknames only to my exes."

CHAPTER TWENTY-TWO

Bright and early the next morning, their car was fixed and they were on their way to the mountain. By midmorning they were on foot following hundreds of angels up barely discernible game trails and slipping on pine needles, praying neither one of them twisted an ankle. At least Abby was praying. Hiking was not something she did for fun, and this was a seriously steep slope.

Several hours of hiking later, they hadn't encountered a single human being. The angels were singing yet another round of some Roman marching song, but Abby didn't have the breath to join in—especially not in Latin.

She unsnapped her pack and let it slide to the ground, then collapsed beside it. Gwynne sat next to her and dug out Abby's water bottle and opened it for her.

"Drink," said Gwynne.

Abby had to wait until she stopped panting before she could attempt to swallow her water without choking. "If I survive this, I'm going to start going to the gym."

"I'll join you," Gwynne said, breathing hard herself.

"You have softball."

"What…I can't do both?"

"Maybe I should try softball too." Abby paused. It was hard to talk without wheezing. "Because I never want to be this out of shape again. I can't…" She gulped some more air. "…breathe."

Gwynne gingerly pulled off one of her boots and showed Abby the painful-looking blister on her heel.

Abby winced. "Does it hurt?"

"Yup." Gwynne found moleskin and stuck it on while angels flitted through the pines, leaping, spinning and somersaulting, laughing with barely contained excitement, waiting for them to get back on their feet. "You know what would be annoying? If it turns out Elle's taking us the back way and there's a road we don't know about on the other side."

Elle separated herself from her friends and hovered above Abby and Gwynne. "There is no road. This is the trail other people take—the UFO hunters and the peak baggers—although why anyone would want to bag this modest a peak is beyond my comprehension."

A hawk cried overhead and Elle glanced up sharply, as did several other angels. They watched it circle until at some unknown signal they all returned to what they'd been doing before.

"If it makes you feel any better," Elle said, "we're almost there."

Gwynne put her boot back on and they continued up the mountain.

An hour later they emerged from a stand of aspen into a clearing with a panoramic view of the plains far below. The air smelled like ozone, poisonously sweet. A faint trace of shimmering, iridescent blue-gray and lavender arced high in the sky, touching down on the mountain and wavering in and out of sight.

"Can you see it?" Abby breathed.

Gwynne took her hand. "It's beautiful."

She raised her hand to her lips and kissed her palm with only the barest touch. Abby shivered. So gentle, but intense.

And that had better not have been a kiss goodbye. Because this was it. They were at the bridge and there was no more time to debate the wisdom of what they were about to do. Abby laced her fingers with Gwynne's.

A songbird flew past, trilling as it headed straight for the angels' dazzling, nearly invisible bridge, and dropped dead from the sky.

Another bird careened out of the way.

In the dirt, an angel cradled the small, broken body.

* * *

They positioned themselves on the bridge, one on each node, countless angels holding hands to form one long chain that stretched farther than anyone could see, disappearing into the sky like a stairway of stars toward the heavens.

Way at the other end, where the bridge was anchored in the Angelic Realm, was an angel who formed the first link of the chain. Here on earth, Elle and Sapphire were the last two angels in the chain, leaving one empty node a foot or two off the ground. Sapphire held out her hand, waiting for Abby to join them. Abby gave Gwynne one last squeeze and let go so she could take her place on the last node.

There was no node for Gwynne.

Abby gripped Sapphire's hand, expecting to feel the flicker of connection she'd felt the last time, but there was nothing. She hesitated.

Gwynne approached the bridge, closer than looked safe, and blew her a kiss. It wasn't a jaunty, lighthearted gesture, the way blowing a kiss ought to be. Instead, her eyes were downcast and a muscle worked in her jaw as she pressed her fingers to her lips before she reluctantly raised her eyes, her gaze boring through her, and sent the kiss.

"We can do this," Gwynne said. She reached for her hand but stayed where she was, far enough away that they wouldn't touch unless Abby wanted to.

Abby looked at her outstretched arm and took a deep breath. "We can."

From her position a foot above the ground, Abby bent her knees and started to reach for her. Electricity arced between them, jumping across the space that separated them, shocking them before they even touched. In the split second before Abby could instinctively pull back, Gwynne had already launched herself at her and held her in a fierce hug, her arms tight around Abby's waist, her head to her chest. Abby braced herself for electrical overload, but it never came. Instead, everything around them went still. No birdsong, no angelic choir, no wind whistling through the trees.

"I can hear your heartbeat," Gwynne whispered, still alive.

The angelic link rushed through her like a stream of musical notes forming a chord. The chord wavered, teetering on the cusp of dissonance. Abby held her breath. Her fingers tensed as if they were on harp strings and could physically wrest the vibration under control. Her lungs screamed and the chord reasserted itself and stabilized. Abby reeled with light-headedness, sure that she would fall if Gwynne weren't holding her.

Gwynne was alive. Gwynne was alive and Sapphire was beside her and they were part of this endless chain of angels. The rightness of that filled her with an overwhelmingly pure, aching sweetness. And deep within that sweetness, a whisper of angelic essence woke inside her, tingling in her spine. The essence spiraled and hummed and spread through her whole body and finally she gave in to the unbearable urge to stretch her arms out to the sides, still part of the chain, until the muscles between her shoulder blades reached their limit. Huge wings, immeasurable times the size of her body, swept open like a cascading fan with ribs of blinding white light. Silence echoed in a vast white emptiness.

Eternity passed.

Then out of the silence, the mountain began to hum, chanting an ancient, volcanic melody. The sound rose from the depths of the earth, up through layers of molten rock and crystal, and rumbled in the clear, dry air.

The bridge glowed. The angels' unearthly love filled her again as it had before, but this time Gwynne was there too, clinging to her with legs, chest, arms, joining them in the link. She could feel Gwynne's love pouring into her, modulating her energy, maintaining the phase shift, supporting her.

Abby melted into her, allowing their energies to merge. Everything she was merged with everything Gwynne was, and the rush nearly shook her apart. Together they gasped for breath and became a churning dynamo that generated more power, and more love, than either of them could alone.

Beneath her and into the distance, the bridge rippled with currents of energy, shimmying and realigning itself. Through her link with the others, she sensed breaks in the structure disappear.

It was working. The bridge was repairing itself.

* * *

Gwynne knew she held Abby in her arms because she could feel the shape and warmth of her body, but, engulfed by the bridge's electrical maelstrom, all she could see of her was an explosive field of white light crackling with sparks of gold. Abby was magnificent. She was a fierce, determined conduit powerful enough to handle the energy of the bridge, and of the angels, plus everything Gwynne could throw at her.

Gwynne didn't hold back. She surrendered everything. It was unlike anything she'd ever experienced, to feel Abby welcome her energy and integrate it into her own and use it. Her thoughts merged with Abby's thoughts; her edges blurred. They were both completely open. A whisper of angelic essence floated through the link, and Gwynne reached for it with everything she had.

A jolt of electrical current slammed into her with unimaginable force.

A scream pierced the air. The sound reverberated in her jaw and bounced around in her head. Was she the one who screamed? Would she scream, if she was dead?

Like a smashed Christmas ornament, her mind splintered into jagged, weightless, silver shards flashing in the glow of a thousand twinkling lights before the world flattened out into stark white oblivion.

* * *

Gwynne felt like she'd been slammed to the ground by a two-ton truck. Everything ached. Worse than ached. If she opened her eyes, would she still be on the mountain? Or would she find herself hooked up to life support in a hospital bed? Or not on earth at all? She went for it and noted with relief that she was flat on her back a few yards from the bridge. Abby sat at her side, holding her hand, surrounded by angels who were as somber as if they were keeping watch over a deathbed. She knew the look—she'd seen them like this once before, watching over her dying mother. She wasn't dying, was she? She hoped not. Reflexively, she shut her eyes against the angels' brightness and groaned in pain.

Abby's small, gentle hand touched her forehead. Hesitantly, as if she were afraid her feather-light touch might hurt her.

She should let Abby know she was okay. Reassure her, even if it was a lie. She made an effort to open her eyes again. Squinting, this time. It wasn't so bad.

Abby smiled wanly, deepening the worry lines around her eyes. "How do you feel?"

"I'll live," Gwynne said. "I am alive, right?"

Abby squeezed her hand. "Sorry I don't have a butterscotch for you."

It seemed so long ago that Abby had been the one who collapsed and Gwynne had given her candy and made the stupid-ass move of confirming for her that angels were real. Maybe it hadn't been such a bad move after all.

"There's one in my pocket. Left side," Gwynne said.

"Do you want it?"

"I wouldn't mind your hand in my pocket."

Abby obliged with a mischievous twinkle in her eye, and Gwynne, satisfied that Abby was no longer worried about her, gave up the fight to keep her eyes open. Getting hit by a truck was exhausting.

She didn't realize she'd fallen asleep until she woke and found that Abby's hand was resting on the center of her chest, pouring love into her, filling her heart with warm sunshine that eased the aches in her body and seeped into her soul. Gwynne was so used to being the one who helped other people that she'd never fully allowed herself to receive what others had to give. What Abby had to give. And what Abby had to give was astonishingly powerful, a flood of love and aliveness that touched every molecule of her being and awakened an almost unbearable joy. Her chest expanded with a deep, effortless breath that went on and on and on. Abby was her life.

* * *

The next time Gwynne woke, she felt surprisingly fine. She sat up and the world swayed to the left but it didn't tip her over, so she tried to stand. Abby was there, gripping her arm to steady her.

"You okay?" Abby said.

"Yeah." The world stabilized but the air was thinner, brighter, more sparkly. Even her body seemed to glow. And there were angels absolutely everywhere, spinning and tumbling and dancing. "Did we do it?"

Abby laughed, a sound of relief mixed with the thrill of accomplishment. "Look how happy they are. Of course we did it."

One of angels approached. A very familiar angel. Or…not. No, it was her. It was. The world slipped and Gwynne swayed against the support of Abby's body.

How she recognized her mother, she couldn't say. But it was her. Her aura was different, but the same. Brighter, clearer, free of the mask of human form. It felt like her. A warm ache lodged in her heart. Could it really be her?

"Gwynne, my little star."

"Mom?" She threw her arms around her. She looked like an angel, but she felt as solid and alive as ever.

"I'm so proud of you, Gwynne."

"Mom? You're an angel? What..." Her head reeled. It didn't make sense.

And then it did.

"Like Abby? You incarnated? How...Oh my God. You killed yourself. Elle asked you to kill yourself. And you believed her."

She couldn't accept that her mother was that naïve. Sure, it was obvious at this point that Elle had been right, but nothing had been obvious back then. Her mother was worse than Abby.

"It's not wrong to believe others, Gwynne. I'd been talking to angels all my life, just like you. I trusted her."

She trusted her. And that was enough? "Why didn't you tell me?"

Abby stepped forward and hugged her mother before she could respond—just jumped in and flung her arms around her like they were long-lost friends who'd known each other forever. Come to think of it, if they were both angels, they *had* known each other forever—except Abby couldn't remember. Or had that changed?

"It's an honor to meet you," Abby said. "Gwynne may not act like it, but she's happy to see you."

Her mother's smile was warm and welcoming, and as Abby stepped out of the embrace she gripped both of Abby's hands. "She's lucky to have found you."

"Thank you for raising her and helping her grow up to be a wonderful person." Abby drew their clasped hands together and toward her heart in a gesture of gratitude. "Thank you."

Gwynne squirmed with embarrassment. Abby was so nice. Leave it to Abby to find the exact right thing to say to her mother and to sincerely mean every word.

They stepped apart and her mother turned to Gwynne. "You're upset that I hid the truth from you."

Was it time for questions? She'd be happy to continue to watch Abby be her amazing self, but she did have questions. "I wish you'd said something."

"I wish I could have, but it wasn't possible. You know I couldn't have told you."

"Why? Why couldn't you tell me? Or Dad? We could at least have said goodbye."

Her mother shook her head sadly. "You would have tried to stop me. I couldn't afford to risk that."

Gwynne thought of all those angels hovering over her mother's hospital bed, watching over her but refusing to help.

"That's why they wouldn't help me heal you." It was so clear now. "They *wanted* you to die." She rubbed her forehead, trying to get at the headache lodged firmly behind her eyes.

"Nobody planned for it to happen that way—for you to see me in the hospital."

Of course nobody planned it that way. Why plan for the interfering daughter to get in the way?

"I cried over you." She felt so stupid. "You let me believe you were dead!"

"My human form is dead. That wasn't a lie."

"But your spirit…" And it wasn't her only lie. "All this time I thought you died trying to save Heather."

Her mother shrank and her light dimmed. "I did try to save her. I wanted to save her more than anything. I was willing to give my life for it. Yes, I was planning to help Elle anyway, but in that instant I wasn't thinking about that. All I wanted to do was save my child. Not that it didn't occur to me that I could save Heather's life and then slip away afterward under the ice, make it look like an accident. But I miscalculated. In the end it really was an accident."

It was impossible to stay mad at her when she looked so defeated. Gwynne gave her another hug, but this time her arms passed right through the illusion of her mother's form, nothing but air and a lingering essence. "Can I tell Dad, or will that just upset him?"

"He…" Her voice was a quiet, hesitant tinkling of glass. "He…knows. I'm not supposed to show myself to him, but…I do, sometimes. I can make him see. Even when I don't, he senses my presence."

"Wow, that's good." Her dad had been devastated by her mother's death, still in love with her despite their divorce.

Anything that could help him was great, even if it meant that her mother had been visiting her father but had apparently been hiding from her daughter. She was surprised Elle hadn't forced her to make an appearance to convince Gwynne to put pressure on Abby. "You could have maybe told me."

"I couldn't let you see me. I was trying to protect you. I was afraid that if you knew what I was, you'd think you were something you're not, and you'd do something foolish and end up like your sister."

"You mean like help with the bridge?" The pieces suddenly fell into place. "If you're an angel, that makes me half angel. That's why the bridge didn't kill me. You must have known it wouldn't kill me." She rubbed at the diffuse, white light that, although gradually fading, still glowed from her forearms. An aftereffect of touching the bridge, she guessed. Abby had it too. "You must have known. *Elle* must have known."

All that arguing. All that crap about fools rushing in where angels fear to tread, about Abby being the only one who could help.

"Elle knows you're my mother, right?"

"She knows."

"She didn't act like it."

"Humans cannot touch the bridge."

Gwynne's irritability seemed to have triggered the angel's parental instinct to keep her in line. She'd been relatively easygoing as a mother, but when she got that look on her face, Gwynne knew she was in for a lecture.

"But—"

"You have to understand, we know very little about our children, what they are. We've always assumed you were just like any other human being, although the genetics are highly unpredictable."

"You really didn't know?"

"I wanted to stop you. I didn't think it would work."

"So Heather's not…"

"Heather's dead," her mother said softly, her voice cracking. "Her spirit moved on."

"But not to the Angelic Realm."

"No. Hybrids have an angelic signature in their energy field, but in every other way you're human."

"Except that I can see angels," Gwynne pointed out.

"As can some humans."

And Heather couldn't. Because the genetics were unpredictable, and an accident of birth saddled Heather with a blindness she could never accept.

But why would people like Megan McLaren be born with the ability to see angels when half angels like Heather weren't? Unless Megan had angel's blood too. Genes didn't always show up where you expected them to.

"There could be people who are one-quarter angel, one-sixteenth angel, one untraceable fraction from generations ago," Gwynne said. "There must be hundreds of us. Thousands."

Elle swept in and joined their small circle. "As a matter of fact, no, there aren't. Even if you look at the entire history of humankind, there have been very few angel-human unions that resulted in children. We're a female society. Not female in quite the same way you think of it, but laying with a man…" She shuddered. "That's something only a human would want to do. Very few angels have the stomach for it. Even you, being only half angel, wouldn't do it. Artemisia was an exception."

Gwynne stared. Her mother, a sexual renegade. It was almost more bizarre than her being an angel.

"We didn't know what you were capable of. Helping to fix the bridge…" Her mother's wings became a blur of movement. "I thought it *would* kill you. Half human or one hundred percent human, the human part of you shouldn't have been able to handle the high voltage. And fifty percent dead becomes one hundred percent dead pretty much immediately."

"We didn't know it would transform you," Elle said.

"It transformed me?"

"You're an angel now," her mother said.

Abby stiffened at her side. Gwynne was sure she'd done the same thing.

"What?"

"Look at yourself."

Gwynne rubbed her arms. Sure, they glowed a little, but that was temporary, right? As far as she could tell, she still had solid form. Her energy field did feel different, but it was hard to be sure what exactly was different about it, considering the dizziness hadn't completely gone away.

"I have human form." Glowing human form, but still. She knew that much, at least.

"Human form, yes. Human thoughts. The appearance of human karma. But inside, you're an angel." Her mother brightened with pride. "When the energy of the bridge and the energy of all of us surged through you, it magnified your angelic DNA and burned out your old identity. It turned you into an angel."

"An incarnated angel," Elle said. "We're thrilled to have you onboard."

An angel. She didn't know how she felt about that.

"Is this glow going to wear off?"

"Eventually. And look," Elle said. "The bridge has an extra node. A new one, just for you."

Perfect. Gwynne narrowed her eyes at the happy angel. "I never, ever want to hear about this bridge ever again. If it gets damaged again it is staying broken, do you hear me?"

Her mother sparkled with indulgent, maternal laughter. "Okay, honey. We'll discuss it in a few decades when you join us in the Angelic Realm."

"I cannot believe this is happening to me," Gwynne muttered.

Abby put her arm around her waist. "I'm just glad we'll be together."

They would be, wouldn't they? Gwynne softened. Together forever in the Angelic Realm. She leaned into the comfort of Abby's arm and pointedly did not look at the two angels who blazed with unbearable light. She didn't want them to know how happy they'd made her.

Or maybe she did. She squinted in their direction. "I look forward to it."

They blinked out.

Gwynne pressed her forehead to Abby's shoulder. "Having you around will make it worth putting up with my mother for eternity."

EPILOGUE

Abby stepped out the front door onto the wraparound porch of Gwynne's cozy, hundred-year-old beach cottage—their beach cottage—and discovered a jumping cardboard box with air holes punched in the top. Gwynne had warned her this would happen—that bunnies had a way of appearing at her doorstep. She hadn't told her about their evasive maneuvers, though. She scooped up the panicked box and brought it inside before it could hurt itself.

"Gwynne!" she called into the house, setting the box on the entryway's slate floor and carefully opening the flaps.

Gwynne padded in from the bedroom. When she saw what Abby was doing, she ran the last few steps.

Abby lifted the black-and-white rabbit out of the box. "I've never seen one with Dalmatian spots," she said, depositing the overweight bundle of fur into Gwynne's arms. "And black ears. So cute."

Gwynne cuddled the rabbit close to her chest and did her rabbit whisperer thing, petting and crooning and calming the animal down. Abby felt a little rabbit-whispered herself, watching Gwynne glow with love for the abandoned creature, making it feel safe.

"Where did you come from?" Gwynne asked softly. With the rabbit settled in the crook of her arm, she checked out the empty box. "Looks like there was a note in here, but our busy guy ripped it to shreds."

"Oh!" Abby said, realizing he could have been trapped all night on their porch without food. "He must be hungry."

She ran to the fridge and pulled out a handful of carrot tops and lettuce and met Gwynne in the backyard where they had a rabbit pen. She placed the greens on the ground, careful not to startle their guest. The rabbit eyed his new family suspiciously from the farthest corner of the pen, but it didn't take him long to dart out to snatch some leafy goodness and retreat to his corner with it.

"This is so exciting," Abby said. "If he's a boy, let's name him Peter the Sixteenth."

"I like it." Gwynne stood behind her and wrapped her arms around her waist. "You're not going to ask what I need another bunny for?"

"What?"

"You're not going to say *Not another one? Again?*"

The small hitch in Gwynne's voice was painful to hear. She squeezed Gwynne's arms and a fierce protectiveness swept through her, making her sway.

"I love that you want to help them. You love them. And they need you."

She leaned back, cradled in the circle of Gwynne's arms. This was where she belonged—in the embrace of this beautiful being who had a caring heart worthy of both a woman and an angel. She didn't have to join the angels in the Angelic Realm to find home—she already had a place where she belonged, right here on earth.

Gwynne rubbed her hands around Abby's waist, over her hip bones, up her ribcage. "I can't believe you weren't mad when Nimbus chewed a hole in your blouse—the blouse I wasn't supposed to be wearing because you told me you didn't want to get rabbit hair on it."

Oh, Gwynne. If Gwynne had any sense of self-preservation she wouldn't remind her that Nimbus had landed himself firmly in the doghouse with that stunt, and yet she couldn't find it within herself to stay mad at either of them.

"I promise I'll make it up to you." Gwynne's hands moved lower.

"It was just the hem. The patch won't even show."

"I love you." Gwynne nuzzled the back of her neck with an appreciative purr. "You know you're never going to get rid of me now that I can follow you to the Angelic Realm."

Abby turned in her arms to look at her. "I can't imagine anything I'd enjoy more."

Gwynne smiled seductively. "I can." Surviving near-death had made her insatiable.

"It's the middle of the day, Gwynnosaurus."

"So?"

"So, we both have to go to work."

Gwynne had an evening shift at Sea Salt and Abby had an afternoon wedding to play, and afterward she'd stop by the spa and Gwynne would take a break from healing everyone who asked and she'd rub the soreness out of Abby's shoulders. They'd go home together and they'd check on Peter the Sixteenth and Gwynne would chase the other rabbits away from the harps and Abby would practice her rapidly improving bra-unhooking skills and they'd go to bed in their huge bed that was twice the size of her old one and still end up on top of each other.

"We don't have to leave for work just yet," Gwynne argued.

Abby gave her a quick kiss. "I'm playing a wedding. I can't be late."

"Speaking of…" Gwynne said a little too casually. "Do you have any musician friends who play weddings?"

"Why?" Was Gwynne seriously going to…

"Because if I asked you to marry me, and if you made me the happiest girl in the world and said yes, we'd need to find someone who's not you to do the music."

That was so Gwynne. Charming and wonderful. She wiped a tear from her eye. "That is so corny."

"I know. Will you marry me?"

"Only if I get to pick the music."

"I wouldn't dare have it any other way."

Abby laughed, because who was she kidding? She'd be willing to marry her to Pachelbel's Canon and the Wedding March and "Another One Bites the Dust" and anything else Gwynne came up with, and she'd be too excited to hear any of it.

"The bunnies can be ring bearers." That seemed like the sort of thing Gwynne would want. If she could train them to do magic shows, she could maybe train them to hop down the aisle, right? Or they'd find bridesmaids willing to hold the furry guys. Not that they needed to do an aisle or bridesmaids or any of it to feel married. Their real marriage had already happened, on the angels' bridge, when their souls were irrevocably seared together in the glow of the angelic link. But if Gwynne wanted a ceremony…

Gwynne gave her a fierce hug, trembling all over, burying her face in her hair.

Abby rubbed between her shoulder blades and pulled her close. "I love you," she whispered.

"I love you too."

"Do you like my plan?"

"Have I told you how much I love you?" Gwynne threaded her fingers through Abby's hair with an intimacy that made Abby want to come up with more wedding plans she would like.

"You really think including the bunnies in the ceremony would work?"

"I think it'll be chaos, but who cares? Although I have to say, if the boys are going to dress up, they'd rather be flower girls so they can go in drag."

Gwynne wanted them to wear *clothes*? Well, okay, she could sew them little outfits. She loved costumes, and a skirt should be easy enough to put on a rabbit—easier than pants, anyway. Would sequins work? Or would they chew those off and make themselves sick? Maybe lace skirts with matching pointy princess hats. That would look nice—if lace could be made of rabbit-proof, indestructible material. Because as far as she could tell, those handfuls of cuddle-bun cuteness were willing to gnaw on just about anything. Including the flower girl baskets.

Which gave her an idea. "They can eat the rose petals on their way down the aisle. They'll like that."

Gwynne beamed. "They will! I can't wait."

Gwynne's kiss convinced her she had more time before she needed to leave for work than she'd thought.

Forever was going to feel wonderful.

Bella Books, Inc.

Women. Books. Even Better Together.

P.O. Box 10543
Tallahassee, FL 32302

Phone: 800-729-4992
www.bellabooks.com